Alexander Balloch Grosart, John Davies

The Complete Poems of Sir John Davies

Vol. 2

Alexander Balloch Grosart, John Davies

The Complete Poems of Sir John Davies
Vol. 2

ISBN/EAN: 9783337397869

Printed in Europe, USA, Canada, Australia, Japan

Cover: Foto ©Andreas Hilbeck / pixelio.de

More available books at **www.hansebooks.com**

Early English Poets.

THE
COMPLETE POEMS

OF

SIR JOHN DAVIES.

EDITED,

WITH

Memorial-Introduction and Notes,

BY THE

REV. ALEXANDER B. GROSART.

IN TWO VOLUMES.—VOL. II.

London:
CHATTO AND WINDUS, PICCADILLY.
1876.

Contents.

Those marked with [*] are either printed for the first time, or for
the first time published among Davies' Poems.

CONTENTS.
ix.

EPIGRAMS, WITH ADDITIONS.

B

NOTE.

I am indebted to the Bodleian copy—among Malone's books —for my text of these ' Epigrams.' I have preferred this edition to the two others that preceded, inasmuch as, while it, like them, bears the imprint of ' Middlebourgh,' there seems no reason to doubt that it was printed in London : therefore most probably under the author's eye. The volume is a small 12mo. and the following is the title-page :—

All
OVIDS ELEGIES
3 Bookes
By C. M.
EPIGRAMS BY J. D.
At Middlebourgh.

Malone has filled in in MS. ' Christopher Marlowe and John Davis.' Cf. Collier's Bibliographical Account of Early English Literature : Vol I. *s.n.*

The Rev. Alexander Dyce in his collective edition of the Works of Marlowe, has given Davies' " Epigrams" *in extenso*, with a painstaking collation of the various readings from the other two editions (both undated) together with similar various readings from a Manuscript discovered by him in the Harleian Collection (1836.) Mr. Dyce with reference to his reprint of the ' Epigrams,' and the foregoing MS. says, " I have given them with the text considerably improved by means of one of the Harleian MSS" (' Some

Account of Marlowe and his Writings : p. xl : edition 1862.)
I must demur to this alleged 'improvement.' The MS.
has no authority whatever, the Scribe being an extremely
ignorant and blundering one. These nine examples out of
many, taken at random, will suffice to prove this :

[1] Epigram 1, line first.

    ' Fly, merry Muse unto that merry towne &c.
he actually reads, spite of its heading ' Ad Musam '

        ' Fly, merry Newes. . . .

[2] Epigram 2, line 14

    ' And stands, in Presence, stroaking up his haire '
he gives, to neglect of the rhyme with ' yeare '

    '. . . . . stroaking up his heade '

[3] Epigram 3, line 5, for ' fry ' he stupidly reads ' cry.'

[4] Epigram 13, line 9, for ' sectaries ' he gives nonsen-
sically ' scituaries.'

[5] Epigram 15, line 3.

    ' Thou with harsh noise the ayre doth rudely breake,'
he transmogrifies into

    '. . . . . horse nor sea the ayre doth.'

[6] Epigram 26, line 11, he substitutes ' sweete ' for ' hot '
oblivious of the rhyme with ' petticoat.'

[7] Epigram 36, line 19, for ' rarifie ' he reads ' ratiffie ' [!]

[8] Epigram 41, line 2,

    ' Paulus, in spite of enuy, fortunate '
he gives thus

        Paulus, in fight of envy '. . . . .

[9] Epigram 43, line 3, for 'Paris-garden' he has 'Parish-garden;' and so on ludicrously, with numerous proper names.

Any one capable of perpetrating such stupidities as these, ought not in my opinion, to be allowed to displace a text printed for the Author, more especially his cannot for a moment be allowed to over-bear the third edition, our text.

From a confused inscription on the first page of the MS. its probable writer is ascertained. It is as follows " Ex spoliis Richardi Wharfe, ex . . . . . . It is much trouble and much . . . . Ex spoliis R. W." Underneath is the book-plate of John, Duke of Newcastle. The general title runs " Epigramma in Musam, like Buckminster's Allmanacks servinge generallie for all England : but especiallic for the meridian of this famous Cittie of London." I regret that besides these (mis-called) ' improvements,' so admirable an Editor should have *modernized* throughout, the ORTHOGRAPHY equally of MARLOWE and of DAVIES : and all the more, that in his ' Notes ' he adheres to the original orthography whenever he quotes from his wealth of illustrative extracts. The annotation condemns the text. Without any hesitation therefore, I have set aside Mr. Dyce's reprints, and returned (as *supra*) to Davies' own text and orthography, saving a slight reduction of capitals and italics. None the less do I owe thanks to Mr. Dyce for his kind permission kindly given, to use any ' Notes ' that might be deemed interesting.

Those that I have taken are marked with his initial, D. I have to add another important correction of Mr. Dyce. After describing the HARLEIAN MS. he observes " Though it is of a date considerably posterior to the first appearance in print of *Epigrams by I. D.*, perhaps ALL THE PIECES WHICH IT EXHIBITS ARE FROM THE PEN OF DAVIES. (page 353.) HOMER nods here : for on reading these additional ' Epigrams ' thus assigned to Davies, I at once discovered that they consisted merely of a like blundering transcript of the " Satyricall Epigrams " of HENRY HUTTON, Dunelmensis, that were appended to his " Follie's Anatomie or Satyres " (1619.) The oversight is the more noticeable in that all these were reprinted in 1842, (edited by Rimbault), for the Percy Society, whereof Mr. Dyce was one of the most effective members of Council.

I confess that it was far from a disappointment to find that the ' Epigrams ' of Davies were not to be increased to the extent they would have been had I accepted Mr. Dyce's opinion, and failed to discover the Hutton-authorship of nearly all those in the Manuscript, additional to his acknowledged ones. Nevertheless in the Appendix to our reprint of the ' Epigrams ' I give certain additions from this Manuscript, that are found neither in Davies's nor Hutton's publications, but which seem to me to have the *ring* of Davies in them. The remainder—prefixed and affixed—may well be left in Manuscript. See the Memorial-Introduction for more on these Epigrams. G.

Epigrammes.

Ad Musam. i.

Fly, merry Muse unto that merry towne,
Where thou maist playes, revels, and triumphs see ;
The house of Fame, and theater of renowne,
Where all good wits and spirits loue to be.
Fall in betweene their hands that loue and praise thee,[1]
And be to them a laughter and a jest :
But as for them which scorning shall reproue thee,
Disdaine their wits, and thinke thine one [2] the best :
But if thou finde any so grose [3] and dull,
That thinke I do to priuate taxing [4] leane,
Bid him go hang, for he is but a gull,
And knows not what an Epigramme does meane ;

---

[1] MS. "seeme to loue thee." D.   [2] Own. G.   [3] Gross. G.
[4] Blaming, censure. G. [i.e. censuring of individuals. MS.
" priuate talkinge." Compare the Induction to The Knight of the
Burning Pestle :
> " Fly from hence
> All private taxes ! " &c.

Beaumont and Fletcher's Works, ii., 136, ed. Dyce. D.]

Which taxeth,[5] under a peculiar name,[6]
A generall vice, which merits publick blame.

OF A GULL. 2.

Oft in my laughing rimes, I name a Gull :
But this·new terme will many questions breed ;
Therefore at first I will expresse [7] at full,
Who is a true and perfect Gull indeed :
A Gull is he who feares a veluet gowne,
And, when a wench is braue,[8] dares not speak to her ;
A Gull is he which trauerseth the towne,
And is for marriage known a common woer ;
A Gull is he which while he proudly weares,
A siluer-hilted rapier by his side ;
Indures the lyes and knocks about the eares,
Whilst in his sheath his sleeping sword doth bide :
A Gull is he which weares good handsome cloaths,
And stands, in Presence, stroaking up his haire,
·And fills up his unperfect speech with oaths,
But speaks not one wise word throughout the yeare :

---

[5] MS. "carrieth." G.   [6] Other editions "particular" : and so
MS. G.
[7] MS. "Wherefore . . . . disclose." D.   [8] ' Fine, richly dressed.' D.

But to define a Gull in termes precise,—
A Gull is he which seemes, and is not wise.[9]

[9] In our Introductory-Note it is stated that the original edition of
the 'Epigrams' is undated. From contemporary allusions the
date is determined to have been prior to 1598. Among these allusions is an ' Epigram ' by E. Guilpin in his ' Skialetheia ' [1598]
on the same subject with this by Davies. It follows here:

TO CANDIDUS [EPIGRAM.] 20.

" Friend Candidus, thou often doost demaund
What humours men by gulling understand :
Our English Martiall hath full pleasantly,
In his close nips describde a gull to thee :
I'le follow him, and set downe my conceit
What a gull is: oh word of much receit !
He is a gull, whose indiscretion
Cracks his purse strings to be in fashion ;
He is a gull, who is long in taking roote
In baraine soyle, where can be but small fruite :
He is a gull, who runnes himselfe in debt,
For twelue dayes wonder, hoping so to get ;
He is a gull, whose conscience is a block,
Not to take interest, but wastes his stock :
He is a gull, who cannot haue a whore,
But brags how much he spends upon her score :
He is a gull, that for commoditie
Payes tenne times ten, and sells the same for three :
He is a gull, who passing finicall,
Peiseth each word to be rhetoricall :
And to conclude, who selfe conceitedly,
Thinkes al men guls : ther's none more gull then he." G.

In Ruffum. 3.

Rufus the Courtier at the theater,

Leaving the best and most conspicuous place,

Doth either to the stage[1] himselfe transferre,

Or through a grate[2] doth shew his double[3] face :

For that the clamorous fry of Innes of Court,

Fills up the priuate roomes of greater price :

And such a place where all may haue resort,

He in his singularity doth dispise.

Yet doth not his particular humour shun

The common stews and brothells of the towne,

Though all the world in troops doe hither[4] run,

Cleane and uncleane, the gentle and the clowne :

    Then why should Rufus in his pride abhorre,

    A common seate, that loues a common whore.

In Quintum. 4.

Quintus the dancer useth euermore,

His feet in measure and in rule to moue :

---

[1] See Note on Epigram 28. G.

[2] Malone has cited this passage (Shakespeare by Boswell iii. 81) and, if he explains it rightly, the allusion is to one of the two boxes (sometimes called *priuate boxes)* which were situated on each side of the balcony or upper stage. D.

[3] Other editions (as the Isham) ' doubtfull.' G .

[4] Other editions (as the Isham) ' thither.' G.

Yet on a time he call'd his Mistresse, ' whore '
And thought[5] with that sweet word to win her loue :
  Oh had his tongue like to his feet beene taught
  It neuer would haue uttered such a thought.

IN PLURIMOS.[6] 5.

Faustinus, Sextus, Cinnæ, Ponticus,
With Gella, Lesbia, Thais, Rhodope,
Rode all to Stanes[7] for no cause serious,
But for their mirth, and for their leachery :
Scarce were they setled in their lodging, when
Wenches with wenches, men with men fell out :
Men with their wenches, wenches with their men ;
Which straight dissolues[8] their ill-assembled rout.[9]
But since the Deuill brought them thus together,
To my discovrsing[1] thoughts it is a wonder,
Why presently as soone as they came thither,
The selfe same deuill did them part asunder.
  Doubtlesse it seemes it was a foolish deuill,
  That thus did[2] part them e're they did some euill.

<hr>

[5] MS. " Thinkinge." D.   [6] MS. " In meritriculas [*sic*]
Londinensis." D.
[7] MS. " Ware." D. [8] MS. " dissolv'd." D.
[9] " Rabble, set." D.   [1] MS. " discerninge." D.
[2] MS. " straight would." D. Isham ' thus would.' G.

Titas, the braue and valorous[4] young gallant,
Three yeares together in this towne hath beene ;
Yet my Lord Chancellor's tombe[5] he hath not seene
Nor the new water-worke,[6] nor the Elephant.[7]
    I cannot tell the cause without a smile,—
    He hath beene in the Counter[8] all this while.

In Faustum. 7.

Faustus, nor lord, nor knight, nor wise, nor old,
To euery place about the towne doth ride ;
He rides into the fields, Playes to behold,
    He rides to take boat at the water side :

---

[3] Mr. Dyce corrects (as Isham) to ' Titum ' and line 1st 'Titus.' G.

[4] MS. " Valient." G.

[5] Viz., of Sir Christopher Hatton, whose huge and splendid mon-umental-tomb was long one of the London sights for country cousins. Col. Cunningham *(in loco)* adds " It was erected in St. Paul's Cathedral, and Bishop Corbet says was " higher than the host and altar." G.

[6] Recently described by Smiles in his Lives of the Engineers. *s. v.* G.

[7] It is curious to find the article *' the '* Elephant. Coriat later gave his own portrait showing himself on the back of an elephant, as a great wonder, in one of his travel title-pages. But query—Is it the famous inn named by Shakespeare : " I could not find him at

He rides to Pauls',[9] he rides to th' Ordinary
He rides unto the house of bawdery too,—
Thither his horse doth him so often carry,
That shortly he will quite forget to goe.

In Katum.[1] 8.

Kate being pleas'd wisht that her pleasure could
Indure as long as a buffe-jerkin would :
Content thee, Kate ; although thy pleasure wasteth,
Thy pleasure's place like a buffe-jerkin lasteth,

---

the Elephant " (Twelfth Night, iv. 3) ?   Col. Cunningham (as before) assuming it is the animal that is meant, annotates thus : " The Elephant was an object of great wonder and long remembered. A curious illustration of this is found in *The Metamorphosis of the Walnut Tree*, written about 1645, where the poet [William Basse] brings trees of all descriptions to the funeral, particularly a gigantic oak—

> The youth of these our tymes that did behold
>   This motion strange of this unwieldy plant,
> Now boldly brag with us that are more old,
>   That of our age they no advantage want,
>   Though *in our youth we saw an elephant.* G.

[8] Debtors' prison. G.

[9] Other editions " Powles," and Isham ' Poules.' G.   MS. " Powels." D.

[1] Mr. Dyce reads ' Katam ' : being feminine the poet is here put right. G.

For no buffe-jerkin hath beene oftner worne,
Nor hath more scrapings or more dressings borne.

In Librum. 9.

Liber doth vaunt how chastly he hath liu'd,
Since he hath bin seuen yeares in towne, and more,[2]
For that he sweares he hath four onely swiude ;[3]
A maid, a wife, a widdow, and a whore :
    Then, Liber, thou hast swiude all women-kinde,
    For a fifth sort, I know thou canst not finde.

In Medontem. 10.

Great captaine Maedon weares a chaine of gold,
Which at fiue hundred crownes is valuèd ;
For that it was his grand sire's chaine of old,
When great King Henry, Bulloigne conquerèd.
And weare it Mædon, for it may ensue,
That thou, by vertue of this [4] massie chaine,
A stronger towne than Bulloigne maist subdue,
If wise men's sawes be not reputed vaine ;

---

[2] MS. "Knowne this towne 7 years." Isham "he hath beene in towne 7 yeeres." G.
[3] 'Swiude' from Isham : other editions ——. G.
[4] MS. "wearing of that." D.

For what said Philip king of Macedon?
There is no castle so well fortified,
    But if an asse laden with gold comes on,
    The guard will stoope, and gates flye open wide.

In Gellam. 11.

Gella, if thou dost loue thy selfe, take heed,
Lest thou my rimes [5] unto thy louer read;
    For straight thou grin'st, and then thy louer seeth
Thy canker-eaten gums and rotten teeth.

In Quintum. 12.

Quintus his wit [6] infused into his braine,
Mislikes [7] the place, and fled into his feet;
And there it wandered [8] up and downe the street,
Dabled in the dirt, and soakèd in the raine:
    Doubtlesse his wit intends not to aspire,
    Which leaues his head, to travell in the mire.

In Severum. 13.

The Puritan Severus oft doth read
This text, that doth pronounce vain speech a sin,—

---

[5] MS. "lynes." D.

[7] Mislikt? G.

[6] = Quintus's wit. G.

[8] Isham 'wanders.' G.

" That thing defiles a man, that doth proceed,
From out the mouth, not that which enters in."
Hence it is,[9] that we seldome heare him sweare :
And thereof as a Pharisie he vaunts ;
But he devours more capons in one [1] yeare,
Then would suffice an hundred [2] Protestants.
And sooth, those sectaries are gluttons all,
As well the thred-bare cobler, as the knight ;
For those poore slaues which haue not wherewithall,
Feed on the rich, till they devour them quite ;
    And so, as [3] Pharoe's kine, they eate up clean,
    Those that be fat, yet still themselues be lean.

In Leucam.   14.

Leuca, in Presence once, a fart did let ;
Some laught a little ; she refus'd [4] the place ;
And mad with shame, did then [5] her gloue forget,
Which she return'd to fetch with bashfull grace ;

---

[9] Isham ' Hence is it.'   G.   [1] Isham ' a.'   G.
[2] Isham ' a hundreth.'   G.   [3] Isham ' like.'   G.
[4] Isham ' forsook.'   G.
[5] Isham ' eke.'   G.

And when she would haue said, " I've lost my gloue," [6]
My fart (qd. she :) which did more laughter moue.

In Macrum. 15.

Thou canst not speake yet, Macer, for to speake,
Is to distinguish sounds significant :
Thou with harsh noise the ayre dost rudely breake ;
But what thou utterest common sence doth want,—
Halfe English words, with fustian termes among
Much like the burthen of a Northerne song.

In Fastum.[7] 16.

" That youth," saith Faustus, "hath a lyon seene,
Who from a dicing-house comes money-lesse " :

[6] Mr. Dyce says here "something has dropt out," the line being
a foot short, I have supplied ' I've lost.' G.

[7] *Sic*, but should be Faustum (1st line) and is so given by Mr.
Dyce and Isham. G.

But when he lost his haire, where had he beene?
I doubt me he had seene a Lyonesse?

In Cosmum.   17.

Cosmus hath more discoursing in his head
Then Ioue, when Pallas issued from his braine;
And still he strives to be delivered
Of all his thoughts at once, but all in vaine;
For, as we see at all the play-house doores,
When ended is the play, the dance, and song,
A thousand townesmen, gentlemen, and whores,
Porters and serving-men, together throng,—
So thoughts of drinking, thriuing, wenching, warre,
And borrowing money, raging,[8] in his mind;
 To issue all at once so forward are,
 As none at all can perfect passage find.

In Flaccum.   18.

The false knave Flaccus once a bribe I gaue:
 The more foole I to bribe so false a knaue:
 But he gaue back my bribe; the more foole he,
 That for my folly did not cousen me.

---

[8] MS. "ranging."   G.

In Cineam. 19.

Thou doggèd Cineas, hated like a dogge,
For still thou grumblest like a masty [9] dogge,
Compar'st thyself to nothing but a dogge ;
Thou saith [1] thou art as weary as a dogge,
As angry, sicke, and hungry as a dogge,
As dull and melancholly as a dogge,
As lazy, sleepy,[2] idle as a dogge :
But why dost thou compare thee to a dogge
In that, for which all men despise a dogge ?
I will compare thee better to a dogge :
Thou art as faire and comely as a dogge,
Thou art as true and honest as a dogge,
Thou art as kind and liberall as a dogge,
Thou art as wise and valiant as a dogge.
But Cineas, I have [often] [3] heard thee tell,
Thou art as like thy father as may be ;
   'Tis like enough ; and faith I like it well ;
   But I am glad thou art not like to me.

---

[9] Mastiff. D. [This is an error. A 'mastiff' is not a grumbling dog, and 'masty' is = fatted, and here answers apparently to the over-fed vicious pet. See *Maste*, Prompt. Parv. & p. 151 (Way's ed.) G.   [1] Isham 'saist.' G.

[2] 'And as' not in Isham. and being superfluous left out. G.

[3] Supplied from MS. by Mr. Dyce. Isham 'oft.' G.

In Gerontem. 20.

Geron's[4] mouldy memory corrects

Old Holinshed, our famous Chronicler,

With morall rules; and policy collects

Out of all actions done these fourscore yeare;[5]

Accounts the times of euery old [6] event,

Not from Christ's birth, nor from the Prince's raigne,

But from some other famous accident,

Which in mens generall notice doth remaine,—

The siege of Bulloigne and the Plaguy Sweat,

The going to St. Quintin's and New-haven,

The rising in the North, the Frost so great

That cart-wheeles' prints on Thamis face were graven,[7]

The fall of money, and burning of Paul's steeple;

The blazing starre, and Spaniard's ouerthrow:

By these events, notorious to the people,

He measures times, and things forepast doth show:

---

[4] MS. 'Geron, his.' D. Isham 'Geron whose.' G.

[5] Isham corrects the misprint 'yeares,' and of 'time ' in next line. G.   [6] Isham 'odde.' G.

[7] The reading in our text, and in all the editions, including Isham, is 'seene': but above from MS, as rhyming with New-haven seems preferable. Newhaven was formerly called Havre Grace. All the date-events are commonplaces of History. G.

But most of all, he chiefly reckons by

A priuate chance,—the death of his curst [8] wife ;

This is to him the dearest memory,

And the happiest accident of all his life.

IN MARCUM. 21.

When Marcus comes from Minnes,[9] hee still doth
   sweare,

By "come on[1] seauen," that all is lost and gone ;

But that's not true ; for he hath lost his haire,—

Onely for that he came too much at one.

IN CIPRUM.[2] 22.

The fine youth Ciprius is more tierse and neate,

Then the new garden of the Old Temple is ;

[8] Ill-natured. D. [This is a good-natured explanation. I fear that in this place it means more and worse, though in the Taming of the Shrew we have Kate the curst, without the slightest imputation on her moral character, or any allusion to anything but her vixen temper. G.]

[9] MS. "for newes."—The first edition [and Isham] reads 'from Mins' : the other two as above. Mins' (which perhaps should be written Min's) is, I presume, the name of some person who kept an Ordinary where gaming was practised. D.   [1] Isham 'a.' G.

[2] Sic : but should be, as Isham, Ciprium; Mr. Dyce reads Cyprium. G.

And still the newest fashion he doth get,
And with the time doth change from that to this;
He weares a hat of the flat-crowne block,
The treble ruffes, long cloake, and doublet French;
He takes tobacco, and doth weare a lock,
And wastes more time in dressing then a wench:

 Yet this new fangled youth, made for these times,
 Doth aboue all praise old George Gascoine's[3] rimes?

In Cineam. 23.

When Cineas comes amongst his friends in morning,
He slyly spies[4] who first his cap doth moue;
Him he salutes, the rest so grimly scorning,
As if for euer they had lost his loue.
I seeing[5] how it doth the humour fit
Of this fond[6] gull to be saluted first,
Catch at my cap, but moue it not a whit:
Which to[7] perceiuing, he seemes for spite to burst:

---

[3] Died October 7th, 1577.   His Works have been worthily collected by Mr. W. C. Hazlitt in his Roxburghe Library.   G.

[4] MS. "notes."   D.   [first edition and Isham "lookes": others as *above*.   G.]

[5] In first edition and Isham " Knowing " and MS.   G.

[6] Foolish.   G.

[7] Dyce's text is ' he': but ' to ' is often in Davies' time printed for 'too.'   Isham ' Which perceiuing.'   G.

But Cineas, why expect you more of me,
Then I of you ? I am as good a man,
And better too by many a quality,
For vault, and dance, and fence and rime I can :
  You keep a whore at your own charge, men tell me,
  Indeed friend (Cineas) therein you excell me.

In Gallum. 24.

Gallas hath beene this Summer-time in Friesland,
And now return'd, he speaks such warlike words,
As, if I could their English understand,
I feare me they would cut my throat like swords :
He talkes of counter-scarfes [8] and casomates,
Of parapets, of curteneys, and palizadoes ;
Of flankers, ravelings, gabions he prates,
And of false-brayes,[9] and sallies [1] and scaladoes.

---

[8] Isham ' scarphes.' G.

[9] Isham ' false brayes.' In this place I have restored the reading
' false-brayes ' of the 1st edition and of the MS, rejecting ' false-
baits ' of 2nd and 3rd editions. There is no such word in military
engineering or fortification ; but there is ' fausse-braye ' or ' false-
braye.' There is a not very intelligible description in Bailey's
Dictionary. G.

[1] With this passage compare the following lines :
    " See Captaine Martio he i' th' ' Renounce me ' band,
    That in the middle region doth stand

But, to requite such gulling tearmes as these,
With words of my profession I reply;
I tell of fourching,[2] vouchers, and counterpleas,
Of withermans,[3] essoynes, and Champarty.
    So, neither of us understanding [4] one another,
    We part as wise as when we came together.

In Decium. 25.

Audacious painters have Nine Worthies made;
But poet Decius,[5] more audacious farre,
Making his mistris march with men of warre,

> Wo' th' reputation steele ! Faith, lets remoue
> Into his ranke (of such discourse you loue) :
> Hee'l tell of basilisks, trenches, retires,
> Of pallizadoes, parapets, frontires,
> Of caluerins, and baricadoes too.
> What to bee harquebazerd, to lie in perdue," &c.

Fitzgeoffrey's *Notes from Black-Friars'* Sig. E 7, a portion of the
volume entitled *Certain Elegies,* &c., ed. 1620. See our Memorial-
Introduction for an impudent appropriation of this epigram. G.

    [2] MS. "forginge." D. Isham 'foorching.' G.

    [3] Other editions and MS. "Withernams": Isham 'whither
names.' G.

    [4] Isham 'vnderstanding either.' G.

    [5] Drayton is here meant. [Malone's Manuscript-note in Bodleian
copy. G.]

With title of "Tenth Worthy"[6] doth her lade.[7]

Me thinks that gull did use his tearmes as fit,

Which tearm'd his loue "a gyant for her wit."

[6] [Ben] Jonson told Drummond "That S[ir] J[ohn] Davies played in ane Epigrame on Drayton's, who in a sonnet, concluded his Mistress might [have] been the Ninth [Tenth] Worthy; and said, he used a phrase like Dametas in [Sir Philip Sidney's] Arcadia, who said For wit his Mistresse might be a gyant." 'Notes of Ben Jonson's conversations with William Drummond, of Hawthornden,' p. 15 (Shakespere Society). The sonnet by Drayton, which our author here ridicules, is as follows :

"TO THE CELESTIALL NUMBERS.

"Vnto the World, to Learning, and to Heauen,
Three Nines there are, to euery one a Nine,
One Number of the Earth, the other both Diuine;
One Woman now makes three odde numbers euen :
Nine Orders first of Angels be in Heauen,
Nine Muses doe with Learning still frequent,
These with the Gods are euer Resident ;
Nine Worthy Ones vnto the World were giuen :
My Worthy One to these Nine Worthies addeth,
And my faire Muse one Muse vnto the Nine,
And my good Angell (in my soule Diuine)
With one more Order these Nine Orders gladdeth :
My Muse, my Worthy, and my Angell, then,
Makes euery one of these three Nines a Ten."

[7] Isham reads badly 'woorthly.' 'Laide.' G. *Idea* : Sonnet 18 ed. 8vo. n. d. D.

In Gellam. 26.

If Gella's beauty be examinèd,
She hath a dull, dead eye, a saddle nose,
And[8] ill-shap't face, with morphew ouer-spread,
And rotten teeth, which she in laughing shows ;
Briefly, she is the filthiest wench in towne,
Of all that doe the art of whoring use :
But when she hath put on her sattin gowne,
Her cut[9] lawne apron, and her velvet shooes,
Her greene silke stockins and her petticoat
Of taffaty, with golden fringe a-round,
And is withall perfumed with civet hot,[1]
Which doth her valiant stinking breath confound,—
    Yet she with these additions is no more
    Than a sweet, filthy, fine, ill-favoured[2] whore.

---

[8] The other editions, as Isham and MS., 'an.' G.

[9] MS. 'cut.' D. [This is unquestionably the right word, not 'out.' Whether 'cut-lawne apron' meant curiously shaped like "the sleeves curiously cut" of Katharine's dress : or whether it was cut-wove lawn, lawn embroidered by cutting out holes and sewing them round, seems uncertain,—probably the latter. G.

[1] MS. 'sweete.' D.   [2] Isham again badly 'ilfauoted.' G.

In Syllam. 27.

Sylla is often challenged to the field,
To answer as a gentleman, his foes :
But then he doth this[3] answer onely yeeld,—
That he hath livings and faire lands to lose.
  Silla, if none but beggars valiant were,
  The King of Spaine would put us all in feare.

In Sillam. 28.

Who dares affirme that Silla dares not fight ?
When I dare sweare he dares adventure more
Than the most braue and all-daring[4] wight,[5]
That euer armes with resolution bore ;
He that dares [6] touch the most unwholsome whore
That euer was retir'd into the Spittle [7]
And dares court wenches standing at a doore,
(The portion his wit being passing little) ;

---

[3] In first edition and Isham, "then doth he this." G. [MS. "he doth all this." D.]

[4] MS. "valiant and all-daring." D. [First edition, "braue, most all daring." G.]

[5] MS. "Knight." D.   [6] Isham, 'dare.' G.

[7] Hospital : or query prison ? So late as Thomson's "Castle of Indolence" (c 1. 77) we have the word : "all the diseases which the *spittles* know." G.

He that dares give his dearest friends offences,
Which other valiant fooles doe feare to doe :
And when a feaver doth confound his sences,
Dare eate raw beefe, and drink strong wine thereto : ·
He that dares take tobacco on the stage,[8]
Dares man a whore at noone-day through the street :
Dares dance in Paul's and in this formall age,
Dares say and doe whateuer is unmeet ;
   Whom feare of shame could neuer yet affright,—
   Who dares affirme that Sylla dares not fight ?

---

[8] Probably most readers are aware that it was formerly the custom of gallants to smoke tobacco on the stage, during the performance, either lying on the rushes or sitting upon hired stools. D. [In Hutton's 'Satyres' and 'Epigrams' (1619) well edited by RIMBAULT for the Percy Society, there are various passages illustrative of above, *e.g.*

> " Dine with Duke Humfrey in decayed Paules'
> Confound the streetes with chaos of old braules,
> Dancing attendance on the Black-friers stage
> Call for a stoole with a commanding rage, &c.
>   [pp. 68, 69.] Cf.

Also Ben Jonson's *Devil is an Ass* (1616) who censures the conduct of the gallants allowed seats on the stage. G.]

Haywood, that did[1] in Epigrams excell,

Is now put downe since my light Muse arose ;

As buckets are put downe into a well,

Or as a schoole-boy putteth downe his hose.[2]

---

[9] Mr. Dyce spells Heywodum.   John Heywood's Epigrammes accompany his Proverbs : 1562.   G.

[1] 1st edition, ' which in epigrams did ;' Isham ' which did.' [The Epigrams of John Heywood are well known.   An allusion to this epigram of Davies occurs in Sir John Harington's *Metamorphosis of Ajax*, 1596: " This Heywood for his proverbs and epigrams is not yet put down by any of our country, though one [*Marginal Note*, M[aster] Davies] doth indeed come near him, that graces him the more in saying he puts him down," p. 41, edition 1814.   (In the same work we find, " But, as my good M. Davies said of his epigrams, that they were made, like doublets in Birchin-lane, for every one whom they will serve, &c. p. 133.   D.]   [I add from T. Bastard's 'Chrestoleros ' [Lib. ii : Epigram 15] an answer to this :

> Heywood goes downe saith Dauis, sikerly,
> And downe he goes, I can it not deny :
> But were I happy did not fortune frowne
> Were I in heart I would sing Dauy downe.

Cf. also lib. iii. Ep. 3.   Mr. Dyce also quotes from Freeman's *Rubbe and a great Cast*, 1614.   G.]

[2] Breeches.   D.

In Dacum.[3] 30.

Amongst the poets Dacus numbred is,
Yet could he neuer make an English rime ;
But some prose speeches I haue heard of his,
Which haue been spoken many an hundreth time :
The man that keeps the Elephant hath one,
Wherein he tells the wonders of the beast :
Another Bankes pronouncèd long agon,[4]
When he his curtailes[5] qualities exprest :
He first taught him that that keeps the monuments
At Westminster, his formall tale to say ;
And also him which Puppets represents,
And also him which with the Ape doth play :
   Though all his Poetry be like to this,
   Amongst the poets Dacus numbred is.

---

[3] This is not Decius of Epig. 25, who was Drayton, but (eheu !) Samuel Daniel. Cf. Epig. 45, and relative note. On the elephant (l. 5) see note on Epig. 6. G.

[4] Isham badly ' a goe.' G.

[5] Id est, horse's [the word means properly—a docked horse.] So much may be found in various books concerning Banks and his wonderful horse, that any account of them is unnecessary here. D. [The ' wonderful horse ' is referred to by Shakespeare. G.]

In Priscum. 31.

When Priscus, rais'd from low to high estate,
Rode through the street in pompous jollity ;
Caius, his poore familiar friend of late,
Bespake him thus : " Sir, now you know not me.'
   " 'Tis likely friend," (quoth Priscus) " to be so,
   For at this time myselfe I do not know."

In Brunum. 32.

Brunus, which deems himselfe a faire sweet youth
Is thirty nine yeares of age at least ;
Yet was he neuer, to confesse the truth,
But a dry starveling when he was at best :
This gull was sicke to shew his night-cap fine,
And his wrought pillow over-spread with lawne ;
   But hath been well since his griefe's cause hath line [6]
   At Trollup's by Saint Clement's Church, in pawne.

In Francum. 33.

When Francus comes to sollace with his whore,
He sends for rods, and strips himselfe stark naked ;
For his lust sleeps and will not rise before,
By whipping of the wench it be awakèd.

---

[6] Lien, lain. D.

I enuie him not, but wish I had the powre
To make myselfe[7] his wench but one halfe houre.

In Castorem. 34.

Of speaking well why doe we learne the skill,
Hoping thereby honour and wealth to gaine ;
    Sith rayling Castor doth, by speaking ill,
    Opinion of much wit and gold obtaine?

In Septimium. 35.

Septimus liues, and is like garlick scene,
For though his head be white, his blade is greene :
    This old mad coult deserves a Martyr's praise,
    For he was burnèd in Queene Marie's daies.

Of Tobacco. 36.

Homer, of Moly and Nepenthe sings :
Moly, the gods' most soueraigne hearb diuine,
Nepenthe, Heauen's[8] drinke, most[9] gladnesse brings,

    Col. Cunningham emends 'himself' for 'myself'; but the
'whipping of' (l. 4) is = by: and Davies' wish is that he wielded
the rods on Francus. G.
    [8] Mr. Dyce reads ' Helen's ' and confirms from Milton's Comus
(1675)—

Heart's griefe expells, and doth the wits refine.
But this our age another world hath found,
From whence an hearb of heauenly power is brought;
Moly is not so soueraigne for a wound,
Nor hath Nepenthe so great wonders wrought :[1]
It is Tobacco, whose sweet substantiall[2] fume
The hellish torment of the teeth doth ease,
By drawing downe, and drying up the rheume,
The mother and the nurse of each disease :
It is Tobacco, which doth cold expell,

Not that Nepenthes, which the wife of Thone
In Egypt gave to Jove-born Helena, &c.

In first edition there is a misprint " Hekens " : in the other editions,
as *above* " Heauens" : in MS. "helvs " : Isham ' Heuens.' Helen
is admissible, but ' Heavens ' what Davies himself printed. See
the poem on Tobacco among the hitherto unpublished poems, of
which the Epigram seems only a first rough draft—and relative
note.

⁹ Isham ' which.' G.   ¹ Isham badly ' brought.' G.

² MS. 'subtle.' D. [Substantial is here = partaking of the
substance or essence, or, as we say, properties peculiar to tobacco—
a fume holding in it the virtues or substance of the tobacco. The
MS. 'subtle' may be regarded as an Author's variant, especially as
it is also found in ' Tobacco ' among the hitherto unpublished
poems, onward. G.

And cleares the obstructions of the arteries,
And surfeits, threatning death, dijesteth well,
Decocting all the stomack's crudities :
It is Tobacco, which hath power to clarifie
The cloudy mists before dimme eyes appearing :
It is Tobacco, which hath power to rarifie
The thick grosse humour which doth stop the hearing ;
The wasting hectick, and the quartaine feuer,
Which doth of Physick make a mockery ;
The gout it cures, and helps ill breaths for euer,
Whether the cause in teeth or stomack be ;
And though ill breaths were by it but confounded,
Yet that vile medicine it doth farre excell,
Which by Sir Thomas Moore[3] hath beene propounded :

---

[3] Mr. Dyce quotes an ' Epigramma ' of Sir Thomas More, which,
is headed

"*Medicinæ ad tollendos fœtores, anhelitus, provenientes a cibis
quibusdam.*"

"Sectile ne tetros porrum tibi spiret odores,
  Protenus a porro fac mihi cepe vores.
Denuo fœtorem si vis depellere cepæ,
  Hoc facile efficient allia mansa tibi.
Spiritus at si post etiam gravis allia restat,
  Aut nihil, aut tantum tollere *merda* potest."
      T. Mori Lucubrationes, &c., p. 261, edition 1563. G.

For this is thought a gentleman-like smell.

O, that I were one of those Mountebankes,

Which praise their oyles and powders which they sell !

My customers would giue me coyne with thanks;

I for this ware, for sooth [4] a tale would tell :

Yet would I use none of these tearmes before;

I would but say, that it the Pox will cure :

This were enough, without discoursing more,

All our braue gallants in the towne t'allure,

In Crassum. 37.

Crassus his lyes,[5] are not pernicious lyes,

But pleasant fictions, hurtfull unto none

But to himselfe; for no man counts him wise

To tell for truth that which for false is knowne.

He sweares that Gaunt is three score miles about,

And that the bridge at Paris on the Seyn

Is of such thicknesse, length and breadth throughout,

That sixe score Arches can it scarce sustaine ;

He sweares he saw so great a dead man's scull

At Canterbury, dig'd out of the ground,

That would containe of wheat three bushels full;

And that in Kent are twenty yeomen found,

---

[4] Isham 'so smooth.' G.   [5] That is, Crassus's lies. G.

Of which the poorest euery yeare dispends,
Fiue thousand pounds : these and fiue thousand mo,
So oft he hath recited to his friends,
That now himselfe perswades himselfe 'tis so.
But why doth Crassus tell his lyes so rife,
Of Bridges, Townes, and things that haue no life?
   He is a Lawyer, and doth well espie,
   That for such lyes an Action will not lye.

IN PHILONEM.   38.

Philo the Lawyer[6] and the Fortune-teller;
The Schoole-master, the Midwife, and the Bawd,
The conjurer, the buyer, and the seller
Of painting, which with breathing will be thaw'd,
Doth practise Physicke ; and his credit growes,
As doth the Ballad-singer's auditory,[7]
Which hath at Temple-barre his standing chose,
And to the vulgar sings an Ale-house story :
First stands a Porter ; then an Oyster-wife
Doth stint her cry, and stay her steps to heare him ;

---

⁶ Isham ' Gentleman.'   G.

⁷ See our Memorial-Introduction with reference to Wordsworth's
splendid filling up of this earlier sketch.   G.

Then comes a Cut-purse ready with a[8] knife,
And then a Countrey clyent passeth neare him ;
There stands the Constable, there stands the whore,
And, listening[9] to the song, heed[1] not each other ;
There by the Serjeant stands the debitor,[2]
And doth no more mistrust him then his brother :
Thus Orpheus to such hearers giueth musick,
And Philo to such patients giueth physick.

In Fuscum. 39.

Fuscus is free, and hath the world at will ;
Yet in the course of life that he doth lead,
He's like a horse which, turning round a mill,
Doth always in the self-same circle tread :
First, he doth rise at ten ; and at eleuen
He goes to Gyls,[3] where he doth eate till one ;
Then sees a Play till sixe, and sups at seven ;
And after supper, straight to bed is gone ;
And there till ten next day he doth remaine,
And then he dines, and[4] sees a Comedy ;

---

[8] Isham ' his.' G.   [9] Isham ' hearkening.' G.
[1] 1st edition and Isham, ' marke.' G. [2] Isham 'debter poore.' G.
[3] No doubt some Ordinary near St. Giles, Cripplegate. Isham
' Gilles.' G.   [4] Isham ' then.' G.

And then he suppes, and goes to bed againe :
Thus round he runs without variety,
   Saue that sometimes he comes not to the Play,
   But falls into a whore-house by the way.

In Afram. 40.

The smell-feast Afer, trauailes to the Burse[5]
Twice euery day, the newest[6] newes to heare ;
Which, when he hath no money in his purse,
To rich mens tables he doth often beare :
He tells how Gronigen[7] is taken in,[8]
By the braue conduct of illustrious Vere,[9]
And how the Spanish forces Brest would win,
But that they doe victorious Norris feare.
No sooner is a ship at sea surpris'd,
But straight he learnes the news, and doth disclose it :

---

[5] Bourse,=Exchange. G.   [6] 1st edition and Isham and MS.
'flying.' G.   [7] Groningen. G.

   [8] Conquered and added to or 'taken in' with other conquests. G.

   [9] To the truly 'illustrious' VERE—one of the noblest of England's
earlier generals—DR. RICHARD SIBBES dedicated his 'Soul's Con-
flict' in very loving words to him and his Lady. See my edition of
SIBBES *in loco.* G.

No sooner hath the Turk a plot deuis'd
To conquer[1] Christendom, but straight he knows it :[2]
Faire written in a scrowle he hath the names
Of all the widdows which the Plague hath made ;
And persons, times, and places still he frames,
To euery tale, the better to perswade :
We call him Fame, for that the wide-mouth slaue
Will eate as fast as he will utter lies ;

 For Fame is said an hundred mouths to haue,
 And he eates more than would fiue score suffice.

In Paulum. 41.

By lawfull mart, and by unlawfull stealth,
Paulus in spite of enuy, fortunate,
Deriues out of the Ocean so much wealth,
As he may well maintaine a lord's estate ;
 But on the land a little gulfe there is,
 Wherein he drowneth all the wealth of his.

[1] Isham once more badly ' conquerie.' G.
[2] This couplet is given by Mr. Dyce from the MS. : the Isham has
it. G.

In Licum. 42.

Lycus, which lately[3] is to Venice gone,
Shall if he doe returne, gaine three for one :[4]
But ten to one, his knowledge and his wit
Will not be bettered or increas'd a whit.

In Publium. 43.

Publius [a] student at the Common-law,
Oft leaves his Bookes, and for his recreation,
To Paris-garden[5] doth himselfe withdrawe ;

---

[3] Recently : the MS. reads ' that is of late.' G.

[4] In our author's days, it was a common practice for persons, before setting out on their travels, to deposit a sum of money, on condition of receiving large interest for it on their return: if they never returned, the deposit was forfeited. Innumerable allusions to 'putters out' occur in the works published during the reigns of Elizabeth and James. D.

[5] That is, to the Bear-Garden on the Bank-side, Southwark. D. [Near the Globe Theatre: referred to as Palace garden by Hutton, as before. Isham reads badly ' parish.' The Theatre at Paris Garden stood almost exactly at what is now the Surrey starting place of Blackfriars Bridge. In 1632 Donald Lupton in his *London and the Country Carbonadoed* says of it, " Here come few that either regard their credit or loss of time ; the swaggering Roarer ; the amusing Cheater; the swearing Drunkard ; and the bloody Butcher have their rendezvous here, and are of the chiefe place and respect." (Col. Cunningham's Marlowe, p. 365). G.

Where he is rauisht with such delectation,

As downe among[6] the beares and dogges he goes ;

Where, whilst he skipping cries " to head to head,"

His satten doublet and his veluct hose[7]

Are all with spittle from aboue be-spread :

When he is like his father's countrey Hall,[8]

Stinking with dogges, and muted[9] all with haukes ;

And rightly too on him this filth doth fall,

Which for such filthy sports his bookes forsakes ;[1]

Leaving old Ployden,[2] Dyer, Brooke alone,

To see old Harry Hunkes, and Sacarson.[3]

In Sillam. 44.

When I this proposition had defended,

"A coward cannot be an honest man,"

Thou Silla, seem'st forthwith to be offended,

And holds the contrary, and sweares he can ;

---

[6] Isham ' amongst the dogges and beares.' G.   [7] Breeches.   G.

[8] Misprinted ' countrey shall ' :   Qu—country-Hall, as above ?
Isham ' country Hall.' G.   [1] Dunged. D.

[9] Isham badly ' forsake.' G.   [3] Plowden. D.

[2] Harry Hunkes and Sacarson were two bears at Paris-garden :
the latter was the more famous, and is mentioned by Shakespeare
in The Merry Wives of Windsor, Act I., sc. 1 .D. Isham ' Saker-
sone.' G.

But when I tell thee that he will forsake
His dearest friend, in perill of his life ;
Thou then art chang'd, and sayst thou didst mistake,
And so we end our argument and strife :
　Yet I think oft, and thinke I thinke aright,
　Thy argument argues thou wilt not fight.

IN DACUM.[4] 45.

Dacus with some good colour and pretence,
Tearmes his love's beauty "silent eloquence :"
　For she doth lay more colour on her face
　Than ever Tully us'd his speech to grace.

[4] Daniel, I believe: [Malone's Manuscript note in Bodlean copy.
See Epigram 30. G.]   Mr. Dyce adds here, "I am sorry
to believe that by Dacus (who is spoken of with great contempt in
Epigram xxx.) our author means Samuel Daniel : but the following
lines in that very pleasing writer's *Complaint of Rosamond* (which
was first printed in 1592) certainly would seem to be alluded to here,

"Ah beauty syren, faire enchanting good,
Sweet, silent rhetorique of perswading eyes,
Dumb eloquence, whose power doth moue the blood
More then the words or wisdom of the wise, &c.

1611, p. 39,—Daniel's *Certaine Small Works*, &c. 1611.") G.

Why dost thou, Marcus, in thy misery,
Raile and blaspheame, and call the heauens unkind?
The heauens doe owe no kindnesse unto thee,
Thou hast the heauens so little in thy minde;
  For in thy life thou neuer usest prayer
  But at primero, to encounter faire.

Meditations of a Gull. 47.

See, yonder melancholy gentleman,
Which, hood-wink'd with his hat, alone doth sit!
Thinke what he thinks, and tell me if you can,
What great affaires troubles his little wit.
He thinks not of the warre 'twixt France and Spaine,
Whether it be for Europe's good or ill,
Nor whether the Empire can itselfe maintaine
Against the Turkish power encroaching still;
Nor what great towne in all the Netherlands,
The States determine to beseige this Spring;
Nor how the Scottish policy now stands,
Nor what becomes of the Irish mutining.
But he doth seriously bethinke him whether
Of the gull'd people he be more esteem'd
For his long cloake or for his great black feather,

By which each gull is now a gallant deem'd ;
Or of a journey he deliberates,
To Paris-garden,[5] Cock-pit or the Play ;
Or how to steale a dog he meditates,
Or what he shall unto his mistriss say :
 Yet with these thoughts he thinks himself most fit
 To be of counsell with a king for wit.

AD MUSAM. 48.

Peace,[6] idle Muse, haue done ! for it is time,
Since lousie Ponticus enuies my fame,
And sweares the better sort are much to blame
To make me so well knowne for my[7] ill rime :
Yet Bankes his horse,[8] is better knowne then he.
So are the Cammels and the westerne hogge,[9]
And so is Lepidus his printed Dog :[1]

[5] See note on this under Epigram 43. G.
[6] Isham ' Pease.' G.   [7] Isham 'so.' G.
[8] See note on this under Epigram 30. G.
[9] Isham corrects ' Hay ' here with ' hogge.' G.
[1] That is ' Lepidus's printed dog.' The following epigram by Sir
John Harington determines that he is the Lepidus of this passage,
and that his favourite dog Bungey is the " printed dog." In a com-
partment of the engraved title-page to Harington's *Orlando Furioso*,

Why doth not Ponticus their fames enuie ?

Besides, this Muse of mine, and the blacke feather

1591, is a representation of Bungey (see too the Annotations on Book xli. of that poem); and hence he is termed by Davies the " printed dog."

"AGAINST MOMUS, IN PRAISE OF HIS DOG BUNGEY."

Because a witty writer of this time
Doth make some mention in a pleasant rime
Of Lepidus and of his famous dog,
Thou, Momus, that dost loue to scoffe and cog,
Prat'st amongst base companions, and giv'st out
That unto me herein is meant a flout.
Hate makes thee blind, Momus: I dare be sworn,
He meant to me his loue, to thee his scorn.
Put on thy envious spectacles, and see
Whom doth he scorn therein, the dog or me ?
The dog is grac'd, comparèd with great Banks,
Both beasts right famous for their pretty pranks ;
Although in this I grant the dog was worse,
He only fed my pleasure, not my purse :
Yet that same dog, I may say this and boast it,
He found my purse with gold when I haue [had] lost it.
Now for myself: some fooles (like thee) may judge
That at the name of Lepidus I grudge :
No sure ; so far I think it from disgrace,
I wisht it cleare to me and to my race.
Lepus, or Lepos, I in both haue part ;
That in my name I beare, this in mine heart.

Grew both together fresh[2] in estimation :

And both growne stale, were cast away together :

What fame is this that scarce lasts[3] out a fashion?

Onely this last in credit doth remaine,

That from henceforth, each bastard cast-forth rime,

Which doth but savour of a libell vaine,

Shall call me father, and be thought my crime ;

  So dull, and with so little sence endu'd,

    Is my grose-headed Judge, the multitude.

     But Momus, I perswade myself that no man

     Will deigne thee such a name, English or Roman.

       Ile wage a but of Sack, the best in Bristo,

       Who cals me Lepid, I will call him Tristo."

Epigrams, Book iii. Ep. 21. edition folio. D.

   [2] In other editions as Isham, but dropped out inadvertently from our text. G.   [3] Isham badly 'last.' G.

𝕱𝖎𝖓𝖎𝖘. I. D.

Appendix to Epigrams:

(FROM THE HARLEIAN MSS. 1836.)

As explained in the Note, page 6 *ante*, I have gleaned a few additions to these Epigrams. At close of those of HUTTON,—in the MS. marked 60 and in Hutton's own volume 56,—on folio 15*d*, is the word 'finis.' Immediately under this, the MS. is continued in the same handwriting on to folio 19, whereon 'finis' is again placed : and on folios 19 and 20 Lines 'of Tobacco' with 'finis' once more. These Lines on 'Tobacco' are curious : and somewhat resemble those on 'Moly' given in the Hitherto Unpublished Poems of Davies, onward.   G.

1.   IN SUPERBIAM.   Epi. 4.

I tooke the wall, one thrust me rudely by,
And tould me the King's way did open lye.
I thankt him y^t he did me so much grace,
to take the worse, leave me the better place ;
   For if by th' owners wee esteeme of things,
   the wall's the subjects, but the way's the King's.

2. Epi. 5.

NIX		SNOW
IX	{	9
CORNIX		A CROW.

NIX :.   I that the Winter's daughter am
       whilst thus my letters stand,
       Am whiter then the plumbe[1] of swan
       or any ladye's hand ;

IX :.   Take but away my letter first,
       and then I doe encline
       That stood before for milke white snowe
       to be the figure nine.
       And if that further you desire
       by change to doe som trickes,
       As blacke as any bird I am.

CORNIX : by adding COR to NIX.

3. Epi. 6.

Health is a jewell true, which when we buy
Physitians value it accordingly.

4. IN AMOROSUM. Epi. 7.

A wife you wisht me (sir) rich, faire and young
with French, Italian, and the Spanish tongue :

---

[1] =plumage. G.

I must confesse yor kindnesse verie much
but yet in truth, Sir, I deserve none such.
for when I wed—as yet I meane to tarry—
A woman of one language i'le but marry,
and with that little portion of her store,
expect such plenty, I would wish no more.

5. Epi. 9.

Westminster is a mill that grinds all causes, ˙ ˙
but grinde his cause for mee there, he y^t list:
For by demures and errours, stayes and clauses,
the tole is oft made greater then the grist.

6. Epi. 10.   ˒ ˙˙

He that doth aske St. James they [?] say, shall speed
O y^t Kinge James would answere to my need.

V. GULLINGE SONNETS.

NOTE.

These 'Gullinge Sonnets' were first printed in my re-production of the Dr. Farmer MS. for the Chetham Society (2 vols. 4to., 1873) in Part I. pp. 76-81. There seems no question that these Sonnets belong to Sir John Davies. Besides the " J. D." and " Mr. Dauyes" of the MS., his most marked turns of thought and epithet are readily discernible in them. See critical remarks on them and their probable *motif* in Memorial-Introduction.

The Sir Anthony Cooke to whom these Sonnets are dedicated descended from the Sir Anthony who was Pre-ceptor to King Edward VI., and for Letters from whom whoso cares may consult the " Reformation" corres-pondence of the Parker Society. His daughter Mildred was second wife of Lord Burleigh, and his daughter Anne was mother of *the* Bacon. His son and heir, Richard Cooke, died in 1579, and was succeeded by his son Anthony (this Sir Anthony), who was knighted in 1596 by the Earl of Essex at the sacking of Cadiz. He was buried at Romford, Essex, on the 28th December, 1604. G.

[Dedicatory Sonnet.]

TO HIS GOOD FREINDE S^R ANTH.
COOKE.

HERE my Camelion Muse her selfe doth chaunge
  to diuers shapes of gross absurdities,
and like an Antick[1] mocks wth fashion straunge
the fond[2] admirers of lewde gulleries.
Your iudgement sees wth pitty, and wth scorne
The bastard Sonnetts of these Rymers bace,
W^{ch} in this whiskinge age are daily borne
To their own shames, and Poetrie's disgrace.
Yet some praise those and some perhappes will praise
euen these of myne : and therefore thes I send
to you that pass in Courte yor glorious dayes ;
Y^t if some rich rash gull these Rimes commend
Thus you may sett this formall witt to schoole,
Vse yor owne grace, and begg him for a foole.

J. D.

[1] = motley-dressed jester or fool. G.   [2] = foolish. G.

Gullinge Sonnets.

1 THE Louer Vnder burthen of his M^ris love
     W^ch lyke to Ætna did his harte oppreffe:
did giue fuch piteous grones y^t he did moue
the heau'nes at length to pitty his diftreffe
but for the fates in theire highe Courte aboue
forbad to make the greuous burthen leffe.
the gracous powers did all confpire to proue
Yf miracle this mifcheife mighte redreffe;
therefore regardinge y^t ye loade was fuch
as noe man mighte wth one man's mighte fuftayne
and y^t mylde patience[3] imported much
to him that fhold indure an endles payne:
By there decree he foone transform'd was
into a patiente burden-bearinge Affe.

2 As when ye brighte Cerulian firmament
     hathe not his glory wth black cloudes defas'te,

---

[3] A trisyllable. G.

Soe were my thoughts voyde of all difcontent ;
and wth noe myfte of paffions ouercaft
they all were pure and cleare, till at the laft
an ydle carcles thoughte forthe wandringe wente
and of y^t poyfonous beauty tooke a tafte
W^{ch} doe the harts of louers fo torment :
then as it chauncethe in a flock of fheepe
when fome contagious yll breedes firft in one
daylie it fpreedes & fecretly doth creepe
till all the filly troupe be ouergone.
So by clofe neighbourhood wth in my breft
one fcuruy thoughte infecteth all the reft.

3 What Eagle can behould her funbrighte eye,
  her funbrighte eye y^t lights the world wth loue,
  the world of Loue wherein I liue and dye,
  I liue and dye and diuers chaunges proue,
  I chaunges proue, yet ftill the fame am I,
  the fame am I and neuer will remoue,
  neuer remoue vntill my foule dothe flye,
  my foule dothe fly, and I furceafe to moue,
  I ceafe to moue wch now am mou'd by you,
  am mou'd by you y^t moue all mortall hartes,
  all mortall hartes whofe eyes yor eyes doth veiwe,
  Yo^r eyes doth veiwe whence Cupid fhoots his darts,

whence Cupid fhootes his dartes and woundeth thofe
that honor you and neuer weare[4] his foes.

4 The hardnes of her harte and truth of myne
  when the all feeinge eyes of heauen did fee
  they ftreight concluded y^t by powre devine
  to other formes our hartes fhould turnèd be.
  then hers as hard as flynte, a Flynte became
  and myne as true as fteele, to fteele was turned,
  and then betwene o^r hartes fprange forthe the flame
  of kindeft loue, wch vnextinguifh'd burned ;
  And longe the facred lampe of mutuall loue
  inceffantlie did burne in glory brighte ;
  Vntill my folly did her fury moue
  to recompence my feruice wth defpighte,
  and to put out wth fnuffers of her pride
  the lampe of loue wch els had neuer dyed.

5 Myne Eye, mine eare, my will, my witt, my harte
  did fee, did heare, did like, difcerne, did loue :
  her face, her fpeche, her fafhion, iudgem^t, arte,
  wch did charme, pleafe, delighte, confounde and moue.
  Then fancie, humo^r, loue, conceipte, and thoughte
  did foe drawe, force, intyfe, perfwade, deuife,

that fhe was wonne, mou'd, caryed, compaft, wrought
to thinck me kinde, true, comelie, valyant, wife ;
that heauen, earth, hell, my folly and her pride
did worke, contriue, labor, confpire and fweare
to make me fcorn'd, vile, caft of, bace, defyed
W^th her my loue, my lighte, my life, my deare :
So that my harte, my witt, will, eare, and eye
doth greiue, lament, sorrowe, difpaire and dye.

6 The facred Mufe that firfte made loue deuine
 hath made him naked and w^thout attyre,
 but I will cloth him wth this penn of myne
 that all the world his fafhion fhall admyre.
 his hatt of hope, his bande of beautye fine,
 his cloake of crafte, his doblett of defyre,
 greife for a girdell, fhall aboute him twyne,
 his pointes of pride, his Ilet holes of yre,
 his hofe of hate, his Cod peece of conceite,
 his ftockings of fterne ftrife, his fhirte of fhame,
 his garters of vaine glorie gaye and flyte ;
 his pantofels of paffions I will frame,
 pumpes[5] of prefumption fhall adorne his feete
 and Socks of fullennes excedinge fweete.

---

[5] = slipper-shoes. G.

7 Into thc midle Temple of my harte
the wanton Cupid did himfelfe admitt
and gaue for pledge yor Eagle-fighted witt
Y^t he wold play noc rude vncivill parte :
Longe tyme he cloak'tc his nature wth his artc
and fadd and grauc and fober he did fitt,
but at the laſt he gan to reuell it,
to breake good rules, and orders to peruerte :
Then loue and his younge plcdge were both conuented
before fadd^6 Reafon, that old Bencher grauc,
who this fadd fentence vnto him prefented
by dilligence, y^t ſlye and fecreate knauc
That loue and witt, for cuer ſhold departe
out of the midle Temple of my harte.

8 My cafe is this, I louc Zepheria brighte,
Of her I hold my hartc by fealtyc :
W^ch I difcharge to her perpetuallyc,
Yet ſhe thereof will neuer me accquite.
for now fuppofinge I wth hold her righte
ſhe hathe diftreinde my harte to fatisfie

---

⁶ = serious; and so 'sadly'=seriously, e. g. Skelton :
      " I have not offended, I trust,
        If it be *sadly* discust." G.

the duty wch I neuer did denye,
and far away impounds it wth defpite ;
I labor therefore iuftlie to repleaue⁷
my harte wch fhe vniuftly doth impounde
but quick conceite wch nowe is loue's highe Sheife
retornes it as efloynde, not to be founde :
Then wch the lawe affords I onely craue
her harte for myne in wit her name to haue.

9 To Loue my lord I doe knightes feruice owe
and therefore nowe he hath my witt in warde,
but while it is in his tuition foe
me thincks he doth intreate it paffinge hard ;
for thoughe he hathe it marryed longe agoe
to Vanytie, a wench of noe regarde,
and nowe to full, and perfect age doth growe,
Yet nowe of freedome it is moft debarde.
But why fhould loue after minoritye
when I am paft the one and twentith yeare
perclude my witt of his fweete libertye,
and make it ftill y^e yoake of wardfhippe beare.
I feare he hath an other Title gott
and holds my witte now for an Ideott.

Mr Dauyes.

⁷ = recover (a legal term)   G.

VI. MINOR POEMS.

Minor Poems.

I. *Yet other Twelve Wonders of the World.*[1]

I. *The Courtier.*

LONG haue I liu'd in Court, yet learn'd not all this
    while,
To sel poore sutors, smoke : nor where I hate, to smile :
Superiors to adore, Inferiors to despise,
To flye from such as fall, to follow such as rise ;
To cloake a poore desire vnder a rich array,
Not to aspire by vice, though twere the quicker way.

---

[1] This and the three following, are from the celebrated collection of early English poetry called the ' Poetical Rhapsody ' by Davison. Our text is from the third edition (1621) which in our case is preferable, as having presumably been revised (in his contributions) by Sir John : It is to be noted that in this edition the original simple I. D. is in the second poem changed to Sir I. D., and that to the third his name is given in full. I have included the Hymn on Music, though the initials I. D. have been assigned to Dr. John Donne by Sir Egerton Brydges and others. It seems to me that as (1) I. D. is our Poet's designation in the 'Rhapsody' throughout, and as (2) the

II. *The Divine.*

My calling is Diuine, and I from God am sent,
I will no chop-Church be, nor pay my patron rent,
Nor yeeld to sacriledge ; but like the kind true mother,
Rather will loose all the child, then part it with another;
Much wealth, I will not seeke, nor worldly masters serue,
So to grow rich and fat, while my poore flock doth sterue.

Lines were not claimed for Donne by himself, or by his son when he collected his father's Poems—we are warranted in assigning them to Sir John Davies. Sir Egerton favours their Donne authorship simply because " they seem rather to partake of the conceits of Donne than of the simple vigour of Davies " but he forgot the ' Hymnes to Astræa ' and ' Orchestra '; which are in the same vein. It is to be regretted that Sir Nicholas Harris Nicolas *modernized* the text in his reprint of the 'Rhapsody' : (2 vols. crown 8vo. 1826, Pickering): and perhaps equally so, that Mr. Collier in his careful and beautiful private one, has selected the first incomplete edition. The following is the title-page of the edition of the 'Rhapsody' used by us:

DAVISONS

POEMS,

OR

A POETICALL RAPSODIE.

Deuided into sixe Bookes.

The first, *contayning Poems and Deuises.*
The second, *Sonets and Canzonets.*
The third, *Pastoralls and Elegies.*
The fourth, *Madrigalls and Odes.*

III. *The Souldier.*

My occupation is, the noble trade of Kings,
The tryall that decides the highest right of things :
Though *Mars* my master be, I doe not *Venus* loue,
Nor honour *Bacchus* oft, nor often sweare by *Ioue ;*
Of speaking of my selfe, I all occasion shunne,
And rather loue to doe, then boast what I haue done.

III. *The Lawyer.*

The Law my calling is, my robe, my tongue, my pen,
Wealth and opinion gaine, and make me Iudge of men.
The knowne dishonest cause, I neuer did defend,
Nor spun out sutes in length, but wisht and sought an end :

The fift, *Epigrams and Epitaphs.*
The sixt, *Epistles and Epithalamions.*

For variety and pleasure, the like neuer
published.
The Bee and Spider by a diuers power,
Sucke hony and poyson from the selfe same flower.
The fourth Impression,
Newly corrected and augmented, and put into
a forme more pleasing to the Reader.
London,
Printed by B. A. for *Roger Iackson,* 1621 (small 12°.) See our
Preface for account of an autograph MS. of "Yet other Twelve Won-
ders of the World." G.

Nor counsell did bewray, nor of both parties take,
Nor euer tooke I fee for which I neuer spake.

V. *The Physition.*

I study to vphold the slippery state of man,
Who dies, when we haue done the best and all we can.
From practise and from bookes, I draw my learnèd skill,
Not from the knowne receipt of 'Pothecaries bill.
The earth my faults doth hide,[2] the world my cures doth
    see,
What youth, and time effects, is oft ascribde to me.

VI. *The Merchant.*

My trade doth euery thing to euery land supply,
Discouer vnknowne coasts, strange Countries to ally;
I neuer did forestall, I neuer did ingrosse,
No custome did withdraw, though I return'd with losse.
I thriue by faire exchange, by selling and by buying,
And not by Iewish vse,[3] reprisall, fraud, or lying.

---

[2] 'The earth my faults doth hide.' This recalls the somewhat irate remonstrance of a bibulous Sexton under the reproaches of a medical church-warden at a parish-meeting: "O Sir, *you* are the last that ever I expected to expose me, seeing I have covered up many of your faults" (i.e. in the graves of his patients.) G.

[3] =usury. G.

VII. *The Country Gentleman.*

Though strange outlādish spirits praise towns, and
    country scorn,
The country is my home, I dwel where I was born :
There profit and command with pleasure I pertake,
Yet do not Haukes and dogs, my sole companions make.
I rule, but not oppresse, end quarrels, not maintaine ;
See towns, but dwel not there, t'abridge my charg or train.

VIII. *The Bacheler.*

How many things as yet are deere alike to me,
The field, the horse, the dog, loue, armes or liberty.
I haue no wife as yet, whom I may call mine owne,
I haue no children yet, that by my name are knowne.
Yet if I married were, I would not wish to thriue,
If that I could not tame the veriest shrew aliue.

IX. *The Married Man.*

I only am the man, among all married men,
That do not wish the Priest, to be unlinckt agen.
And thogh my shoo did wring,[4] I wold not make my mone,
Nor think my neighbors chance, more happy then mine
    own,

---

[4] = pinch. G.

Yet court I not my wife, but yeeld obseruance due,
Being neither fond[5] nor crosse, nor iealous, nor vntrue.

X. *The Wife.*

The first of all our Sex came from the side of man,
I thither am return'd, from whence our Sex began ;
I doe not visite oft, nor many, when I doe,
I tell my mind to few, and that in counsell too :
I seeme not sick in health, nor sullen but in sorrow,
I care for somewhat else of, then what to weare to morrow.

XI. *The Widdow.*

My dying [6] husband knew, how much his death would
       grieue me,
And therefore left me wealth, to comfort and relieue me.
Though I no more will haue, I must not loue disdaine,
Penelope her selfe did sutors entertaine ;
And yet to draw on such, as are of best esteeme,
Nor yonger then I am, nor richer will I seeme.

---

[5] = foolish. G.
[6] In Sir Egerton Brydges edition of the Rhapsody this line stands
"My *dying* husband knew," &c.
an interpolation which, though perhaps called for by the metre, does
not appear to be justified by either of the four editions supposed to
have been printed during the life-time of the original editor. Nicolas.
[True, but as it *is* found in an autograph MS. of the poem, it is inserted. See our Preface. G.]

XII. *The Maid.*

I marriage would forsweare, but that I heare men tell,

That she that dies a maid, must leade an Ape in Hell;

Therefore if fortune come, I will not mock and play,

Nor driue the bargaine on, till it be driuen away.

Tithes and lands I like, yet rather fancy can,

A man that wanteth gold, then gold that wants a man.

(pp. 1—4.)

II. A CONTENTION

Betwixt a Wife, a Widdow, and a Maide.[7]

Wife.   Widdow, well met, whether goe you to day ?
Will you not to this solemne offering go ?
You know it is *Astreas* holy day :
The Saint to whom all hearts deuotion owe.

Widow.   Marry, what else ? I purpos'd so to doe :
Doe you not marke how all the wiues are fine?
And how they haue sent presents ready too,
To make their offering at *Astreas* shrine ?

See then, the shrine and tapers burning bright,
Come, friend, and let vs first ourselues advance,

[7] See Introductory Note to the first of these Minor Poems, *ante.*
In Mr. Collier's History of English Dramatic Poetry, Vol. I. p. 323
seqq. interesting details are given of an Entertainment to the Queen
at Sir Robert Cecil's " newe house in the Strand," at which she was
" royally entertained." From Extracts from a Barrister's Diary
among the Harleian MSS. adduced herein, we glean a notice of the
present Poem, *e. g.* " Sundry devises at hir entrance : three women,
a maid, a widow and a wife, eache contending [for] their own
states, but the virgin preferred." In Nichols' Progs. of Elizabeth
(iii. 601) the poem is also ascribed on authority of John Chamber-

We know our place, and if we haue our right,
To all the parish we must leade the dance.

But soft, what means this bold presumptuous
maid,
To goe before, without respect of vs ?
Your forwardnesse (proude maide) must now
be staide :
Where learnd you to neglect your betters
thus ?

Maide. Elder you are, but not my betters here,
This place to maids a priuiledge must giue :
The Goddesse, being a maid, holds maidens
deare,
And grants to them her own prerogatiue.

Besides, on all true virgins, at their birth.
Nature hath set [8] a crowne of excellence,

lain to Davies (6th December, 1602). See Letters of Chamberlain
published by Camden Society, p. 169 : December 23rd, 1602. Miss
Sarah Williams, in her careful edition of Chamberlain's Letters for
the Camden Society, by an oversight, has annotated this reference *in
loco* as to Davies of Hereford. Chamberlain calls it a " pretty dialogue." The Barrister's Diary *supra* [Manningham] has been
edited for the Camden Society by the late lamented Mr. John
Bruce of London. G.   [8] Misprinted ' sent.' G.

That all the wiues and widdowes of the earth,
Should giue them place, and doe them reuer-
ence?

Wife. If to be borne a maid be such a grace,
So was I borne and grac't by nature to,
But seeking more perfection to embrace
I did become a wife as others doe.

Widow. And if the maid and wife such honour haue,
I haue beene both, and hold a third degree.
Most maides are Wardes, and euery wife a .
slaue,
I haue my liuery sued,[9] and I am free.

Maid. That is the fault, that you haue maidens
beene,
And were not constant to continue so :
The fals of Angels did increase their sinne,
In that they did so pure a state forgoe :

But Wife and Widdow, if your wits can make,
Your state and persons of more worth then
mine,

---

[9] A legal phrase = freedom or liberty. G.

Aduantage to this place I will not take ;
I will both place and priuilege resigne.

Wife. Why marriage is an honourable state.
Widow. And widdow-hood is a reuerend degree :
Maid. But maidenhead, that will admit no mate,
Like maiestic itselfe must sacred be.

Wife. The wife is mistresse of her family.
Widow. Much more the widdow, for she rules alone :
Maid. But mistresse of mine owne desires am I,
When you rule others wils and not your owne.

Wife. Onely the wife enjoys the vertuous pleasure.
Widow. The widow can abstaine from pleasures known :
Maid. But th' vncorrupted maid preserues[1] such
measure,
As being by pleasures wooed she cares for none.

Wife. The wife is like a faire supported vine.
Widow. So was the widdow, but now stands alone :
For being growne strong, she needs not to in-
cline.
Maid. Maids, like the earth, supported are of none.

[1] Nicolas, as before, has 'observes.' G.

Wife. The wife is as a Diamond richly set ;
Maid. The maide vnset doth yet more rich appeare.
Widow. The widdow a Iewel in the Cabinet,
    Which though not worn is stil esteem'd as deare.

Wife. The wife doth loue, and is belou'd againe.
Widow. The widdow is awakt out of that dreame.
Maid. The maids white minde had neuer such a staine,
    No passion troubles her cleare vertues streame.

    Yet if I would be lou'd, lou'd would I be,
    Like her whose vertue in the bay is seene :
    Loue to wife fades with satietie,
    Where loue neuer enioyed is euer greene.

Widow. Then whats a virgin but a fruitlesse bay ?
Maid. And whats a widdow but a rose-lesse bryer ?
    And what are wiues, but woodbinds which decay
    The stately Oakes by which themselues aspire?

    And what is marriage but a tedious yoke ?
Widow. And whats virginitie but sweete selfe-loue ?
Wife. And whats a widdow but an axell broke,
    Whose one part failing, neither part can mooue?

Widow. Wiues are as birds in golden cages kept.

Wife. Yet in those cages chearefully they sing :

Widow. Widdowes are birds out of these cages lept,
Whose ioyfull notes makes all the forrest ring.

Maid. But maides are birds amidst the woods secure,
Which neuer hād could touch, nor yet[2] could take;
Nor whistle could deceiue, nor baite allure,
But free vnto themselues doe musicke make.

Wife. The wife is as the turtle with her mate.

Widow. The widdow, as the widdow doue alone ;
Whose truth shines most in her forsaken state.

Maid. The maid a Phœnix, and is still but one.

Wife. The wifes a soule vnto her body tyed.

Widow. The widdow a soule departed into blisse.

Maid. The maid, an Angell, which was stellified,
And now t' as faire a house descended is.

Wife. Wiues are faire houses kept and furnisht well.

Widow. Widdowes old castles voide, but full of state :

Maid. But maids are temples where the Gods do dwell,
To whom alone themselues they dedicate.

---

[2] Nicolas, as before, reads 'net.'   G.

But marriage is a prison during life,
Where one way out, but many entries be :

Wife. The Nun is kept in cloyster, not the wife,
Wedlocke alone doth make the virgin free.

Maid. The maid is ever fresh, like morne in May :
Wife. The wife with all her beames is beautified,
Like to high noone, the glory of the day :
Widow. The widow, like a milde, sweet, euen-tide.

Wife. An office well supplide is like the wife.
Widow. The widow, like a gainfull office voide :
Maid. But maids are like contentment in this life,
Which al the world haue sought, but none
enioid :

Go wife to Dunmow, and demaund your flitch.
Widow. Goe gentle maide, goe leade the Apes in hell.
Wife. Goe widow make some younger brother rich,
And then take thought and die, and all is well.

Alas poore maid, that hast no help nor stay.
Widow. Alas poore wife, that nothing dost possesse ;
Maid. Alas poore widdow, charitie doth say,
Pittie the widow and the fatherlesse.

Widow.   But happy widdowes haue the world at will.

Wife.   But happier wiues, whose ioys are euer double.

Maid.   But happiest maids whose hearts are calme and
         still,
         Whom feare, nor hope, nor loue, nor hate doth
         trouble.

Wife.   Euery true wife hath an indented[3] heart,
         Wherein the couenants of loue are writ,
         Whereof her husband keepes the counterpart,
         And reads his comforts and his ioyes in it.

Widow.   But euery widdowes heart is like a booke,
         Where her ioyes past, imprinted doe remaine,
         But when her iudgements eye therein doth
         looke ;
         She doth not wish they were to come againe.

Maid.   But the maids heart a faire white table is,
         Spotlesse and pure, where no impressions be
         But the immortal Caracters of blisse,
         Which onely God doth write, and Angels see.

[3] The reference is to the wavy or vandyked cutting of the vellum
MS. whereby the one copy fits into the other. Recently two very
ancient MSS. were thus unexpectedly brought together in H. M
Public Record Office. G.

Wife. But wiues haue children, what a ioy is this?

Widow. Widows haue children too, but maids haue none.

Maid. No more haue Angels, yet they haue more blisse
Then euer yet to mortall man was knowne.

Wife. The wife is like a faire manured[4] field ;

Widow. The widow once was such, but now doth rest.

Maid. The maide, like Paradice, vndrest, vntil'd,
Beares crops of natiue vertue in her breast.

Wife. Who would not dye as wife, as Lucrece died?

Widow. Or liue a widdow, as Penelope?

Maid. Or be a maide, and so be stellified,[5]
As all the vertues and the graces be.

Wife. Wiues are warme Climates well inhabited ;
But maids are frozen zones where none may
dwel.

Maid. But fairest people in the North are bred,
Where Africa breeds Monsters blacke as hell.

Wife. I haue my husbands honour and his place.

Widow. My husbands fortunes all suruiue to me.

---

[4] =cultivated. G.

[5] Cf. 'Orchestra,' Vol. I., page 192, with relative note. G.

Maid.   The moone doth borrow light, you borrow grace,
When maids by their owne vertues gracèd be.

White is my colour ; and no hew but this
It will receiue, no tincture can it staine.
Wife.   My white hath tooke one colour, but it is
My honourable purple dyed in graine.[6]

Widow.   But it hath beene my fortune to renue
My colour twice from that it was before.
But now my blacke will take no other hue,
And therefore now I meane to change no more.

Wife.   Wiues are faire Apples seru'd in golden dishes.
Widow.   Widows good wine, which time makes better
            much.
Maid.   But Maids are grapes desired by many wishes,
            But that they grow so high as none can touch.

Wife.   I haue a daughter equals you, my girle.
Maid.   The daughter doth excell the mother then :
           As pearles are better then the mother of pearle
           Maids loose their value whē they match with
               men.

6 = in the fabric.   **G.**

Widow. The man with whō I matcht, his worth was
         such   .

        As now I scorne a maide should be my peare : [7]

Maid. But I will scorne the man you praise so much,
        For maids are matchlesse, and no mate can
        beare.

        Hence is it that the virgine neuer loues,
        Because her like she finds not anywhere ;
        For likenesse euermore affection moues,
        Therefore the maide hath neither loue nor peere.

Wife. Yet many virgins married wiues would be.

Widow. And many a wife would be a widdow faine.

Maid. There is no widdow but desires to see,
        If so she might, her maiden daies againe.

Widow.[8] There neuer was a wife that liked her lot :

Wife. Nor widdow but was clad in mourning weeds.

Maid. Doe what you will, marry, or marry not,
        Both this estate and that, repentance breedes.

---

[7] = peer. G.

[8] In the previous editions of the Rhapsody, this line has always been imputed to the Wife, and the following one to the Widow ; but as throughout the Contention each party praises her own state, whilst she ridicules that of the other, the transposition in the text appeared to be imperiously called for. Nicolas.

Wife.   But she that this estate and that hath scene,
   Doth find great ods betweene the wife and girle.

Maid.   Indeed she doth, as much as is betweene
   The melting haylestone and the solid pearle.

Wife.   If I were Widdow, my merry dayes were past.

Widow   Nay, then you first become sweete pleasures
    guest,

Wife.[9]   For mayden-head is a continuall fast,
   And marriage is a continual feast.

Maid.   Wedlock indeed hath oft comparèd bin
   To publike Feasts where meete a publike rout ;
   Where they that are without would faine go in,
   And they that are within would faine go out.

   Or to the Iewell which this vertue had,
   That men were mad till they might it obtaine,
   But when they had it, they were twise as mad,
   Till they were dipossest of it againe.

Wife.   Maids cannot iudge, because they cannot tell,
   What comforts and what ioyes in marriage be :

 [9] By the rule of note 8, Wife seems necessary to be here prefixed;
but see our Memorial-Introduction for a critical notice of this and
other portions.   G.

Maid.   Yes, yes, though blessed Saints in heauen do
        dwell,
    They doe the soules in Purgatory see.

Widow. If euery wife do liue in Purgatory.
    Then sure it is, that Widdowes liue in blisse :
    And are translated to a state of glory,
    But Maids as yet haue not attain'd to this.

Maid.   Not Maids ? To spotlesse maids this gift is
        giuen,
    To liue in incorruption from their birth;
    And what is that but to inherit heauen
    Euen while they dwell vpon the spotted earth ?

    The perfectest of all created things,
    The purest gold, that suffers no allay ;[1]
    The sweetest flower that on th' earths bosome
        springs,
    The pearle vnbord, whose price no price can
        pay :

    The Christall Glasse that will no venome hold,[2]
    The mirror wherein Angels loue to looke,

---

[1]   alloy. G.   [2] It was long a " Vulgar Error" that certain 'christall glasses' flew into bits on poison being put into them. G.

Dianaes bathing Fountaine cleere and cold,
Beauties fresh Rose, and vertues liuing booke.

Of loue and fortune both, the Mistresse borne,
The soueraigne spirit that will be thrall to none ;
The spotlesse garment that was neuer worne,
The Princely Eagle that still flyes alone.

She sees the world, yet her cleere thought doth take
No such deepe print as to be chang'd thereby;
As when we see the burning fire doth make,
No such impression as doth burne the eye.

Wife. No more (sweete maid) our strife is at an end,
Cease now : I fear we shall transformèd be
To chattering Pies, as they that did contend
To match the Muses in their harmony.

Widow. Then let us yeeld the honour and the place,
And let vs both be sutors to the maid ;
That since the Goddesse giues her speciall
grace,
By her cleere hands the offring be conuaide.

Maid.　Your speech I doubt hath some displeasure
　　　mou'd,
　　Yet let me haue the offring, I will see;
　　I know she hath both wiues and widdowes
　　　lou'd,
　　Though she would neither wife nor widdow
　　　be.

(pp 5—15.)

III. A LOTTERY.[1]

Presented before the late Queenes Maiesty at the Lord Chancelors House, 1602.[2]

A Marriner with a Boxe vnder his arme, contayning all the seuerall things following, supposed to come from the Carrick,[3] *came into the Presence, singing this Song:*

Cynthia Queene of Seas and Lands,
That fortune euery where commands,

---

[1] See Introductory-note to the preceding poem. G.

[2] This Lottery was presented to the Queen in the year 1602, at York House, the residence of Thomas Egerton, Lord Keeper, not in 1601, as stated in Nichols' *Progresses*, vol iii. p. 570. See our Memorial-Introduction for authority for this correction, and for the names of the ladies who drew the successive 'lots,' and also other points. COLLIER, as before, in a strangely curious remark, supposes these lottery verses may be Samuel Rowland's "When gossips meet," and as strangely does not connect them with Davies' name at all. He, however, supplies interesting *memorabilia* relating to these Elizabethan Entertainments. He mis-names the poet-compiler of the 'Rhapsody' throughout, Davidson.

[3] Or *Caract*, a large ship. Chaucer speaks of Satan having " a tayle, broder than of a Carrike is the sayl.' Sir Walter Raleigh,—a contributor to the *Rhapsody*,—observes " in which river the largest *Carack* may, &c." Nicolas.

Sent forth fortune to the Sea,

To try her fortune euery way.

There did I fortune meet, which makes me now to sing,

There is no fishing to the Sea, nor scruice to the King.

All the Nymphs of *Thetis* traine

Did *Cinthias* fortunes entertaine :

Many a Iewell, many a Iem,

Was to her fortune brought by them.

Her fortune sped so well, as makes me now to sing,

There is no fishing to the Sea, nor scruice to the King.

Fortune that it might be seene,

That she did serue a royall Queene,

A franke and royall hand did beare,

And cast her fauors euery where.

Some toyes fell to my share, which makes me now to
sing,

There is no fishing to the Sea nor seruice to the King.[4]

---

[4] Mr. Nichols, in his *Progresses of Queen Elizabeth*, cites the following passage from a speech made at her entertainment at Cowdray, to prove that the line in the text was an "olde saying." "Madame it is an olde saying ' *There is no fishing to the sea, nor service to the King ;*' but it holds when the sea is calm, and the King virtuous." . . . . Vol. iii., pp. 95—571. Nicolas. The sense is that there is no fishing to be compared (in result) to sea-fishing, nor any service to be compared with the king's. G.

And the Song ended, he vttred this short Speech :

God saue you faire Ladies all : and for my part, if euer I be brought to answere for my sinnes, God forgiue my sharking, and lay vsury to my charge. I am a Marriner, and am now come from the sea, where I had the fortune to light upon these few trifles. I must confesse I came but lightly by them, but I no sooner had them, but I made a vow, that as they came to my hands by Fortune, so I would not part with them but by Fortune. To that end I haue euer since carried these Lots about me, that if I met with fit company I might deuide my booty among them. And now, (I thanke my good Fortune,)! I am lighted into the best company of the world, a company of the fairest Ladyes that euer I saw. Come Ladies try your fortunes, and if any light upon an unfortunate Blanke, let her thinke that Fortune doth but mock her in these trifles, and meanes to pleasure her in greater matters.

The Lots.

1. *Fortunes Wheele.*

Fortune must now no more in triumph ride,
The wheeles are yours that did her Chariot guide.

2. *A Purse.*

You thriue, or would, or may, your Lots a Purse
Fill it with gold, and you are nere the worse.

3. *A Maske.*

Want you a Maske? heere Fortune gives you one,
Yet nature giues the Rose and Lilly none.

4. *A Looking-Glasse.*

Blinde Fortune doth not see how faire you be,
But giues a glasse that you your selfe may see.

5. *A Hankerchiefe.*

Whether you seeme to weepe, or weepe indeed,
This Hand-kerchiefe will stand you well in steed.

6. *A Plaine Ring.*

Fortune doth send[5] you, hap it well or ill,
This plaine gold Ring, to wed you to your will.

7. *A Ring, with this Poesie:*

As faithfull as I find.

Your hand by Fortune on this Ring doth light,
And yet the words[6] do hit your humour right.

---

[5] Manningham, in the original MS., has these variants: l. 1,
'hath sent'; l. 2, 'A plaine.' ˙G.

[6] Manningham, as before, has 'word doth'—a reading which

8. *A Pair of Gloues.*

Fortune these Gloues to you in challenge sends,
For that you loue not fooles that are her friends.[7]

9. *A Dozen of Points.*[8]

You are in euery point a louer true,
And therefore Fortune giues the points to you.

10. *A Lace.*

Giue her the Lace that loues to be straight lac'd,
So Fortunes little gift is aptly plac'd.

11. *A Paire of Kniues.*

Fortune doth giue this paire of Kniues to you,
To cut the thred of loue, if 't be not true.

12. *A Girdle.*

By Fortunes Girdle you may happy be,[9]
But they that are lesse happy are more free.

---

brings it more into accord with the language of the times, 'word'
being then used for a sentence of import, impressa, or posy.   He has
also 'fit' for 'hit.'   G.

 [7] Manningham again reads here:—

    . . . . "to you in double challenge sends
    For you hath fools and flatterers hir best friends."   G.

 [8] A tagged lace used for attaching and keeping up or together
various parts of the dress.   G.

 [9] Manningham reads, "With Fortune's . . . . happy may you
be."   G.

13. *A Payre of Writing-Tables.*

These Tables may containe your thoughts[1] in part,
But write not all, that's written in your heart.

14. *A Payre of Garters.*

Though you haue Fortunes Garters, you must be
More staid and constant in your steps then she.

15. *A Coife and Crosse-Cloth.*

Frowne in good earnest, or be sick in iest,
This Coife and Cross-Cloth will become you best.

16. *A Scarfe.*

Take you this Scarfe, bind *Cupid* hand and foote,
So loue must aske you leaue before hee shoote.

17. *A Falling Band.*

Fortune would haue you rise, yet guides your hand,
From other Lots to take the falling band.

18. *A Stomacher.*

This Stomacher is full of windowes[2] wrought,
Yet none through them can see into your thought.

---

[1] *Ibid,* 'thought.' G.   [2] = worked openings in the dress. G.

19.   *A Pair of Sizzers.*[3]

These sizzers do your huswifery bewray,
You loue to work though you are borne to play.

20.   *A Chaine.*

Because you scorne loue's Captiue to remaine,
Fortune hath sworne to leade you in a Chaine.

21.   *A Prayer-Booke.*

Your Fortune may prooue[4] good another day,
Till Fortune come, take you a booke to pray.

22.   *A Snuftkin.*[5]

'Tis Summer yet, a Snuftkin is your Lot,
But 'twill be winter one day, doubt you not.

23.   *A Fanne.*

You loue to see, and yet to be vnseen,
Take you this Fanne to be your beauties skreene.

---

[3] Manningham has ' scisser case,' which shows the scissors were in a case. He also reads ' you be borne.'   G.

[4] *Ibid,* ' may be.'   Then l. 2 was first as in text, but over ' Till that day ' is inserted above ' Till Fortune come,' though the latter is not erased.   G.

[5] A small muff for Winter-wear.   *Ibid* in heading and l. 1, 'Muf-kin ': in l. 2 ' It will be.'   G.

24.   *A Pair of Bracelets.*

Lady, your hands are fallen into a snare,
For *Cupids* manicles these Bracelets are.

25.   *A Bodkin.*

Euen with this Bodkin you may liue unharmed,
Your beauty is with vertue so well armed.

26.   *A Necklace.*

Fortune giues your faire neck this lace to weare,
God grant a heauier yoke it neuer beare.

27.   *A Cushinet.*

To her that little cares what Lot she wins,
Chance giues a little Cushinet to stick pinnes.

28.   *A Dyall.*

The Dyal's your's, watch time least it be lost,
Yet they most lose it that do watch it most.[6]

29.   *A Nutmeg with a Blanke Parchment in it.*

This Nutmeg holds a Blanke, but chance doth hide it :
Write your owne wish, and Fortune will prouide it.

---

[6] *Ibid,* this variant :—
   " And yet they spend it worst that watch it most."   G.

30. *Blanke.*

Wot you not why Fortune giues you no prize,
Good faith she saw you not, she wants her eyes.

31. *Blanke.*

You are so dainty to be pleaz'd, God wot,
Chance knowes not what to giue you for a Lot.

32. *Blanke.*

Tis pitty such a hand should draw in vaine,
Though it gaine nought, yet shall it pitty gaine.

33. *Blanke.*

Nothing's your Lot, that's more then can be told,
For nothing is more precious then gold.

34. *Blanke.*

You faine would haue, but what, you cannot tell.
In giuing nothing, Fortune serues you well.

Sir I. D. (pp. 42—46.

IV. CANZONET.

A Hymne in Praise of Musicke.[7]

PRAISE, pleasure, profite, is that threefold band,
   Which ties mens minds more fast then Gordions
      knots :
Each one some drawes, all three none can withstand,
Of force conioynd, Conquest is hardly got.
   Then Musicke may of hearts a Monarch be,
   Wherein prayse, pleasure, profite so agree.

Praise-worthy Musicke is, for God it praiseth,
And pleasant, for brute beasts therein delight,
Great profit from it flowes, for why it raiseth
The mind ouerwhelmed with rude passions might :
   When against reason passions fond rebell,
   Musicke doth that confirme, and those expell.

If Musicke did not merit endlesse praise,
Would heauenly Sph_eares_ delight in siluer round ?[8]

---

[7] See Introductory-Note to the first of these Minor Poems. I
include this 'Canzonet' because originally it bore the initials
of Davies' other pieces in the Rhapsody,' viz., I. D.—G.

[8] Qu : sound ? or it may be = their circular movement (supposed). G.

If ioyous pleasure were not in sweet layes
Would they in Court and Country so abound ?
  And profitable needes we must that call,
  Which pleasure linkt with praise, doth bring to all.

Heroicke minds with praises most incited,
Seeke praise in Musicke and therein excell :
God, man, beasts, birds, with Musicke are delighted,
And pleasant t'is which pleaseth all so well :
  No greater profit is then self-content,
  And this will Musicke bring, and care preuent.

When antique Poets Musick's praises tell,
They say it beasts did please, and stones did moue :
To proue more dull then stones, then beasts more fell,
Those men which pleasing Musicke did not loue ;
  They fain'd, it Cities built, and States defended
  To shew the profite great on it depended.

Sweet birds (poor men's Musitians) neuer slake
To sing sweet Musickes praises day and night :
The dying Swans in Musicke pleasure take,
To shew that it the dying can delight :
  In sicknesse, health, peace, warre, we do it need,
  Which proues sweet Musicks profit doth exceed.

But I by niggard praising, do dispraise
Praise-worthy Musicke in my worthlesse Rime :
Ne can the pleasing profit of sweet laies,
Any saue learnèd Muses well define :
 Yet all by these rude lines may clearely see,
 Praise, pleasure, profite in sweet musicke be.

[pp. 138—9.]
(No sig. but in 1602. I. D.)

V. TEN SONETS TO PHILOMEL.[1]

SONNET I.

Vpon Loues entring by the eares.

OFT did I heare our eyes the passage weare,
    By which Loue entred to assaile our hearts :
Therefore I garded them, and void of feare,
Neglected the defence of other parts.
Loue knowing this, the vsuall way forsooke :
    And seeking found a by-way by mine eare.
At which he entring, my heart prisoner tooke,
    And vnto thee sweete Phylomel did beare.
Yet let my heart thy heart to pitty moue,
    Whose paine is great, although small fault appeare.
First it lies bound in fettring chaines of loue,
    Then each day it is rackt with hope and feare.
And with loues flames tis euermore consumed,
Only because to loue thee it presumed.

[1] In my edition of Donne I have assigned these Ten Sonnets to
him, but for reasons given in Memorial-Introduction now reclaim
them for Davies. Our text is as with the others from the ' Rhapsody ' of 1621, where they are numbered in the class of sonnets
xxxiv. to xlii. They were originally signed Melophilus. The
various readings are merely orthographical. G.

O why did Fame my heart to loue betray,
    By telling my Deares vertue and perfection?
    Why did my Traytor eares to it conuey
    That Syren-song, cause of my hearts infection?
Had I been deafe, or Fame her gifts concealed,
    Then had my heart beene free from hopelesse Loue:
    Or were my state likewise by it reuealed,
    Well might it Philomel to pitty moue.
Than should she know how loue doth make me languish,
    Distracting me twixt hope and dreadfull feare :
    Then should she know my care, my plaints and anguish,
    All which for her deare selfe I meekely beare.
Yea I could quietly deaths paines abide,
So that she knew that for her sake I dide.

Of his owne, and his Mistresse sicknesse
at one time.

SICKNESSE entending my loue to betray,
    Before I should sight of my deere obtaine :
    Did his pale colours in my face display,
    Lest that my fauour might her fauours gaine.
Yet not content herewith, like meanes it wrought,
    My Philomels bright beauty to deface :

And natures glory to disgrace it sought,
That my conceiuèd loue it might displace.
But my firme loue could this assault well beare,
Which vertue had, not beauty for his ground.
And yet bright beames of beauty did appeare,
Through sicknesse vaile, which made my loue abound;
If sicke (thought I) her beauty so excell,
How matchlesse would it be if she were well.

Another of her sicknesse and recovery.

PALE Death himselfe did loue my Philomell,
 When he her vertues and rare beauty saw,
Therefore he sicknesse sent : which should expell
 His riuals life, and my deare to him draw.
But her bright beauty dazled so his eyes,
 That his dart life did misse, though her it hit :
Yet not therewith content, new meanes he tries,
 To bring her vnto Death, and make life flit.
But Nature soone perceiuing, that he meant
 To spoyle her onely Phœnix, her chiefe pride,
Assembled all her force, and did preuent
 The greatest mischiefe that could her betide.
So both our liues and loues, Nature defended :
For had she di'de, my loue and life had ended.

Allusion to Theseus voyage to Crete, against the Minotaure.

M Y loue is sail'd against dislike to fight,
  Which like vile monster, threatens his decay :
 The ship is hope, which by desires great might,
 Is swiftly borne towards the wishèd bay :
The company which with my loue doth fare,
  (Though met in one) is a dissenting crew :
  They are ioy, griefe, and neuer-sleeping care,
  And doubt, which neere beleeues good newes for true :
Blacke feare the flag is, which my ship doth beare,
  Which (Deere) take downe, if my loue victor be :
  And let white comfort in his place appeare.
  When loue victoriously returnes to me :
Least I from rock despaire come tumbling downe,
And in a sea of teares be for'st to drowne.

Vpon her looking secretly out at a window as he passed by.

O NCE did my Philomel reflect on me,
  Her Cristall pointed eyes as I past by ;
 Thinking not to be seene, yet would me see :
 But soone my hungry eies their food did spy.

Alas, my deere, couldst thou suppose, that face
    Which needs not enuy Phœbus chiefest pride,
    Could secret be, although in secret place,
    And that transparent glasse such beames could hide?
But if I had been blinde, yet Loues hot flame,
    Kindled in my poore heart by thy bright eye,
    Did plainly shew when it so neere thee came,
    By more the vsuall heate then cause was nie,
So though thou hidden wert, my heart and eye
Did turne to thee by mutuall Sympathy.

When time nor place would let me often view
    Natures chiefe Mirror, and my sole delight;
    Her liuely picture in my heart I drew,
    That I might it behold both day and night;
But she, like Philips Sonne, scorning that I
    Should portraiture, which wanted Apelles Art,
    Commanded Loue (who nought dare her deny)
    To burne the picture which was in my heart.
The more loue burn'd, the more her Picture shin'd:
    The more it shin'd, the more my heart did burne:
    So what to hurt her Picture was assign'd,
    To my hearts ruine and decay did turne.
Loue could not burne the Spirit, it was divine,
And therefore fir'd my heart, the Saints poor shrine.

To the Sunne of his Mistresse beauty eclipsed with frownes.

WHEN as the Sunne eclipsèd is, some say
    It thunder, lightning, raine, and wind portendeth;
And not vnlike but such things happen may,
    Sith like effects my Sunne eclipsèd sendeth !
Witnesse my throat made hoarse with thundring cries,
    And heart with loues hot flashing lightnings fired :
    Witnesse the showers which still fall from mine eies,
    And breast with sighes like stormy winds neare riued.
O shine then once againe sweet Sunne on me,
    And with thy beames dissolue clouds of despaire,
    Whereof these raging Meteors framèd be,
    In my poore heart by absence of my faire.
So shalt thou prooue thy beames, thy heate, thy light,
To match the Sunne in glory, grace, and might.

Vpon sending her a gold ring with this Posie.

Pure and Endlesse.

IF you would know the love which I you beare,
    Compare it to the Ring which your faire hand

Shall make more precious, when you shall it weare :
So my loues nature you shall vnderstand.
Is it of mettall pure ? so you shall proue
  My loue, which ne're disloyall thought did staine.
  Hath it no end ? so endlesse is my loue,
  Vnlesse you it destroy with your disdaine.
Doth it the purer waxe the more tis tride ?
  So doth my loue : yet herein they dissent,
  That whereas gold the more t'is purifide
  By waxing lesse, doth shew some part is spent :
My loue doth waxe more pure by your more trying,
And yet encreaseth in the purifying.

The hearts captivitie.

M Y cruell deere hauing captiu'de my heart,
    And bound it fast in chaines of restlesse loue :
  Requires it out of bondage to depart,
  Yet is she sure from her it cannot moue.
Draw backe (said she) your helpelesse loue from me,
  Your worth requires a farre more worthy place :
  Vnto your suite though I cannot agree,
  Full many will it louingly embrace.
It may be so (my deere) but as the Sunne,
  When it appeares doth make the starres to vanish !

So when your selfe into my thoughts do runne,
All others quite out of my heart you banish.
The beames of your perfections shine so bright,
That straight-way they dispell all other light.

I. D.

VI. TO GEORGE CHAPMAN ON HIS OVID.[2]

I. D. of the Middle Temple.

ONELY that eye which for true loue doth weepe,
 Onely that hart which tender loue doth pierse,
May read and vnderstand this sacred vierse—
For other wits too misticall and deepe :
Betweene these hallowed leaues *Cupid* dooth keepe
 The golden lesson of his second Artist ;
 For loue, till now, hath still a Maister mist,
Since *Ouids* eyes were closed with iron sleepe ;
But now his waking soule in *Chapman* liues,
 Which showes so well the passions of his soule ;
 And yet this Muse more cause of wonder giues,
 And doth more Prophet-like loues art enroule :
For Ouids soule, now growne more old and wise,
Poures foorth it selfe in deeper misteries.

---

[2] From " Ovid's Banquet of | sence. | A Coronet for his Mistresse Philosophie, and his amorous | *Zodiacke.* | With a translation of a Latine coppie, | written by a Fryer, Anno Dom. 1400. | *Quis leget hæc? Nemo Hercule Nemo,* | *vel duo vel nemo.* Persius. | At London, | Printed by J. R. for Richard Smith. *Anno Dom.* 1595. | "
See our Memorial-Introduction. G.

VII.　REASON'S MOANE.[3]

WHEN I peruse heauen's auncient written storie,
　　part left in bookes, and part in contemplation :
I finde Creation tended to God's glory :
　　but when I looke upon the foule euasion,
Loe then I cry, I howle, I weepe, I moane,
　　and seeke for truth, but truth alas ! is gone.

Whilom of old before the earth was founded,
　　or hearbs or trees or plants or beasts, had being,
Or that the mightie Canopie of heauen surrounded
　　these lower creatures ; ere that the eye had seeing :
Then Reason was within the mind of Ioue,
　　embracing only amitie and loue.

The blessed angels' formes and admirable natures,
　　their happie states, their liues and high perfections,
Immortall essence and vnmeasured statures,
　　the more made known their falls and low directions.
These things when Reason doth peruse
　　she finds her errors, which she would excuse.

---

[3] From close of ' A New Post ' consisting of ' Essayes ' by Sir
John Davies.　See Prose Works in Fuller Worthies' Library.　G.

But out alas ! she sees strife is all in vaine ;
   it bootes not to contend, or stand in this defence.
Death, sorow, grief, hell and torments are her gaine,
   and endlesse burning fire, becomes our recompence.
Oh heauie moane ! oh endlesse sorrowes anguish,
   neuer to cease but euer still to languish.

When I peruse the state of prime created man,
   his wealth, his dignitie and reason :
His power, his pleasure, his greatnesse when I scan,
   I doe admire and wonder, that in so short a season,
These noble parts, should haue so short conclusion :
   and man himselfe, be brought to such confusion.

In seeking countries far beyond the seas, I finde,
   euen where faire Eden's pleasant garden stood :
And all the coasts vnto the same confinde,
   gall to cruell wars ; men's hands embru'd in blood,
In cutting throats, and murders, men delight :
   so from these places Reason's banisht quite.

O Ierusalem ! that thou shouldst now turn Turke,
   and Sions hil, where holy rites of yore were vs'd :
Oh ! that within that holy place should lurke
   such sacrilege : whereby Ioue's name's abusde.

What famous Greece, farewel : thou canst not bost
thy great renowne : thy wit, thy learning's lost.

The further search I make, the worse effect I finde :
All Asia swarmes with huge impietie :
All Affrick's bent vnto a bloody minde :
all treachers [4] gainst Ioue and his great deitie.
Let vs returne to famous Britton's king,
whose worthy praise let all the world goe sing,

Great Tetragramaton, out of thy bounteous loue
let all the world and nations truely know,
That he plants peace, and quarrell doth remoue :
let him be great'st on all the earth belowe.
Long may he liue, and all the world admire,
that peace is wrought as they themselues desire.

What Vnion he hath brought to late perfection,
twixt Nations that hath so long contended :
Their warres and enuies by him receiue correction,
And in his royal person all their iars are ended.
And so in briefe conclude, ought all that liue
giue thanks to him for ioy that peace doth giue.

----

[4] =traitors [treacherous].   **G.**

By power and will of this our mightie king
   reason doth shew that God hath wroght a wonder :
Countries distract he doth to Vnion bring
   and ioynes together States which others sunder :
God grant him life till Shiloe's comming be
   in heauen's high seate he may enthronized be.

VIII. ON THE DEATH OF LORD CHAN-
CELLOR ELLESMERE'S SECOND WIFE
IN 1599.[5]

YOU, that in Judgement passion never show,
  (As still a Judge should without passion bee),
So judge your selfe ; and make not in your woe
Against your self a passionate decree.
Griefe may become so weake a spirit as mine :
  My prop is fallne, and quenchèd is my light :
But th' Elme may stand, when with'red is the vine,
And, though the Moone eclipse, the Sunne is
  bright.

---

[5] I take this Sonnet from Collier's 'Bibliographical Catalogue'
sub nomine (Vol. I. p. 192). It is thus introduced by him: " It is
stated correctly by the biographers of [Sir] John Davys that he was
patronized by Lord Ellesmere, and among the papers of his lordship
is preserved the following autograph Sonnet, which appears to have
been addressed to the Lord Chancellor, on the death of his second
wife in 1599." Further : " The following note is appended, also in
the hand-writing of Sir John Davys :—"A French writer (whom I
love well) speakes of 3 kindes of Companions, Men, Women, and
Bookes : the losse of this second makes you retire from the first :
I have, therefore, presumed to send yr. Lp one of the third kind, wch
(it may bee), is a straunger to your Lp. yet I persuade me his con-
versation will not be disagreeable to yr Lp." See Memorial-Introduction for notices of Ellesmere and his wives. G.

Yet were I senselesse if I wisht your mind,
  Insensible, that nothing might it move ;
As if a man might not bee wise and kind.
  Doubtlesse the God of Wisdome and of Loue,
As Solomon's braine he doth to you impart,
So hath he given you David's tender hart.

  Yr. Lps in all humble Duties
  and condoling with yr. Lp. most affectionately
                          Jo. Davys.

IX. TITYRUS *TO HIS FAIRE* PHILLIS.[6]

THE silly Swaine whose loue breedes discontent,
    Thinkes death a trifle, life a loathsome thing,
        Sad he lookes, sad he lyes.

But when his Fortunes mallice doth relent,
Then of Loues sweetnes he will sweetly sing,
        thus he liues, thus he dyes.

Then *Tityrus* whom Loue hath happy made,
Will rest thrice happy in this Mirtle shade.
    For though Loue at first did greeue him :
    yet did Loue at last releeue him.

                    I. D.

[6] From " Englands Helicon :
          Casta placent superis
          pura cum Veste venite,
          Et manibus puris
          sumite fontis aquam.
            At London
      Printed by I. R. for *Iohn Flasket*, and are
    to be sold in St. Paules Church-yard, at the
      signe | of the Beare. 1600. | [40.]
            E 3 (verso)
The Davies authorship of this little lilt, is confirmed by a contemporary (Harleian) MS. list of contributors to England's Helicon
(280), wherein his name is placed against it. G.

UPON A COFFIN BY S. J. D.

There was a man bespake a thing
Which when the owner home did bring,
He that made it did refuse it ;
And he that brought it would not use it,
And he that hath it doth not know
Whether he hath it, ay or no.

    From " The Curtaine-Drawer of the Worlde . . .

        by W. Parkes, Gentleman . . . 1621.[7]

[7] In my Fuller Worthies' Library edition of Davies, I inserted above Riddle as kindly sent me by Mr. W. C. Hazlitt, from the " Philosopher's Banquet : 2d edition, 1614, p. 261. In its text l. 6 'he' is spelled ' hee,' and 'ay' is 'yea.' G.

X.　EPITAPH AND EPIGRAM.

Sir John Davies had a son who became, if he were not born, an idiot. Anthony-a-Wood states " The son dying, Sir John made an epitaph of four verses on him, beginning

Hic in visceribus terræ &c."

It is much to be wished that these 'four verses' were recovered. Further, he had a daughter named 'Lucy'; and of her the same authority writes: "So that the said Lucy being sole heiress to her father, Ferdinando, Lord Hastings, (afterwards Earl of Huntingdon) became a suitor to her for marriage; whereupon the father made this Epigram :

LUCIDA VIS oculos teneri perstrinxit amantis
Nec tamen erravit nam VIA DULCIS erat."

On this WATTS remarks : " This is a remarkable anagram of Lucy Davies. See as remarkable ones on the mother Eleanor Davies, *Reveal O Daniel*, by herself, the other made on her by DR. LAMB,—Dame Eleanor Davies, *Never so mad a Lady*. Heylin's Life of Laud p. 266." Wood's Athenæ, (edn. by Bliss) Vol. II. p. 404. G.

VII. HITHERTO UNPUBLISHED POEMS.

METAPHRASE OF SOME OF THE PSALMS, &c.

NOTE.

The MANUSCRIPT VOLUME from which the following hitherto unpublished POEMS are taken, is the property of DAVID LAING, Esq., LL.D., EDINBURGH, who purchased it, or perhaps obtained it in exchange many years ago from the Rev. John Jamieson, D.D., author of the " Scottish Dictionary" and other learned works—a scholar of full learning and to be held in honour in many respects. It was parted with to his like-minded friend as containing the hitherto unprinted 'Psalms,' &c., by SIR JOHN DAVIES; but no memorial remains to ascertain the quarter from whence Dr. Jamieson obtained the Volume. Mr. Laing states that, if anything was said at the time on the subject, it has escaped his recollection; and this cannot be wondered at, as it must have been from thirty to forty years ago.

Along with eminent Experts I have carefully compared this Manuscript with undoubted holographs of SIR JOHN DAVIES, preserved in Her Majesty's State Paper Office (State Papers : Domestic. James I. Vol. 173. No. 54 : Oct. 18, 1624, etc., etc.) and among the Harleian MSS. in the British Museum—the former being preferable as being of the same year-date with ours : and I feel constrained to pronounce it throughout non-autograph. There are at least FIVE handwritings in the volume—as more particularly

described *in locis :* but none bears a resemblance to SIR
JOHN DAVIES'. The Manuscript, therefore, belongs to a
class that abounds at the Period, viz, a Scribe's transcript
and which closely resembles that of MS. Speeches and
other writings of DAVIES preserved among the HARLEIAN
MSS. This is further, in accord with SIR JOHN DAVIES'
practice, as appears by 'The Egerton Papers' of Mr.
Collier, (Camden Society, 1840, 1 Vol. 4o.) where in a
letter to ELLESMERE (pp. 410-16) he apologizes for his own
'ill hand' and substitutes his 'man's.' The evidence for
DAVIES' authorship of these POEMS is EXTERNAL and
INTERNAL.

(*a*) The existence of the 'Metaphrase of the Psalms'—
which composes the greater portion of the Manuscript—has long been on record. Thus ANTHONY-A-
WOOD in his ATHENÆ states "Besides the before-
mentioned things (as also Epigrams, as 'tis said)
which were published by, and under the name of Sir
John Davies, are several MSS. of his writing and
composing, which go from hand to hand, as (1)
Metaphrase of several of K. David's Psalms . . . . . ."
(edn. BLISS ii., 403.) The original of the Psalms'
MS. was in possession of Sir John's own daughter,
the Countess of Huntingdon, as I found in the Carte
MSS. Bodleian, Oxford.

The others are MSS.—some in part since published—
which WOOD describes as formerly in the Library of Sir

James Ware, and then in that of the Earl of Clarendon.

(*b*) The handwriting of the Manuscript is exactly cor-
respondent with that of its date '1624.' It is
uniform from Psalm I. to L.

(*c*) Throughout the 'Psalms' and other Poems, favourite words of SIR JOHN DAVIES' occur: in part
peculiar to him or used in a peculiar way. I must
refer the Student to the Poems themselves for the
great majority of examples: but note here half-a-
dozen—all the references being to our own edition
of the previous Poems.

1. *'Withall'*: ".... that sinne that we are
borne *withall*." (' Nosce Teipsum ' page 57, stanza
5th, line 4th.) So in the ' Psalms ' :

" Be merciful and hear my prayer *withall*."

(Ps. 4th, line 4th.)

2. *'Wight'*: ".... this World below did need
one *wight*." (page 60 : stanza 4th, line 1st.) So in
the ' Psalms ': ".... measures Iustice vnto euery
wight." (Ps. 9th, line 16th.)

3. *'gray Winter'*: " Here flow'ry Spring-tide
and there *Winter gray*." (page 63, stanza 1st, line
4th.) So in 'A Maid's Hymne in praise of Virginity': " To whome *graye Winter* neuer doth apeare.'
(line 7th.)

4. *'On'* meaning *'o'er'* : " Will holds the royall
scepter *on* the   soul " (' Nosce Teipsum,' page 79,

stanza 2nd, line 3rd.) "And *on* the passions of the heart doth raigne." (page 79, stanza 2d, line 4th.) So in the ' Psalms ' : " Let not my foes trihumph *on* mee againe." (Ps. 35th, line 37th). " In that my foe doth not trihumph *on* me." (Ps. 41st, line 22d.)

5. *'Detruded'* : "... such as me *detruded* downe to Hell." (page 110, stanza 1st, line 1st.) So in the ' Psalms ' : Therefore although my soule *de-truded* were euen to Hell's gates...." (Ps. 23rd, line 7th.)

6. *'Center'* meaning *'Earth'* : " Suruey all things that on this *center* here." (page 25th, stanza 1st, line 4th.) So in the ' Psalms ' : "And all that dwell on his round *Center* here." (Ps. 23rd, line 16th.)

It were easy to multiply these instances from the ' Psalms ' and the other Poems.

(*d*) The secular Poems contain personal allusions that authenticate their authorship. In the 'Elegie of Loue ' and in the lines " To the Kinge vpon his Maties first comming into England " these are of singular interest and value. The latter harmonizes with the fact that SIR JOHN DAVIES proceeded North to meet the King : and it has a direct refer-ence to his ' Nosce Teipsum.' Speaking of his Muse he exclaims,

" Thy sight had once an influence divine
Which gave it power the Soul of man to vew."

Another personal allusion is found in his address to
the " Ladyes of Founthill " in his native Wilts.

(*e*) The "Verses sent to the Kinge with ffiges " is in-
scribed "by Sir John Davis " and the " Elegiacal
Epistle " which immediately follows these ' Verses '
naturally closes a Volume containing the compositions of our Worthy. 'Davis ' is his own spelling in
the 1608 edition of ' Nosce Teipsum,' and in Davison's ' Rhapsody.'

(*f*) Exclusive of the ' Psalms '—the Davies' authorship
of which admits of no doubt—the other Poems have
Sir John Davies' characteristics in choice of subjects
and style, and specific wording, as above. ' Elegie '
is herein used as in the title-page of ' Nosce Teipsum.'

The Manuscript is a thin folio of forty-one leaves and one
page : but *verso* of 35th leaf consists of Memoranda
headed " The State of England before the Conquest,
briefely. By Henry, Lord Hastings, amongst his Notes
found " : and leaves 36 and 37 and page 38 (*verso* blank)
contain ' Notes ' on " William Bastarde, the Norman Con-
querour of England." The former is in a handwriting
different from all the rest : the latter the same as the Poems
that follow " Part of an Elegie in prayse of Marriage."
There are a number of contemporary and of more recent
blank leaves. It is bound in dark calf, with tooled ornament in the centre.

In preparing this Manuscript for the Press, my anxious

endeavour has been faithfully to reproduce the original : only I have extended the contractions ' w^h and w^ch ' for ' with ' and ' which ' and 'o^r. y^r ' for ' our ' and ' your ' and the like. I have somewhat modified the capitals : but in the Divine names (nouns and pronouns) and impersonations, have employed capitals. The punctuation of the Manuscript is almost *nil :* I have adopted present usage on a uniform principle ; and also the apostrophe of the possessive case, &c. Only one point perplexed me a little, viz. the sign of the plural. At the period a peculiar form represented ' es ' as denoting plural, but examination showed our Manuscript as using it with ' e ' immediately before. Hence it is apparent the Scribe used it arbitrarily. My rule has been to represent it simply by ' s ' for our plural, except in the cases—pointed out where they occur—in which ' es ' as an additional syllable is required for the rhythm. Throughout, the orthography is literally preserved : and besides six collations of my transcript with the Original, by myself, I have had the advantage of a minute comparison by my experienced and erudite friend, the late John Bruce, Esq., of London, and in part by W. Aldis Wright, Esq., M.A., Trinity College, Cambridge. So that our first publication of the Manuscript may be relied on as absolutely true to the Original. It may be added that I have adhered to the order in which the several Poems are given, with the single exception of placing the anonymous very noticeable ' Elegiacal Epistle ' on the death of Davies last. The two short pieces that precede it in our Volume, occupy in the MS. the closing page, which is a kind of fly-leaf.

I feel assured that every admirer of Sir John Davies will agree with me that a deep debt of gratitude is due to Mr. Laing for his generous consent to have the Manuscript included in our editions of the 'Poems.' Independent of the interest attaching to their illustrious authorship the 'Psalms' seem to me to possess rare merits, being as a whole strikingly faithfull to the Original, and not paraphrastic—hence Anthony-a-Wood's 'Metaphrase'—simple yet picturesque, 'smooth' but melodious, and in every quality infinitely superior to the attempts of BACON, JEREMY TAYLOR, ROUS, and others. Some of the Versions must find a place in the Church's Psalmody and Hymnology.

I must not omit to acknowledge the courteous attention of Mr. W. Carew Hazlitt in informing me of the existence and ownership of the Manuscript. Anything further requiring to be said, will be found in the footnotes. G.

Hitherto Unpublished Poems.

METAPHRASE OF SOME PSALMS.

PSALM I.[1]

THAT man is blest which hath not walkt aside,
   Takeinge ungodly counsell for his guide ;
Nor in the way of synners stood and staied,
Nor in the couch of Scorners downe him layed,
But in God's Lawe hath plac't his whole delight,
And studieth to performe it, day and night :
Hee, like a plant which by a streame doth growe,
His timely fruite shall in due season showe ;
Whose leafe shall not decay but flourish euer,
And all thinges prosper which hee doth endeauour
But with th'vngodly it shall not bee soe,
But as the dust, which as the whirlewindes to and fro
Uppon the surface of the earth doth driue,
They shall a restless life and fruitles liue ;

---

[1] There is a title here, "The Psalmes translated into verse, Anno
Domini 1624." G.

Nor shall they stand vpright when they are tride,
Nor in the assembly of the just abide :
But in his way God doth the good man cherish,
When wicked men in their bad way shall perish.

PSALM II.

Why doe the nations thus in furie rise ?
Why doe the people such vaine plotts deuise ?
MONARCHES stand vp and PRINCES doe conspire
Against the Lord, and His Annoynted Heire :
' Let vs in sunder breake their bandes,' say they,
' And let vs lightly cast their yokes away.'
But Hee that sitts in Heauen shall them deride,
And laugh to scorne their follie and their pride ;
And in His wrath He shall reproue them sore,
And vex them in His anger, more and more :
Sayinge, ' I sett on SION hill My KINGE,
To preache my LAWE, and shew this heauenly thinge ;
Thou art My SONNE, this day I Thee begott,
Aske, and I will assigne thee for Thy Lott
Of heritage the Landes and Nations all,
Betweene the Sunne's vprisinge & his fall.'
Thou with an iron rodd shall keepe them vnder,
And breake them like an earthen pott in sunder,

Bee wise, yee MONARCHES, and yee PRINCES then ;
Be learnèd, yee that judge the sonnes of men ;
Serue yee the Lord, with humble feare Him serue ;
Rejoyce in Him, yet tremblinge Him obserue ;
Kisse yee the SONNE, lest yee Him angrie make,
And perish, while His just wayes yee forsake,
If His just wrath but once enkinled bee :
Who trust in Him, a blessed man is hee.

PSALM III.

Lord ! how my foes in number doe encrease,
That rise against mee, to disturbe my peace !
MANY there are which to my soule haue said,
His God to him not safety yeilds nor aid ;
But God is my defence, my SUCCOUR nigh,
My glory, and my head Hee lifteth High :
To Him with earnest praier appealèd I,
And from His Holy Hill Hee heard my crie :
I layed mee downe and slept, and rose againe,
For mee the Lord doth euermore sustaine :
Though Thousand of my foes besett mee round,
Noe feare of them my courage shall confound :
Rise Lord ! and saue mee ; Thou hast giuen a stroke
On my foes cheeke, that all his teeth are broke :

SALUATION cometh from this Lord of ours,
Who blessings on His people daily powers.

PSALM IV.

O GOD ! whose righteousnes by grace is mine,
A gracious eare vnto my voyce encline :
Thou that hast set mee free when I was thrall,
Bee mercifull, and heare my prayer withall.
Vaine, worldly men, how long will yee dispise
God's honnour, and His truth, and trust in lies?
God for Himselfe, the good man doth select,
And when I crie Hee doth not mee reject.
Bee angrie, but be angrie without synne ;
Try your owne hearts in silence, close within.
To God, of godly workes, an offeringe make,
Then trust in Him that will not His forsake.
For that which good is, many seeke and pray,
' And who shall shew the same to vs '? say they,
Lord ! shew to vs thy countenance diuine,
And cause the BEAMES thereof on vs to shyne :
Soe shall my heart more joyfull bee and glad,
Then if encrease of corne and wine I had.
To peace therefore lye downe will I and sleepe[2]
For God alone doth mee in safetie keepe.

---

[2] ' rest' is written and erased here.   G.

PSALM V.

LORD weigh my words, and take consideration
Of my sad thoughts and silent meditation :
My God, my KINGE, bowe downe Thine eare to mee,
While I send vp mine humble prayer to Thee.
Early, before the morne doth bringe the day,
I will O Lord, look vp to Thee and pray :
For Thou with synne art neuer pleasèd well,
Nor any [3] ill may with Thy goodnes dwell :
The foole may not before Thy wisdome stand,
Nor shall the impious scape Thy wrathfull hand :
Thou wilt destroy all such as vtter lies ;
Blood and deceit are odious in Thine eyes ;
But, trustinge in Thy manie mercies deare,
I will approch Thy house with holy feare.
Teach me Thy plaine and righteous way to goe,
That I may neuer fall before my foe,
Whose flatteringe tongue is false and heart jmpure,
And throat, an open place of SEPULTURE.
Destroy them, Lord, and frustrate their devices,
Cast out those REBELLS for their manie vices ;
But all that trust in Thee and loue Thy name,
Make them rejoyce and rescue them from shame.

---

[3] An illegible word erased here.   G.

Thou wilt thy blessinge to the righteous yeild
And guard them with Thy grace as with a SHEILD.

PSALM VI.

To iudge me, Lord, in Thy just wrath forbeare,
To punish mee in thy displeasure spare ;
O ! I am weake : haue mercie, Lord, therefore,
And heale my bruisèd bones which payne mee sore.
My SOULE is alsoe trubled and dismayed ;
But, Lord, how long shall I expect Thine aid !
Turne Thee, O Lord, my SOULE from death deliuer,
Euen for Thy mercie's sake which lasteth euer :
They which are dead remember not Thy name,
Nor doth the silent GRAUE thy praise proclaime ;
I faint and melt away with greifes and feares,
And euery night my bed doth swymme with teares.
Myne eyes are suncke and weaknèd is my sight ;
My foes haue vexèd mee with such dispight.
Away from mee, yee sinfull men, away !
The LORD of HEAUEN doth heare mee when I pray.
The Lord hath my petition heard indeed :
Receaue my prayer and I shall surely speed ;
But shame and sorrow on my foes shall light,
They shall be turn'd and put to suddaine flight.

PSALM VII.

O Lord, my God ! I put my trust in Thee,
From all my PERSECUTORS rescue mee :
Lest my proud foe doth like a lyon rend mee,
While there is non to succour and defend mee :
Lord God ! if I bee guilty found in this,
Wherewith my foes haue chargèd mee amisse,
If I did vse my freind vnfreindly soe,
Nay, if I did not helpe my causlesse foe,
Let him preuaile, although my cause bee just,
And lay my life and honnour in the dust.
Vp, Lord ! and stand against my furious foes,
Thy JUDGEMENT against them for mee disclose ;
Soe shall Thy PEOPLE flocke about Thee nigh,
For their sakes therefore lift Thy selfe on high.
Judge of the world, giue sentence on my parte,
Accordinge to the cleannes of my heart:
Let wickednes be brought vnto an end,
And guide the just, that they may not offend.
Thou God art just, and Thou Searcher art
Of hart and raynes, and euery inward part :
My helpe proceedeth from the Lord of Might,
Who saueth those which are of hart vpright ;
A powerfull and a patient JUDGE is Hee,
Though euery day His wrath prouokèd bee :

But, if men will not turne, His sword Hee whets,
And bends His bowe, and to the stringe Hee setts
The INSTRUMENTS of death, His arrowes keene,
GAINST such as rebells to His will haue beene.
The jmpious man conceaues jniquity,
Trauailes with mischief, and brings forth a ly :
The RIGHTEOUS to entrapp hee digs a pitt,
But hee himselfe first falls and sinks in it.
The wicked plotts his workinge braine doth cast,
Light with a mischeife on himselfe at last.
MY THANKES WITH GOD'S GREAT JUSTICE SHALL ACCORD,
AND I WILL HIGHLY PRAISE THE HIGHEST LORD.

PSALM VIII.

O GOD, OUR LORD ! HOW LARGE IS THE EXTENT
Of Thy great name and glorie excellent !
It fills this world, but it doth shyne most bright
Aboue the heauens, in th' vnapproachèd light.
BY SUCKINGE BABES THOU DOST THY STRENGTH DIS-
    CLOSE,
And by their mouth to silence put Thy foes.
When I see HEAUEN wrought by Thy mighty hand,
And all those glorious lights in order stand,
Lord ! what is man that Thou on him dost looke !
Or of the SONNE OF MAN such care hast tooke !

Next ANGELLS in degree Thou hast him plac't,
And with a crowne of honour hast him grac't :
Thou hast him made lord of Thy CREATURES all,
Subjectinge them to his commaund and call ;
All birds and aiery fowles are vnder him,
And fishes all which in the Sea doe swymme.
O Lord, our God ! how large is the extent
Of Thy great name and glorie excellent !

PSALM IX.

Thee will I thanke euer with my hart entire,
And make the world Thy wondrous workes admire ;
In Thee rejoyce, in Thee trihumph will I,
My songs shall praise Thy name, O God, most High !
While my proud foes are put to shamefull flight,
And fall and perish at Thy dreadfull sight.
Thou, righteous JUDGE, dost sitt vpon Thy THRONE
And dost maintaine my rightfull cause alone ;
Thou checkst the HEATHEN ; and the wicked race
Thou dost destroy, and all their names deface.
O ENEMY ! behould thy finall fall,
Thy CITTIES perish and their names withall ;
But God, our Lord, for euer shall endure,
His judgement SEATE, Hee hath establisht sure,

Where Hee judges the World with equall right,
And measures Justice vnto euery weight : [4]
He likewise will become a Bulwarke strong
And tymely aide to them that suffer wrong.
Who knowes Thy name in Thee His trust will place,
Who neuer failest them that seeke Thy face.
O, praise the Lord ! you that in Sion dwell,
His noble Acts among the Nations tell ;
When of oppression Hee enquiry makes,
Of euery poore man's plaint Hee notice takes.
Haue mercy, Lord ! and take into Thy thought
My trubles, which my hatefull foes haue wrought.
Thou from the gates of death my Soule dost raise,
That I in Sion's Gates may sing Thy praise ;
The sweet saluation which Thou dost jmpart
Shall bee the joy and comfort of my heart.
The Infidells make pitts, and sinke therein,
Their feet are caught in their owne proper synne ;
Thy judgement Lord, Thou hast thereby declar'd
When wicked men in their owne workes are snar'd :
Hell is a place for impious men assign'd
And such as doe cast God out of their minde ;

----

[4] = wight. G.

But poore men shall not bee forgotten euer
Nor meeke mens' patience, if they doe perseuér.
Rise Lord ! and let [not]⁵ man aboue Thee rise
And judge the Infidel with angrie eyes :
Strike them with feare, that, though they know not Thee,
Yet they may know that mortall men they bee.

PSALM X.

Why standest Thou O Lord ! so farr away
And hids't Thy face when trubles mee dismay ?
The wicked for his lust the poore man spoyles ;
Lord ! take him in the trap of his owne wiles.
Hee makes his boaste of his profane desires
Contemninge God, while hee himselfe admires :
Hee is soe proud, that God hee setts at naught,
Nay rather, God comes neuer in his thought.
Thy judgements Lord, are farr aboue his sight
This makes him to esteeme his foes soe light,
And in his hart to say, I cannot fall,
Nor can misfortune light on mee at all :
His mouth is full of execrat[i]ons vile ;
Under his tongue doth sit ungodly guile ;

⁵ This ' not ' is self-evidently required.   G.

Close in the corners of the waies he lies,
And lurkes, and waits, the simple to surprize :
Euen as a lyon lurkinge in his den,
To assault and murther innocent poore men ;
Gainst whom his eyes maliciously are sett,
To catch them when they fall into his nett.
Himselfe hee humbles, bowes, and crouchinge stands
Till poore men fall into his powerfull hands ;
Then, in his heart hee sayth ' God hath forgott:
Hee turnes away his face and sees it not.'
Arise O Lord ! and lift Thy hand on high,
The poore forgett not which oppressèd ly :
For why should wicked men blaspheme Thee thus
' Tush ! God is carelesse and regards not us ' ?
Surely Thou seest the wronge which they haue done,
And all oppressions underneath the sunne ;
To Thee alone the poore his cause commends
As th' only freind of him that wanteth freinds.
Lord ! breake the power of the malicious minde
Take ill away, and Thou not ill shalt finde.
The Lord is kinge, and doth for euer raigne,
Nor miscreants shall within His Land remaine ;
Hee hearkeneth to the poore, but first prepareth
Their hearts to pray ; then their petition heareth :

That Hee poore orphans, may both help and saue,
That worldly men on them no power may haue.

PSALM XI.

I TRUST in God : to mee why should you say,
' Fly like a bird to mountaines farr away ' ?
Their bowes and arrowes wicked men prepare,
To peirce the hearts of them that faithfull are :
Euen him whome God hath made a corner-stone
They haue cast downe ; but what hath Hee misdone ?
God in His holy temple doth remaine,
The heauen of HEAUENS : where Hee doth sitt and
    raigne.
Upon the poore He casteth downe His eye,
The sonnes of MEN He doth discerne and trie ;
The just and righteous men Hee doth approue,
But hateth synners which their sinnes doe loue ;
On them He rayneth snares, brimstone and fire,
This is their cup, their wages, and their hire ;
The righteous GOD loues him whose way is right,
And on the just His gracious eye doth light.

PSALM XII.

HELPE Lord ! for all the godly men are gon,
And of the faithfull, fewe there are, or non ;

Each man to other doth vaine things jmpart,
With lipps decceiptfull, and with double hart ;
The Lord will soone cutt of the lipps that lie,
And root out tongues that speake proud words and
      high.
' With mighty words wee will preuale ' say they :
What Lord is Hee that dareth us gainesay ?
' Now for the trubles and oppressions sore
The gronings and the sighings of the poore,
I will arise ' sayth God, ' and quell their foes
That swell with pride ; and them in rest repose.'
God's words are pure, and chaste, like siluer tride
Which hath with seauen fires bene purified.
Thou wilt preserue them Lord ! and guard them still,
From this vile race of men which wish them ill.
The ungodly walke in circles, yet goe free
When such as feare not God, exalted bee.

PSALM XIII.

How long O Lord ! shall I forgotten bee ?
How long wilt Thou Thy bright Face hide from mee ?
How long shall I my thoughts tosse to and fro
And bee thus vext by my insultinge foe ?
Giue ease, O Lord ; giue light unto mine eyes,
Lest death in endlesse sleepe doth mee surprise ;

Lest my proud foe vaunt that hee doth preuaile,
And laugh at mee when I shall faint or faile;
But in Thy mercie all my trust is pight[6]
And thy saluation is my hearte's delight;
Of Thy sweet kindnes therefore sing will I,
And highly praise the name of God, Most High.

PSALM XIV.

'THERE IS NOE GOD,' THE FOOLE SAYTH IN HIS HEART,
Yet dares not with his tongue his thought impart;
All are corrupt and odious in God's sight,
Not one doth good, not one doth well, vpright.
God cast His eyes from Heauen on all mankinde,
And lookt if Hee one righteous man could finde;
But all were wicked, all from God were gone,
Not one did good, in all the world, not one;
Their throat an open graue, their flattering tongue
And lyinge lips, like stinge of wasps haue stung.
With bitter cursing, they their mouthes doe fill;
Their feet are swift the guiltles blood to spill;

---

⁶ = pitched.   Henry More in one of his Hymns uses the word:
   " Lord stretch Thy tent in my straight breast,
       Enlarge it downward, that sure rest
       May there be *pight*."   G.

Sad, wretched mischeife, in their wayes doth lye
But for the wayes of peace they passe them by ;
Noe feare of God haue they before their eyes,
Nor knowledge, while these mischeifes they devise ;
While they God's people doe with might oppresse
And eat them up like bread with greedines ;
And since on God they neuer vse to call,
They fear'd when cause of feare was non at all.
But to the righteous man and to his race,
God present is with His protectinge grace ;
Though fooles doe mocke the counsell of the poore,
Because in God hee trusted euermore.
Who shall saluation out of SION giue
To ISRAELL but God ?   Who shall releiue
His people and of CAPTIUES make them free :
Thou JACOB joyfull, Israell glad shall bee.

PSALM XV.

LORD ! WHO SHALL DWELL IN THY BRIGHT TENT WITH
    THEE

And of Thy rest in heauen pertaker bee ?
Euen hee that is vpright in all his wayes[7]

---

[7] Written here, as elsewhere, not by the contraction-sign of the plural ' es ' but in full.   G.

And from his hart speakes[8] truth in all hee sayes ;
Who hath forborne to doe his neighbour wrong
Nor him deceau'd or slaunderèd with his tong ;
Who of himselfe an humble thought doth beare
But highly valewes them which GOD doe feare ;
Who of his promis doth himselfe acquitt,
Though losse hee suffer by performinge it ;
Nor hath for bitinge vse his monie lent,
Nor tooke reward against the innocent ;
Who shall obserue these poynts, and doe them all,
Assuredly that man can neuer fall.

PSALM XVI.

MEE thy poore seruant Lord ! preserue and saue,
For all my trust in Thee repos'd I haue :
Lord ! said my soule, Thou art my GOD, to Thee
My goods are nothinge when they offered bee ;
But my delight[s] are in those saints of Thine,
Which liue on Earth, and doe in vertue shine ;
But they which runn to worshipp idolls vaine,
Shall multiply their sorrow and their paine.
Of their blood offerings will I not pertake,
Nor of their names shall my lipps mention make.

---

[8] Another example in the MS., of the plural ' es ' in contraction-
sign, preceded by ' e.' G.

The portion of mine heritage and cupp
Is God Himselfe who houlds and keepes [9] mee upp ;
In a faire ground to mee my lott did chance,
Soe I possesse a rich Inheritance :
Thankes [1] bee to God His warninge giues mee light,
My raynes with paine doe chasten me by night ;
I looke to God in my endeauors all,
Hee stands soe neare mee that I cannot fall ;
This hath my heart and tongue with joyes possest,
And now my flesh in hope to rise, shall rest ;
My soule shall not be buryed in the graue,
Nor shall Thy Holy One corruption haue ;
Shew mee the path of life ; for in Thy sight
Doth endles pleasure rest and full delight.

PSALM XVII.

HEARE my just cause Lord ! heare my prayer and crie,
Which come from lipps not vs'd to faine or lie :
Lord, let my sentence from Thy mouth be giuen,
For Thou regards't things only just and euen ; [2]

[9] Another example of ' e ' before the contraction-sign of ' es.'   G.

[1] In full ' es ' here, as before. Having now given several examples of the arbitrary use of the ' s,' and ' es ' in full and by contraction-sign, it will not be needful to note more in the sequel.   G.

[2] A later handwriting substitutes for the respective rhymes of this couplet ' proceed' and ' right indeed.'   G.

In the darke night of my aduersitie,
Thou did'st my heart examine, prouc and trie ;
And yet vpon this triall did'st not finde
My heart or tongue to any ill enclinde :
For that their workes against Thy Word are done
I doe their wayes which tende to ruine, shunn.
Lord ! in Thy pathes doe Thou my goings guide,
Lest in this slippery life my footstepps slide :
Thy name haue I invok't, Thou shalt mee heare
And to my humble words incline Thy care ;
O Sauiour ! of all those that trust in Thee
Thy mercies full of wonder shew to mee ;
Preserue mee as the apple of Thine eye,
Under Thy winges in safetie let me lie ;
Saue mee from them which Thy right hand oppose,
And from my ungodly circumuenting foes ;
Their fatt estates doe them soe fortifie
As they presume to speake proud words and high ;
In all my wayes in wait for mee hee lies,
To cast mee downe hee downewards casts his eyes
Euen like a lyon, watching for his prey,
Or lyon's whelpes which lurke beside the way.
Vp Lord ! defeat, defeat this foe of mine,
That wicked man who is a sword of Thyne ;

From wordly men vouchsafe my soule to saue,
Who in their mortall life their portion haue;
Whose bellies with Thy treasure Thou dost fill,
Who children haue, and leaue them wealth at will ;
But I Thy face in righteousnes shall see
And with Thy presence shall contented bee.

PSALM XVIII.

Thou art my strength, O Lord ! Thee will I loue,
Thou art my Rocke, which nothing can remoue :
My God, in Whome my trust I will repose,
My Sauiour, sheild and horne, against my foes ;
Lord, most praise worthy, pray will I to Thee
Soe shall I from my foes protected bee ;
When deadly sorrowes did besett mee round,
And floods of wickednes did mee surhound[1]
When paines of hell I felt in my descase,
And pangs of death upon my soule did sease ;
On God I call'd in that instant truble,
And my complaints unto the Lord did dubble :
But when His wrath and vengeance kindled were,
The Earth did quake, and mountaines shooke for feare,
And coles grew redd with His inflaminge jre ;

---

[1] = surround : as 'trihumph' for triumph.   Cf. Psalm **xxxv.**
line 37.   G.

Hee bowed the heauens, and did descend withall,
And shadowes darke beneath His feet did fall:
Hee ridinge on the CHERUBINS did fly,
And with the wingèd windes was borne on high;
Darkness His clossett, His pauilion wide
Made of blacke clouds, His face a while did hide;
But at His presence right away they flew
When haile and coles of fire abroad Hee threw;
The Lord from heauen did send His thunder lowd
With fire and haile from out the broken cloud;
A shower of arrowes on His foes did fall,
His thunderboults and lightenings slewe them all;
Fountaines were dride and the earthe's foundation
       mou'd
When synners, in His wrath, the Lord reprou'd;
But Hee from heauen shall send His angell's downe
And take mee vp when waters would mee drowne;
Hee from my foe, too mightie and too strong,
Shall saue mee when Hee doth mee mightie wrong,
Preuentinge mee [in] my disastrous day:
But then the Lord was my support and stay;
When I was captiue, Hee did sett mee free,
And brought mee forth because Hee fauoured mee.

He shall reward mee as my dayes bee right,
And hands be cleane[4] : soe shall Hee mee requite ;
For I still kept his pathes, and did not shunn
To walke therein, as other men haue done :
But euer sett[5] His lawes before mine eyes,
And neuer did His holy words dispise.
My heart was vncorrupt before Him still,
Pursuinge goodnes and eschewinge ill ;
Hee shall reward mee as my deeds bee right,
And hands bee cleane : soe shall He mee requite.
Unto the good Thou wilt Thy goodnes show,
And righteous men Thy righteousnes shall know ;
The pure of heart shall Thee behold most pure
But froward men Thy curses shall endure ;
Them will God raise, which under pressures ly,
And proud men humble which doe looke soe high ;
Hee shall sett up for mee a candle bright,
My God shall turne my darkness vnto light.
Through Thee, an host of men, I conquere shall,
And with Thy helpe transcend the highest wal ;[6]

---

[1] Inadvertently written 'cleare.' G.
[5] 'My' written and erased here. G.
[6] 'Wal' is supplied in a more recent hand. G.

God's way is pure, His word is tride with fire ;[7]
Hee heals all them which unto Him retire ;
For who is God ? or who hath strength and power
Except our Lord, our God and only our ?
Hee girdeth mee with furniture to fight,
And guideth mee, and houldeth mee upright ;
My feet as swift as HART's feet Hee doth make,
And vp to honnor's tower Hee doth mee take ;
Hee giues such strength unto my fingers weake,
As that my arme a bowe of steele shall breake.
Thy hands shall bee my safety and protection,
Thou shalt aduance mee with Thy sweet correction ;
Thou for my feet shalt make a passage wide,
Soe as my steps shall neuer goe aside ;
I shall pursue, and in pursuite outgoe,
And neuer turne till I haue quelld my foe ;

---

[7] In the MS. following on the line " God's way . . . . fire," is
this :
      " All those that trust in Him will He vphold."
The Original enables us to see that this was a variation not settled
on. The first form was evidently as in the text, but the second line,
" Hee heals," &c., not being quite the thought of the Original,
Davies went nearer it in the new line, " All those," &c., thinking
perhaps of varying the first line to " tride as gold ;" but on reflection,
seeing that was bad, left it as at first, albeit he must have neglected
to cancel " All those," &c. I have not hesitated to withdraw a line
the retention of which would leave it without its fellow. G.

When I him smite[8] he shall not rise at all,
If once at my victorious feet hee fall.
Thou hast girded mee with a sword of strength,
Wherewith I shall subdue my foes at length;
For thou shalt turne the stubburne necke about
Of them that hate mee till, I root them out;
Then shall they crie (but helpe there shall be non)
Euen to the Lord, Who shall not heare their mone.
My foes to powder I shall breake and bray
And tread them down like mire amid the way.
Thou my rebellious subjects shalt accord,
And ouer Heathen Nations make mee Lord;
A people whome I knowe not shall mee serue,
And with base adulation mee obserue;
These Aliens all, shall faint and bee dismaied
And in their strongest Castles bee afraid.
Liue Lord! my strength: and blessed bee therefore
And praisèd bee my Sauiour euermore,
Who doth repay my foes with vengeance due,
And unto mee my vassals doth subdue;
Who doth not only saue but sett mee high
Aboue my foes, and there[9] feirce crueltie.

---

[8] The MS. reads 'sute' but as above, Query—contracted for 'smite'? G.   [9] =their. G

For this, both of my thanks and praise to Thee,
The Heathen Nations witneses shall bee ;
For wealth and power and blessings manie moe,
On Dauid and his race Thou shalt bestowe.

PSALM XIX.

THE workmanship of heauen soe bright and faire,
Thy power O Lord, and glorie doth declare ;
One day Thy praise doth to another preach,
One night another doth in order teach ;
Where euer any tongue or voyce doth sound,
In all the world their speech is heard around.
In middest of heauen, the hands of God hath pight[1]
For the sunne's lodgeinge, a pauilion bright ;
Who as a bridegroome from his chamber goes ;
Or GIANT, marchinge forth against his foes,
Hee issues ; and from EAST TO WEST doth runne :
His peircinge heat noe liueinge weight[2] can shun.
God's lawe is perfect and man's soule renues,
And simple mindes with knowledge it endues ;

---

[1] = pitched, as *ante.* G.

[2] A later hand has placed above this, 'wight' : which is only a different spelling. Mr. Bruce, (as before) adds Qu: It seeme to have stood originally ' weigh.' The Corrector added a ' t ' and then perhaps thinking it not quite clear, or not liking the incorrect spelling, wrote ' wight ' above it. G.

Right are His statutes and rejoyce the heart,
Light to the eyes His precepts pure impart ;
His feare is cleane and soe endures for aye ;
His judgements true and righteous euery way ;
More sweet then honie, to bee valewed more
Then many heapes of finest goulden oare.
They rectifie withall Thy seruants minde,
And who soe keeps them, great reward shall finde ;
But Lord who knowes how oft hee doth transgresse ?
O clense mee from my secret wickednes !
Nor let presumptuous sinns beare rule in mee,
Soe shall I from the great offence bee free ;
And Lord ! my strength and Sauiour ! soe direct
My words and thoughts as Thou maiest them accept.

PSALM XX.

The Lord giue eare to thee in thy distresse !
And bee thy Sheilde, when trubles thee oppresse !
And let His help come downe from heauen for thee !
And strength from Syon Hill imparted bee !
Let Him remember, and accept withall,
Thine offerings and thy sacrifices all ;
And of His bountie euermore fulfill
Thy hearts desire ; and satisfie thy will.

But wee will glory in our great God's name
And joy in our saluation through the same ;
And pray unto the Lord our God, that Hee
The effect of all thy prayers will graunt to thee.
Hee now I know will heare, and helpe will bringe,
With His strong hand to His annoynted KINGE ;
On chariots some, on horses some, rely,
But wee inuoke the name of God Most High.
Those others are bowed downe and fall full lowe,
When wee are risen and vpright doe goe.
Saue us O Lord of Heauen ! and heare us thence,
When wee inuoke Thy name for our defence.

PSALM XXI.

Glad is the kinge, and joyfull is his hart,
That Thou O Lord, his strength and safety art ;
That Thou hast giuen him what his heart desired,
And not denied him what his lipps required ;
Preuentinge him with blessings manifould,
And crowninge him with pure refinèd gould.
Hee askt Thee life, Thou gauest him length of daies,
Euen endlesse life, to giue Thee endlesse praise ;
His safety, through Thy prouidence deuine
With honour great and glorie makes him shine ;

Blisse without end Thou wilt to him jmpart,
The sunn-beames of Thy face will cheare his hart :
For in Thy mercy hee doth trust withall,
Which stayes his stepps that hee shall neuer fall ;
But Thy long hand shall reach Thy flyinge foe
And finde him when he most secure doth goe ;
Thine enimies shall (when kindled is Thine ire)
As in a furnace be consumed with fire ;
Their ofspringe from the Earth shall rotted bee,
Their second generation non shall see :
For against Thee and Thine their councell was,
Yet could not bringe their wicked plott to passe,
But turn'd their backes and put themselues to chase,
When Thou hadst bent Thy bowe against their face ;
Bee pleased in Thine owne strength Thyselfe to raise,
Soe shall wee Lord, Thy power and mercie praise.

PSALM XXII.

My God ! my God ! why leauest Thou mee ? and why
Dost Thou soe farr withdraw Thee from my crie ?
I cry all day, but Thou dost not giue eare ;
At night I cease not, yet Thou wilt not heare ;
Yet Thou art holy still, Thou God of might,
Thy people's great renowne and glory bright ;

When our forefathers plac't their hope in Thee
From cruell bondage Thou didst sett them free ;
In Thee they trusted, and to Thee they prayed,
And neuer faild of Thy celestiall aid ;
But as for mee, a worme not man, am I ;
A scorne to euery man that passeth by ;
They laugh and mocke, my poore estate to see ;
They draw their mouth and shake their heads at mee ;
And say, ' hee hop't in God, that Hee should saue
    him,
Now let God rescue him if Hee will haue him.'
But Thou Lord from my mother's wombe didst take
    mee,
And when I suck't her brest, didst not forsake mee ;
Euen from my birth I was to Thee bequeathèd,
And Thou hast bene my God since first I breathèd.
O leaue mee not when trubles doe mee presse,
And there is non to helpe mee in distresse ;
Many strong beasts haue mee invironèd
As fatt and feirce as bulls in BASHAN fedd ;
They runne on mee with open mouthes and wide ;
Like hungry lyons rampinge in their pride.
My soule, like water on the earth is spilt,
My joynts are loosed, my heart like wax doth melt,

My synewes shrunke are, like a potsheard drie,
My tongue cleaues to my jawes, dead dust am I.
For many doggs haue compast me about,
I am besett with a malitious rout ;
They peirce My hands and feet, and stare on Mee,
And euery ribb of My leane bodie see ;
They spoyle Mee of My GARMENTS, and beside,
The parts thereof by lotts they doe deuide.
Lord ! bee not farr, when I Thy help shall need,
Thou art My strength, O succour Mee with speed !
And sheild Mee from the sword, and from the power
Of doggs, which would My dearest SOULE deuoure !
And from the lyon's mouth, and from the hornes
Of many, fearce, insultinge unicornes !
Among My kinn will I declare Thy name,
And in the great Assembly spread the same.
Yee that feare Him His praise and glory tell,
And honnour Him yee seed of ISRAELL ;
Hee scorneth not the poore, nor hides His face,
But heares his suit when hee laments his case.
When all Thy faithfull folke assembled bee,
I sound Thy praise and pay my vowes to Thee.
The Lord shall fully satisfie the meeke,
Their soule shall liue which His light face doe seeke ;

The EAST AND WEST shall turne to their right minde,
And to the true God's worshipp be inclinde;
Who doth, of all the world the SCEPTER beare,
Rules and commaunds the nations euery where;
The fatt shall eate and worshipp Him therefore,
And they that lye in dust shall Him adore.
Euen hee which cannot his own life preserue,
Nor quicken his owne soule, the Lord shall serue.
Their seed, O Lord! shall serue to worshipp Thee,
And with Thy chosen people numbred bee;
And to their children's children, shall expresse
Thine euerlasting truth and righteousnes.

PSALM XXIII.

THE Lord my SHEAPERD is, Hee doth mee feed,
His bounty euermore supplies my need;
When I in pastures greene my fill haue tooke,
He leads mee forth into the siluer brooke;
Hee turnes my soule, when it is gon astray,
For His name's glory, to His right[cous]³ way;
Therefore although my soule detruded were,
Euen to Hell's gates, yet I not ill should feare;

---

³ I add 'cous' to 'right' of the MS. agreeably to the Prayer Book
version—" and bring me forth in the paths of righteousness."   G.

When Thou art with mee, what should mee dismay?
Thy crooke, my comfort is; Thy staffe, my stay;
My table Thou hast spread and furnisht soe,
As glads my heart, and greiues my enuious foe;
Thy balme powr'd on my head, doth sweetly smell;
Thou makst my cup aboue the brimme to swell.
Thy mercy, while I breathe, shall follow mee,
And in Thy house my dwellinge-place shall bee.

PSALM XXIV.

THE Earth, and all things which on the Earth remaine,
Euen all the world, doth to the Lord pertaine;
Amid the Sea, Hee founded hath the Land
And made this GLOBE aboue the floods to stand.
Who shall unto JEHOUAH's MOUNT ascend?
Or who shall in His holy place attend?
Euen hee whose hands are cleane, whose heart is pure,
Whose tongue is true, whose oath is just and sure.
He shall receaue both rightcousnes and blisse
From God, Whose mercy his saluation is.
Such are the seed of JACOB's faithfull race,
Which seeke the Lord, and loue to see His face;
Ye euerlasting GATES, your heads upreare,
And let the King of Glory enter there.

That glorious name, to Whome doth it belong?
To God Most Mightie and in warr most stronge.
Eternall dores, lift [up] your heads, I say
That there, the King of Glorie enter may.
The King of Glory enters, what is Hee?
The Lord of Hosts is knowne that Kinge to bee.

PSALM XXV.

MINE humble soule O Lord! I lift to Thee,
On Whome my trust shall euer fixèd bee;
O suffer not my cheekes with shame to glowe,
Nor make me slaue to my insultinge foe;
For they which hope in Thee incurr noe blame,
But wilfull synners shall bee clothed with shame.
To mee, O Lord! vouchsafe Thy wayes to show,
And Thy right pathes, that I therein may goe;
Teach mee the way of truth, direct my will;
Thou art my SAUIOUR, I attend Thee still;
Receaue mee Lord, and to remembrance call
Thy ould compassions, and Thy mercies all;
But of Thy wonted grace to mee, O Lord
Of the errours of my youth keep noe record;
The Lord is good, and for His goodnes' sake
Hee teaches sinners, godly wayes to take;

Yet Hee His learninge doth to non impart
But to the meeke and to the humble hart ;
His pathes are grace and truth ; that only way
Hee leads all those which doe His will obey.
For Thy name's glorie, I doe Thee intreat
To my great sinns, extend Thy mercie great
To him which feares the Lord, the Lord doth showe
How in his callinge hee may safely goe ;
His soule shall bee at ease and all his race,
Shall in the Land possesse a blessed place ;
His couenant and His counselles neare,[4]
God shewes to them in whome Hee plants His feare ;
My looke to Him shall euer raisèd bee,
Who from the nett my captiue feet doth free.
Haue mercy Lord on mee ! and turne Thy face
To see my desolate and wither'd case ;
Enlargèd is my greife and heauines,
But Lord, enlarge Thou mee from my distresse !
Looke on the wofull STATE that I am in ;
REMITT the cause thereof, which is my synne ;
My foes consider, and their multitude
Which mee with deadly hatred hath pursude ;

---

[4] Though not written with the contraction-sign of 'es' it is
spelled therewith. The measure requires ' neare' to be read as a bi-
syllable. G.

And keepe my soule[5] from sinne,[6] my face from shame,
Who trust in Thee and call upon Thy name.
Let truth and righteousnes without deceipt
Still wait on mee, because on Thee I wait ;
And sett Thy faithfull Israell at rest
From all the trubles which doe him molest.

PSALM XXVI.

Bee thou my Iudge, O Lord ! my cause is just ;
I shall not stagger while in Thee I trust.
Weigh and examine mee, search all my vaines,
The bottom of my heart and inward raines ;
I sett Thy goodnes euer in my sight,
Which in Thy truth doth guide my stepps aright ;
I use not to conuerse with persons vaine,
Nor with dissemblers fellowship retaine ;
My soule the assembly of the wicked hates.
Nor will I sitt among ungodly mates ;
Repentance haueing made my conscience cleare,
Then will I Lord, approach Thine Alter neare ;
That I may thanke [Thee] both with harte and voyce,
And tellinge of Thy wondrous workes rejoyce

---

[5] ' face ' previously written and erased. G.   [6] ' Shame ' for
' sinne : ' but also erased. G.

Thy temple Lord, I loue exceeding well,
Wherein Thy MAJESTIE AND GLORIE dwell.
O let not sinfull men my soule enclose,
Nor of my life let sinfull men dispose ;
Whose hands are foule, their sinnes them foule doe
    make,
And full of guifts which they coruptly take ;
But I to leaue a blamelesse life entend :
O Lord therein with mercie mee defend.
My foot stands right and therefore all my dayes
In all assemblies I the Lord will praise.

PSALM XXVII.

GOD IS MY LIGHT, SALUATION, strength and aid,
Of whome and what shall I then bee afraid?
The wicked came to haue devour'd mee quite,
But stumbled in their way, and fell downe-right.
Though mighty armies in my wayes were laid,
I stand secure, I cannot bee dismaid.
One thinge I wish, euen while I liue to dwell,
In God's faire House, where beauty doth excell ;
His tent, in time of truble, shall mee hide,
And I shall on His rocke of safety bide ;
Now shall Hee lift my head aboue my foes,
Which mee with armèd multitudes, enclose ;

And now will I His praise in trihumph singe,
And joyfull offerings to His temple bringe ;
And let my cries approach Thy gracious care,
Vouchsafe in mercie my complaints to heare ;
My heart doth tell that Thou bidst mee still
Thy face to seeke : Lord ! seek Thy face I will.
Then doe not hide from mee Thy face soe bright,
Nor in Thy wrath exclude mee from Thy sight ;
Thou euer wast mine aid, since I was borne :
God of my safety leaue me not forlorne.
My father and my mother both forsooke mee,
But then the Lord to his tuition tooke mee ;
Teach mee the way that I therein may goe,
Soe shall I neuer fall before my foe ;
Nor fall into their power which doe me hate,
And brought false oathes against mee in the gate.
My heart had fail'd but that my hope to see
God's endlesse blisse in heauen, did comfort mee.
Then stay God's time, Hee shall thee stay at length,
And Hee till then shall arme thy heart with strength.

PSALM XXVIII.

Heare (Lord my strength !) the crie I make to Thee !
I am but dead, if Thou seeme deafe to mee :

Heare, when with humble prayer, I Thee entreat,
With lifted hands before Thy mercy seate.
But rancke me not with those which wicked are,
Whose lipps speake peace, whose hearts are full of warr ;
Accordinge to their actions let them speed,
And as their merrit is, soe make their need ;
For that they see Thy workes, and yet neglect them,
Thou shalt destroy and neuer more erect them :
The Lord bee praisd Who hath vouchsaft to heare,
And lend unto my prayer a gracious eare ;
His SHEILD protects, His strength doth mee aduance ;
My tongue shall sing His praise, my heart shall dance ;
Hee to His seruants, force, and vertue, giues ;
Through Him in safetie His annoynted liues.
Saue Thy peculier people, Lord ! and blesse them,
And lift their heads aboue them that oppresse them.

PSALM XXIX.

Yee kings, since by God's power and grace, yee raigne,
Glory and power ascribe to Him againe ;
Yeild Him the honnour due to His great name,
And in His glorious COURTS, His praise proclaime ;
His voyce doth cause the Seas, to swell and shake,
And in the heauens the dreadfull thunder make ;

JEHOUAH's voice, effects of power doth breed,
It is a stronge and glorious voyce indeed;
His voyce the cedar doth in sunder teare,
The Cedars which MOUNT LEBANUS doth beare;
Makes LEBANUS, and HERMON hill, to tremble
And skippinge CALUES and UNICORNES, resemble;
Doth breake the clouds, and flames of fire deuide,
The deserts shake, euen CADES [7] desert wide;
Makes hindes to calue, for feare makes forrests bare,
While in His temple wee His praise declare;
The Lord vpon the water-floods doth raigne,
The Lord a KINGE for euer doth remaine;
The Lord shall still His people's strength encrease,
And giue to them the blessinge of His peace.

PSALM XXX.

Highly the Lord I praise Who setts mee high
Aboue my proud insultinge enimie;
Sicke to the death, I cried to GOD for ease,
And Hee hath cur'd my dangerous disease;
Hee from the graue hath lifted up my head
And hath reduc't [8] mee from among the dead.

---

[7] The Kadesh of our Authorised Version is spelled Cades in the Prayer Book. G.   [8] = re-led. G.

Yee SAINTS of His in songs His praise expresse,
With thankes [9] make mention of His holines;
For momentarie His displeasure is,
When in His fauour there is life and blisse;
Sad sorrow may continue for a night,
But joy returneth with the morninge light.
When my estate did prosper, then said I
I shall not fall, my seat is fixt on high.
But when Thou Lord, didst turne Thy face aside,
Then was I trubled, and to Thee I cride;
To Thee began I then againe to pray,
And in my humble prayer thus did say:
What profit can there by my death arise,
When buried in the graue my body lies?
Shall dust and ashes celebrate Thy name?
Or shall the silent TOOMBE Thy truth proclaime?
Lord, heare my prayer, and then Thy mercie show
In aidinge mee against my cruell foe!
Loe now to dancinge,[1] Thou hast turn'd my sadnes,
Out [2] of my sackloth girded mee with gladnes.

---

[9] With reference to the 'es' here and elsewhere, it is given only when written in full and not by contraction-sign: the latter, except where the rhythm demands it, is represented by the simple 's' of our modern plural. Cf. prefatory Note to these 'Psalms,' *ante*. G.

[1] 'sadnes' written and erased here. G.

[2] I am uncertain whether this is 'But' or 'Out.' G.

For this shall euerie good man singe Thy praise,
And I shall thanke and blesse Thee all my dayes.

PSALM XXXI.

In Thee, O Lord ! haue I put all my trust,
Then rescue mee from shame, as Thou art just ;
Giue eare, and soone from perill sett mee free ;
Bee Thou a Rocke and stronge defence to mee ;
Thou art my Rocke and Castle when I stray ;
Bee Thou my Guide, and leade mee in the way.
Thou art my strength ; O cleare mee from that net
Which priuily my foes for mee haue sett !
Into Thy hands[3] my soule I doe committ :
Lord God of truth Thou hast redeemèd it.
I hate all those which in vain lies delight,
For all my trust is in the Lord of might.
Thy mercies glad my heart : for in my woe
Thou hast vouchsaft my [weary] soule to knowe.
Thou hast not left mee prisoner with my foe,
But sett me free that I at large may goe.
Yeild to my trubles mercifull releife,
My cares waxe deafe, my heart doth melt with greife.

[3] In MS. another example of the contraction-sign of ' es ' with ' e'
preceding. Cf. prefatory Note, as *supra*. G.

Few are my yeares, in number to be tould,
Yet sorrow, care, and greife, hath made mee ould;
My strength with prayer and anguish doth decay,
My joynts growe weake, my bones consume away;
I am a scorne to all my enimies,
But specially my Neighbours mee dispise;
My very presence did my friends affright,
And all my ould acquaintance shun my sight.
I am forgott as if I buried lay,
And viler then a broken pott of clay.
I heard the waylings of the multitude
And trembled while they did my death conclude;
But all my hope hath beene O Lord in Thee,
Whome I professe my only Lord to bee;
My tyme is in Thy hand, O doe not leaue
Mee in their hands which would my life bereue.
O turne to mee the brightnes of Thy face,
And saue mee through Thy mercy and Thy grace
Make not mee blush which did invoke Thy name,
But put my foes to silence and to shame;
And let the lipps bee dumbe which vtter lyes
Against the righteous in spightfull-wise.
O what blessings, dost Thou keepe in store
For them that feare and loue Thee euermore;

Thou shalt protect them from the great men's pride,
And in Thy Tent from stormes of tongues them hide.
Blest bee the Lord Whose mercies manifold
Doe keepe mee safer then the strongest hold ;
When I with passion was transported quite,
I said I was sequester'd from His sight ;
And yet for all my weaknes, heard was I,
When to my MAKER I did make my crie.
Loue Him yee SAINTS of His who guardeth those
Who trust in Him : and pay'st[4] their proudest foes.
Yee that rely on Him be strong of hart
And Hee to you shall heauenly strength jmpart.

PSALM XXXII.

HAPPIE indeed and truly blest is hee
Whose sinnes remitted and faults couerèd bee ;
To whome the Lord doth not jmpute his sinne,
Whose single heart hath not deceipt therein.
When I was silent I consum'd away,
And pyninge greife did waste mee day by day ;
Thy hand on mee was heauy still, whereby
My moisture grewe like draught in Summer drie.

---

[4] This word has been altered in the MS. by the (original) writer,
and the reading cannot be very certainly made out ; but I read pay'st
=plenteously rewarded. G.

My sinne I will acknowledge Lord to Thee,
My secret faults shall not concealèd bee ;
I said, I will my synnes to God confesse,
And God forthwith forgaue my wickednesse.
If good men seeke Him when Hee may be found,
The world's high waues shall neuer them surround ;
Thou hid'st mee close and sauest mee from annoy,
And dost enuirone mee with songs of joy ;
When Thou hast sett mee in Thyne owne right way,
Thine eye doth guide mee that I doe not stray.
Then must I not be brute, as horse and mule,
Which men with bitt and bridle only rule.
With many whipps, God doth the wicked chase
But doth with mercies faithfull men embrace ;
Bee glad, rejoyce, and glory in the Lord
All yee whose hearts doth with His will accord.

PSALM XXXIII.

REJOYCE yee righteous in the Lord, and singe ;
To giue God thankes, it is a comely thinge :
Singe prayses unto Him and sett your songs
To harpe and lute, that speaketh with ten tongues ;
Singe to the Lord a new composèd songe,
With chearefull heart and with affection stronge ;

For His most holy Word is euer true,
And all His workes His constancie doe shew.
Hee loueth right and justice euermore,
And with His blessinge Hee the earth doth store;
For by His word the heauens created were;
His breath made euery STARR and euery sp'ere;[5]
The Seas, as in a STOREHOUSE Hee doth keepe,
And heapes them up as treasures in the deepe;
The earth before the LORD shall quake for feare,
And all that dwell on His round CENTER here:
Hee spake, and they were made; at His commaund
The heauens began to moue, the earth to stand.
COUNSELLS of princes and of NATIONS great,
And peoples' plotts, His wisdome doth defeat;
But GOD's owne counsell, purpose and decree,
Eternall stand, and cannot frustrate bee.
That NATION hath true happines and blisse,
Whose GOD and LORD, the LORD JEHOUAH is;
Downe from the highest heauen the Lord did looke,
And of all men a full suruey Hee tooke;
From Heauen aboue the Lord did cast His eye,
And all mens wayes and wanderings did espie.

---

[5] Qu: =sphere? G.

Hee formèd all their hearts, and understands
Their thoughts, their words, and workes of all their hands.
The greatest armies cannot saue a KINGE,
Nor strength unto a stronge man safety bringe;
His trust is vaine who trusteth in his horse,
And seckes deliuerance by soe small a force;
With gracious eye the Lord behoulds the just,
Which Him doe feare and in His mercie trust:
In tyme of dearth their hungrie soules to feed
And from deathe's jawes to rescue them with speed.
Our soules with patience for the Lord haue staid,
Who is our only sheild, support and aid;
Our hearts shall Him as our true joy embrace,
For wee our only trust in Him doe place.
Thy mercie Lord to us exceeded bee,
According to the hope wee haue in Thee.

PSALM XXXIV.

Lord euermore will I giue thankes to Thee,
And in my mouth Thy praise shall euer bee;
My soule shall boast that shee Thy scruant is,
The humble shall be glad to heare of this;
Come then, O come, and let vs praise the Lord,
And magnifie His name with sweet accord.

I sought the Lord by prayer which He did heare,
And saued mee from that ill my soule did feare.
Looke towards God, thou shalt enlightenèd bee,
And no foule shame shall euer light on thee.
The poor man's crie, the Lord doth quickly heare,
And doth for all his trubles quitt him cleare ;
Such as feare God His Angell guards them all,
From euery mischeife that may them befall.
O taste the Lord, and see how sweet Hee is,
The man that trusts in Him liues still in bliss.
O feare the Lord, yee that are SAINTS of His,
Who feare the Lord noe needfull thinge shall misse.
Rich become poore, and lyons hungrie bee,
But such as feare the Lord noe want shall see.
Come then yee children, listen and giue eare,
And I will teach you this religious feare :
What man art thou that longest long to liue,
And wouldst that GOD to thee good dayes should giue ;
Refraine thy tongue from speaking ill the while,
And from thy lipps let there proceed noe guile ;
Doe that is good, decline from that is ill,
Seeke peace with God and men, and hould it still.
Upon good men God casts a gentle eye,
And bends a gentle eare unto their crye.

But to the wicked shewes an angrie browe,
Till they bee quite exterpèd, root and bow ;[6]
But when the righteous cry, the Lord doth heare them
And from all trubles absolutely cleare them ;
God's present helpe the Lord['s own folk] doth finde,
And such Hee saues as are of humble minde.
The righteous into many trubles fall,
But God's sweet mercy brings them out of all ;
Their very bones so keepe and count doth Hee,
As not one broken nor one lost, shall bee.
But some foule death shall on the wicked light,
And they which hate the just, shall perish quite ;
But of his seruants, GOD the SAUIOUR is ;
They trust in Him, their hope they cannot misse.

PSALM XXXV.

PLEAD Thou my cause, O Lord my Advocate !
Against all those with whome I haue debate ;
Fight against them that doe against mee fight,
Take up Thy shield, and helpe mee with Thy might ;
Lift up Thy launce, stopp them which mee pursue,
Say to my soule, I am Thy SAUIOUR true ;

[6] = 'bough.'   G.

Let shame on them which seeke my ruin light,
And with confusion turne them all to flight.
Let them bee like the dust before the winde,
With God's feirce angell followinge them behinde;
Set them in slipperie wayes, and darke withall,
And let God's Angell smite them as they fall;
For they have spred a nett and dig'd a pitt,
Euen without cause to catch my soule in it:
But in that pitt let them fall vnawares,
And bee entangled in their proper snares;
But thou my soule, whom God[7] thus guides from ill,
Rejoyce in Him, and His saluation still;
My bones shall say, Lord who is like to Thee?
Who poore weake men men from their strong foe dost
     free:
False witnesses arose with oathes untrue,
And chargèd mee with things I neuer knew;
They to my greife did ill for good requite,
And recompenc't my kindnes with dispight;
Yet in their sicknes I did sackcloth weare,[8]
And fast and pray with many a secret teare;

[7] Written with a small 'g': the Scribe varies much in this. We have given the capital uniformly in Divine names, nouns and pronouns. G.   [8] 'Ware' written and erased. G.

I could not more for friend or brother mourne,
Or if my mother to her graue were borne :
But in my woe they made great mirth and glee,
The very abjects mockt and mowde⁹ at mee ;
Base flatterers and jesters came withall,
[And] gnasht their teeth to show their bitter gall.
How long shall this bee Lord ? my soule withdraw
From these men's wrongs, and from the lyon's jaw :
Soe in Thy Church shall I my thankes proclaime,
And in our Great Assembly praise Thy name ;
Let not my foes trihumph¹ on mee againe,
Nor with their mockinge eyes shew their disdaine ;
They meet and parte, but peace they doe not seeke
But to supplant the peaceable and meeke ;
They gape and drawe their mouthes in scornefull wise,
And cry, fie, fie, wee sawe it with our eyes.
But Thou their deed (O Lord !) dost alsoe see ;
Then bee not silent soe, nor farr from mee.
Awake, stand up O God and Lord of might,
Auenge my quarrell, judge my cause aright ;
To Thy doome rather lett mee fall or stand
Then subject bee to their insultinge hand ;

---

⁹ =to wry the mouth. G.   ¹ Cf. Psalm xviii, l. 8. G.

Then they should say, soe, soe, these things goe right,
We haue our will, and haue deuour'd him quite.
Shame bee to them that joy in my mischance,
And which to cast mee downe themselues aduance ;
Let them bee glad that my wellwishers bee,
And blesse the Lord that hath soe blessèd mee.
As for my tongue it shall sett forth Thy praise,
And celebrate Thy justice all my dayes.

PSALM XXXVI.

THE wicked man's bould sinnes my heart doe tell,
Noe feare of God before his eyes doth dwell ;
Yet flattereth hee himselfe in his owne sight,
Untill his hatefull deeds bee brought to light ;
His words are lies, and most deceiptfull too,
He leaues of[f] quite all honest deeds to doe ;
Hee on his bed doth nought but mischeife muse,
Hee shunns noe ill and noe good way doth choose ;
Thy mercie Lord doth to the heauens extend,
Thy faithfullnes doth to the CLOUDES assend ;
Thy justice stedfast as a MOUNTAINE is,
Thy JUDGEMENTS deepe as is the great Abisse ;
Thy noble mercirs saue all liueinge thinges,
The sonnes of men creepe underneath Thy winges :

With Thy great plenty they are fedd at will,
And of Thy pleasure's streame they drinke their fill;
For euen the well of life remaines with Thee,
And in Thy glorious light wee light shall see ;
To them that know Thee, Lord, bee loveinge still,
And just to them whose heart intends noe ill ;
Let not the foot of pride tread on my Crowne
Nor the hand of the vngodly cast mee downe :
False are the wicked in their slippery wayes,
And haue no power againe themselues to raise.

PSALM XXXVII.

If ill men prosper doe not Thou repine,
Nor enuy them though they[2] in glory shyne ;
For as the grasse they shall be mowen away,
And as greene hearbes shall turne to withered hay :
Trust thou in God and still bee doinge good,
And thou shalt neuer want noe house nor food ;
Delight in Him, Hee shall to thee jmparte,
The full desires and wishes of Thy heart ;
On Him rely, to Him thy way commend,
And Hee shall bringe it to a blessed end ;
Thine vpright light shall shine like the morninge light ;
And Thy just dealinge like the NOONE-day bright ;

[2] Miswritten 'thou' in the MS. G.

Bee still and frett not, but God's leasure stay
Though wicked men doe prosper in their way ;
Suppresse Thine anger, let offences die,
Lest thou be mouèd to offend thereby ;
Expect a while, obserue what will befall ;
Th' ungodly shall bee gon, their place and all.
The Lord shall root out sinners out of hand,
When good men and their heires shall hould their Land.
Meeke persons shall enjoy the earthe's encrease,
And shall abound in plentie and in peace :
Against the just the wicked haue combin'd,
And in dispight their teeth at them they grinde ;
But God with scorne behoulds them from the skie,
For that Hee sees their day of ruin nigh ;
The vngodly drawes his sword and bends his bowe
To slay the just, the weake to ouerthrowe :
But his bent bowe shall breake and make him start,
And his owne sword shall peirce his wicked heart ;
That little which the just enioyes with peace,
'Tis better then th' ungodlie's great encrease ;
For th' armes of jmpious men the LORD will breake,
And giue the righteous strength when they are weake ;
The just man's dayes the LORD doth know and see,
That his inheritance shall endlessse bee ;

The tymes of danger shall not him confound,
And in the dayes of dearth, hee shall abound;
Thy foes O Lord, shall perish and consume
Like fatt of lambes, and vanish into fume;
Th' ungodly want and borrow, but repay not
The good men frankly giue, [and] yet decay not;
Their seat is firme whom God hath best belou'd
But such as Hee doth[3] curse shall bee remou'd.
The good man's goings soe directeth Hee
As it most pleasinge to Himselfe may bee;
Oft falls the just, yet is not cast away,
For God's owne hand is his support and stay;
Though I am ould, the just man or his seed
I neuer sawe forsaken or in need;
Hee doth giue daily almes, and frankly lend,
Which makes his offspringe blessèd in the end;
Shun to doe ill, bee euer doinge well,
And euermore thou shalt in safety dwell;
The LORD who loueth right, forsaketh neuer,
Those that are His, but keepeth them for euer;
His children Hee correcteth now and then,
But roots out quite the race of wicked men.
As long as HEAUEN shall moue and Earth shall stand,
The righteous men inherit shall the Land;

---

[3] 'Shall' written and erased. G.

The just man's mouth is wisedome's flowinge well,
His tongue, of truth and judgement loues to tell ;
And in his heart the lawe of God doth bide,
Which makes him walke vpright and neuer slide ;
The wicked sees the just with enuious eye,
And lies in waite to wound him mortally ;
But God will neuer leaue him to his hands,
Nor him condemne when hee in judgement stands :
Then wait thou on the Lord, and keepe His way,
Hee shall thy patience with promotion pay ;
Thy dwellinge in the Land shall stablisht bee,
When thou the fall shalt of the wicked see.
The vngodly in great power myselfe haue scene,
Soe that he flourisht like a bay-tree greene ;
But soone's⁴ I passèd by, and gon was hee,
His place I sought, but noe where could it see ;
Keepe a cleare conscience, right and truth intend,
For that brings peace and comfort in the end ;
When sinners shall at once together fall,
And in the end shall be extèrpèd all ;
But good mens' safety doth from God proceed,
Who is their strength in truble, helpe at need ;
Against the wicked Hee assists the just,
And recues them, because in Him they trust.

⁴ Another example of ' e ' before ' es ' as *ante.* G.

PSALM XXXVIII.

If for my sinnes Thine anger kindled bee,
Lord ! let not then Thy justice chastise mee ;
Thine arrowes fixèd in my fleshe doe stand,
I feele the pressure of Thy heauie hand ;
I haue noe health Thine anger is soe much,
My bones noe rest ; my greiuous synne is such,
My wickednes doth mount abouc my head
And fallinge presse mee like a load of lead ;
My ulcers are corrupted and doe smell,
Caus'd by my folly, which I blush to tell.
I am with greife soe broken and soe torne,
As I all day in heart and habit mourne.
My loynes are fillèd with a sore descase,
Noe parte of all my bodie feeleth ease ;
I am soe faint, soe feeble, and soe sore,
As paine and anguish make mee crie and roare ;
Thou Lord ! the longings of my heart dost see,
My sighes and groanings are not hidd from Thee.
My heart doth pant, my sinewes faile mee quite,
My weepinge eyes haue lost their power of sight ;
Meane while, my freinds and neighbours they looke on,
My nearest kinsmen farthest of[f] are gon :
And they which seeke my life haue layed their snares
And sett their trapps, to catch mee vnawares.

They that to doe mee mischeife lye in wait,
Doe plott and practise nothinge but deceit ;
But as for mee in silent patience
I seemèd deafe and dumbe and voyde of sence ;
As one whose eare admitts not any sound,
And in whose mouth there[5] is noe answeare found.
For on the Lord I euermore rely,
Though I stand mute, Thou shalt for mee replie :
My suite is that my foes may not preuaile
Who greatly joy to see my footinge faile ;
For in a place of stumblinge sett am I,
My sad estate is still before mine eye ;
But I with sorrow will confesse my synne,
And grieue that I offend my God therein ;
And yet my foes do liue and grow in might,
They grow in numbers which do beare me spight.
They which doe ill for good, doe hate mee too,
Because I loue good turnes for ill to doe :
Lord leaue mee not nor from mee farr depart,
Saue mee with speede : for Thou my safety art.

PSALM XXXIX.

I said I will bee wary in my way ;
Lest I offend in that my tongue should say,

[5] Miswritten 'their.' G.

I will my mouth as with a bridle hould,
While wicked men with enuy mee behould :
I dumb did stand and from all speech refraine,
Euen from good words, which was to mee a paine :
My heart was hott : while I such doubts did cast,
The fire brake out, and thus I spake at last :
' Lord of my life reueale to mee the end,
The period showe, to which my dayes doe tend ' !
My life is but the measure of a spann,
Nought as to Thee, so vaine a thinge is man :
Who dreaminge walks, and toyles for wealth in vaine,
And doth not know to whome it shall remaine.
But what doe I expect ? what is my hope !
Of my desires Thou art the only scope.
Lord ! from my synnes Thine indignation turne
And make mee not to wicked fooles a scorne,
When Thou didst strike I silent was and dum[b]
Because I knewe the blowe from Thee did come.
Remoue Thy hand, withdrawe Thy plague from me
Wherewith my vitall spirrits consumèd bee :
Thy plagues for sinne doth like a moth consume
Man's beauty vaine, which is nought else but fume.
Lord ! heare my prayer, and listen to my cries,
Let not Thy gracious eye my teares dispise :

For I am but Thy guest, and sojourne heare,
On earth a pilgrim as my fathers were ;
O spare a little, and my strength restore
Before I goe from hence to come noe more.

PSALM XL.

Long on the Lord, I waited patiently,
Till He enclin'd His eare, and heard my cry :
Drew mee from out the pitt of mire and clay
Did sett mee on firme ground and guide my way :
Put in my mouth a new and joyfull song
Of thankes[6] and praise, that to Himselfe belong.
Of His great mercie, many shall haue sense,
And of the Lord haue feare and confidence.
Blest is the man who hath on God relide,
Not turninge vnto lies or worldly pride ;
O Lord ! Thy works of wonder, they are such
Thy care and loue to vsward is soe much,
They are soe great, they are soe numberlesse,
As if I would, I could not them expresse.
My sacrifice of meates Thou would'st not take,
But Thou mine eare didst peirce and open make.

---

[6] Another example of ' e ' preceding the contraction ' es,' as also
on line 5th below this, in ' workes,' and in Psalm xli, line 19th,
' evenings.' See prefatory Note to these Psalms. G.

Thou didst not aske burnt-offerings at my hand
Then LORD said I ' I come at Thy commaund ;
Thy Booke eternall, doth of mee record,
That I should come to doe Thy will O Lord !
To doe Thy will, my heart is pleasèd well,
For in my heart Thy lawe doth euer dwell ;
Thy truth I haue to all Thy people tould,
Therein Thou knowest my tongue I cannot hould :
Thy justice in my heart is not conceal'd,
Thy mercy to the world I haue reucal'd ;
I haue not spar'd to make Thy bounty knowne,
But in the Great Assembly haue it showne.
Take not Thy wonted mercy Lord, from mee,
But let Thy goodnes still my safety bee.
My trubles numberlesse such hould haue tooke
On my weake soule, as vp I cannot looke :
My sinnes beinge more then[7] haires upon my head,
Make my heart faint and vitall spirrits dead :
But bee it Lord, Thy pleasure and Thy will,
With speed to saue and rescue mee from ill :
Bringe them to shame that would my life destroy,
Reproue them Lord, that wish my soule's annoy :
Let them bee left to scorne and pride, which blame
Which scorninge say to me, fie, fie, for shame.

[7] ' On my ' written here and erased.   G.

But let all those that seeke their blisse, in Thee
Rejoyce and say, the Lord's name prais^èd bee'.
For mee who am contemtible and poore,
The Lord takes care, and feeds mee euermore:
Thou Lord art my protection, and my aid,
Let not Thy gracious helpe bee long delay'd.

PSALM XLI.

THAT man is blest who doth the poore regard;
In tymes of truble God shall him reward,
Prolong his life, and blesse him in the Land,
And free him from his foes' oppressing hand:
Shall comfort him, when sicke and weake hee lies,
And make his bedd till hee in health doe rise:
My synne hath giuen my soule a greiuous wound,
Apply Thy mercy Lord, and make it sound;
Thus speakes my foe of mee to show his spight,
' When shall his life and honnour perish quite'?
Hee vissitts mee, but with false heart and tongue
And thereof vaunts, his complices amonge:
Euen all my foes against mee doe conspire,
And with one minde my ruin doe desire;
' Let him,' say they of mee, ' in judgement fall
And when hee once is downe not rise at all.'

The freind I trusted, which did eat my bread,
Hath lifted vp his heele against my head.
Thy mercie's winges on mee O Lord display;
Raise mee againe, and I shall them repay.
By this I doe Thy gracious fauour see,
In that my foe doth not trihumph on mee.
Thou in my health uphouldst mee with Thy hand,
And in Thy presence I shall euer stand.
The name of JACOB's GOD bee blessèd then,
From age to age for euermore : Amen.

PSALM XLII.

As for the streames the hunted hart doth bray,
Soe for God's grace my heart doth pant and pray.
My soule doth thirst (O God of life !) for Thee,
When shall I come Thy blessed[8] face to see?
My teares are all my food both night and day,
While ' where is now thy God ?' the wicked say.
I powrèd out my hart, while thus I thought
And to God's House the multitude I brought :
With songs of praise and thankfullnes withall,
To celebrate the Lord's great festiuall :
Then why art thou my soule soe full of woe,
Vnquiet in thyselfe and vexèd soe?

[8] ' Life from thee ' written and erased.   G.

O put thy trust in God and thankfull bee,
For his sweet helpe His presence yields to Thee.
My soule is greiu'd remembringe all the ill
I felt in JORDAN's vale and HERMON hill.
One depth of sorrow doth to another call,
Thy waves O God haue ouergon mee all :
I prais'd at night God's bounty of the day,
And vnto Him that giues mee life did pray.
God of my strength, why hast Thou left mee soe,
With heauy hart oppressèd by my foe ?
My foe doth cut my bones as with a sword,
While hee in scorne repeats this bitter word,
'Where is thy God ? ' his speech to mee is such :
'Where is thy God, of which thou talk'st soe much ? '
But why art thou my soule dejected soe?
Why art thou trubled and soe full of woe ?
Trust thou in God, and giue Him thankfull praise[9]
Who is Thy present helpe in all thy wayes.

PSALM XLIII.

JUDGE thou my[1] cause, [O God !] and right mee then,
Against vngodly and decciptfull men.

---

[9] 'O put thy trust in God and thankfull bee' written and erased. G.
[1] 'Mee' miswritten. G.

O God, my strength, why sett'st Thou mee aside
And leau'st mee to my foes' oppressinge pride?
Send forth Thy light and truth and guide mee still,
In the right way to Thy most holy hill.
God of my[2] joy, before Thine Alter high,
My thankfull harte, my harpe shall justifie.
Then why art thou my soule dejected soe?
Why art thou trubled and soe full of woe?
O put thy trust in God and thankfull bee,
For that sweete aide His presence giues to thee.

PSALM XLIV.

Lord! of Thy workes, our fathers haue vs tould,
Some in their dayes, and former times of ould;
How Thou hast rooted out the PAGAN race,
And Thy choice people planted in their place :
Who did not with their owne sword winne the Land,
Nor make the conquest with their proper hand;
But by Thine Arme, Thy fauour and Thy grace,
Thy countenance and brightnesse of Thy face;
Thou art my KINGE, O God, and royal Guide,
And Thou for JACOB's safety dost prouide.

---

[2] ' Thy ' miswritten and corrected in a later hand. G.

Wee through Thine aid our foes doe bouldly meet,
And by Thy vertue[3] cast them at our feet ;
Therefore my trust I place not in my bowe,
Nor in my sword, to saue mee from my foe.
Thou only sau'st vs from our enimies,
Confoundinge them that doe against vs rise.
Wee boast and glory in our strength therefore,
And to Thy name singe praises euermore ;
But now Thou standest of[f] and leau'st vs quite,
And dost not lead our armies out to fight ;
Thou mak'st vs fly before our foes with feare,
While they from vs rich spoyles away doe beare ;
Like sheepe, to feed them Thy poore flock is giuen,
Or scattered into seuerall NATIONS driuen.
Thyne owne deare people Thou dost sell for naught,
And setts on them noe price when they are bought ;
Thou hast vs made vnto our NEIGHBOURS all,
An object of reproch and scorne withall :
To NATIONS which doe worship Idolls dumbe,
Wee are[4] a byword of contempt become ;
All the day long my shame is in my sight,
Which makes me hide my face and shun the light,

---

[3] =Through the ' vertue' of Thy name, *i.e.*, through Thee. The
original is ' And in Thy name.' G.

[4] ' Become' written and erased. G.

Not able to endure the blasphemies
And scornes of my reuengefull enimies.
For all these ills wee doe not Thee forgett,
Thy blessed COUENANT wee renounce not yet.
Our hearts recede not from the LAWE deuine,
Nor doe our footsteps from Thy pathes declyne ;
Though wee in dennes of dragons haue bene plac't,
And with death's fearefull shadowes⁵ ouercast.
If wee the name of our true GOD forgett,
And Idolls false wee in His place doe sett,
Shall not Hee search [it] out, Whose eye doth see
The heart of man whose thoughts most trubled bee?
But for Thy cause LORD wee are martir'd still,
Like sheep which SLAUGHTER-MEN cull out to kill.
Up Lord ! why dost Thou seeme to slumber thus?
Awake and bee not alwayes farr from vs :
Why hidest Thou from vs Thy blessed face,
Forgettinge our distresse and wretched case?
Our soules euen to the dust are humbled lowe,
Our prostrate bodies to the ground doe growe.
Arise and helpe vs Lord ! defend vs still,
And saue vs for Thy mercie's sake from ill.

---

⁵ Spelled ' Shawdowes ' and corrected.   G.

My heart is mou'd to vtter some good thinge,
Which I entend to offer to the kinge.
My tougue shall bee the pen, and swiftly write
What in my heart deuotion doth endite.
Fairest of men, whose lipps with grace abound,
Whom with eternall blessings God hath crown'd ;
Gird Thy sharp sword vpon Thine armèd thigh,
And shew Thyselfe in power and MAJESTIE.
Ride on with Thy great honnour prosperously,
Raigne and trihumph, and bee Thou mounted high,
Borne vp with justice, truth and meeknes' wings :
And Thy right hand shall teach Thee dreadfull things ;
Thine arrowes sharpe, shall make Thy foes to fall,
Which Thou shalt shoote and peirce their hearts withall.
Eternall is Thy judgement-seat O God !
Thy scepter is a true directinge rod ;
Right hast Thou lou'd and loth'st vnrighteousnes,
And therefore GOD Thy GOD Who doth Thee blesse,
Hath powr'd on Thee O PRINCE OF PRINCES best,
More oyle of gladnes then on all the rest :
Thy garments, which Thy person shall aray,
Brought out of Iuory wardrobes where they lay,

Of Myrrh, of Alloes, and of Casha smell ;
Which odours doe refresh and please Thee well.
The queene, all cladd in gould at Thy right hand,
Daughters of Kings attendinge her, shall stand.
Attend faire daughter, listen and giue eare,
Forgett thy father's house and Cuntry deare.
Soe shall the Kinge take pleasure in thy beautie ;
Hee is thy Lord, yield Him both loue and duty.
The Tyrian virgins shall bringe guifts to thee,
And merchants rich, thy suppliants shall bee.
The daughter of the Kinge is rich without,
Her gownes embroidered all with gould about;
And yet within, shee is more glorious farr,
The jewells of her minde more precious are.
In finest dressinge, with the needle wrought,
Shee with her fellow virgins shall bee brought.
They shall with joy, O Kinge bee brought to Thee,
And in Thy princely Courte receauvèd bee.
Thou in thy father's stead, O Bride shalt gaine
Sonnes, which in sundry Prouinces shall raigne.
Thee Lord, will I remember, all my dayes,
And all the world shall giue Thee endlesse praise.

PSALM XLVI.

God is our hope and strength, which neuer failes ;
Our present helpe, when mischeife vs assailes.

Though the earth remouèd, and the mountaines were
Amid the Ocean cast, wee would not feare.
Though raginge seas a dreadfull noise doe make,
Thou[gh] floodes and tempestes [roaring,] hills doe shake.
There is a streame, which though it bee not great,
Makes glad God's CITTIE, and His holy seate.
God in her CENTER dwells, and makes His place
Unmoueable, by His preuentinge grace.
They were[6] enrag'd which heathen kingdomes sway,
But when God spake, the Earth did melt away.
The Lord of Hosts assists vs with His power,
And JACOB's GOD to vs becomes a Tower.
Come, and behould what workes the Lord hath wrought,
And Hee, His foes hath to destruction brought.
In all the world Hee warr to peace doth turne,
The bowe and speare doe breake and chariotts burne;
Bee quiet then and still, and know that I
Am Lord of the world and God Most High:
The Lord of Hosts assists vs with His power,
And JACOB's GOD to vs becomes a Tower.

PSALM XLVII.

CLAP hands yee people, with applause rejoyce,
Singe to the Lord with loud and chearfull voyce;

---

[6] Miswritten 'warr.' G.

His throne is high, His judgement breedeth feare,
On all the earth Hee doth the SCEPTER beare.
Hee makes much people our commaund obey,
And many NATIONS at our feet doth lay ;
And hath for vs an heritage in store,
Euen JACOB's portion whom Hee lou'd before.
In glorious trihumph GOD is mouuted high,
The Lord with trumpet's sound ascends the SKIE.
Singe, singe, vnto our God, vnto our Kinge,
All praises due, euen all due praises singe.
All KINGDOMES of the earth to Him belonge,
Singe wisely then, and vnderstand your song.
In all the heathen Hee doth raigne alone,
And sitts in judgment in His holy throne.
And heathen princes which were seuerd farr,
To Abraham's faithfull seed now joinèd are.
And God, Whose highnes doth the heauens transcend,
As with a buckler doth the earth defend.

PSALM XLVIII.

Great is the Lord and highly to bee praised,
In God's owne CITTIE, SYON hill is rays'd ;
The beautie and the joy of all the Land,
The great king's CITTIE on the NORTH doth stand ;

In his faire PALLACES God's name is knowne,
Where Hee doth cherish and protect His owne.
Though manie kings against her gathred bee,
They stand astonisht her great strength to see.
As when a woman doth in trauell fall,
A suddaine feare and tremblinge takes them all;
And God shall breake them though they bee combin'd,
As shipps are broken with an EASTERNE winde.
What wee haue heard, wee see Thou dost fullfill,
Thou GOD OF HOSTS vphoulds't Thy CITTIE still :
Amidst Thy Temple Lord, wee doe attend
Till Thou to vs Thy grace and fauour send.
Great is Thy name, O God, Thy praise noe lesse,
And Thy right hand is full of righteousnes.
Rejoyce O Sion, and your joyes renew,
Daughters of JUDAH,[7] for His judgements true.
About the walls of Sion walke yee round,
And tell the towers wherewith that forte is crownd ;
Obserue her bulwarks and her turrets high,
And tell the same to your posterity.
This euer liuinge God our God is Hee,
And shall our Guide while we haue liuinge, bee.[8]

[7] ' Judgement' written here and erased. G.

[8] A later hand substitutes another line, ' And while we live, our only guide shall be.' G.

PSALM XLIX.

HEARE this yee people, all yee people heare;
Listen to[9] mee and giue attentiue eare,
All yee that in the world residinge bee,
Both rich and poore, of high and low degree :
My mouth shall vtter, and my heart deuise,
Matters of greatest skill, profound and wise.
Mine eares to parables will I encline,
And singe vnto my harpe, of things deuine.
Then why should I in ill times fearfull bee,
When mischeife at my heeles doth follow mee.
Howbeit, some doe in their riches trust,
And glory in their wealth, which is but dust;
Yet non from death his brother's life can stay,
Nor vnto GOD for Him a ransome pay.
For it cost more the soule of man to saue,
Then all the wealth is worth, which worldlyngs haue.
Nor may men hope to liue on earth for euer,
Though long they last, ere soule and body seuer.
That fooles and wise men die alike they finde,
And vnto strangers leaue their wealth behinde.
Their houses yet they thinke shall euer stand,
They giue their proper names vnto their land ;

---

[9] 'Unto' written and the 'un' erased.   **G.**

Yet noe man can in honnour euer bee,
But as the brute beast dies, euen so does hee.
This is their follie, this their stumblinge wayes ;
And yet the children doe their fathers praise.
[1]They are shut vp in graues as sheepe in folde,
And hungry Death feeds on their bodies cold,
The just shall rule them when the sunne doth rise,
With them their pride and beauty buried lies ;
But God shall from Deathe's power my soule deliuer,
When Hee shall take it to Himselfe for euer.
Then let not feare and enuy thee surprize,
When thou seest men in wealth and honnour rise,
For to their graues they naught away shall beare,
Nor shall their glory waite vpon them there ;
Yet they themselues thought happie all their dayes,
For him who helps himselfe others will praise:
As his forefathers all are gon before,
Soe shall hee die and see the light noe more.
Soe man on honnour little doth foresee,
But as brute beasts doe perish, soe dies hee.

PSALM L.

The Lord, the God of Gods, the world doth call,
Euen from the sunn's vprisinge to his fall ;

---

[1] The MS. begins here with 'and': but is struck out. G.

From out of SION doth the Lord appeare,
And shewes the brightnes of His beauty cleare.
In trihumph, not in silence come shall Hee,
His vsher fire, His guard a storme shall bee.
Hee by His summons heauen and earth will call,
That Hee [may]² judge at once his creatures all.
To Mee, saith Hee, let all My saints repaire,
Which worshipp Mee with sacrifice and prayer ;
God's justice shall from heauen declarèd bee,
For Who is judge of all the world but Hee ?
Harke ISRAELL ! I am Thy God, giue eare ;
I will against thee speake and witnes beare.
Not for the dailie taske of sacrifice,
Or that burnt-offerings shine not in Mine eyes :
I want them not, nor will I take at all,
Goat from thy fould or bullocke from thy stall ;
All beasts are Mine within the forrest wide,
And cattle on a thousand hills beside ;
I knowe all fowles which in the aire doe fly,
And see all beasts which in the feild doe lye.
If I were hungrie would I begg of thee,
When all things in the world belong to Mee ?

---

² I have filled in ' may ' as evidently overlooked, and as it is the
word of the prose version : a later hand has written 'will' and
another ' for ' in the place of ' That.'   G.

Art thou O man, soe simple as to thinke
That bulls' flesh is My meat, goats' blood My drinke ? [3]

*   *   *   *   *

PSALM LXVII.

Shew us Thy mercy, Lord, and grace diuine :
Turne Thy bright face that it on vs may shine,
That all the men on Earth enlight'ned so
Theire owne saluation and Thy wayes may know.
O let Thy people praise Thy blessed name,
And let all tongues and nations doe the same ;
And let all mortall men rejoyce in this,
That God['s] their judge, and iust His iudgment, is.

[3] The Manuscript thus far is in one handwriting : and since the prefatory Note to these Psalms was written, I have discovered among the Harleian MSS. a very remarkable document by Sir John Davies, viz. his " Plea spoken at the Bar of the House of Lords " on " the King's power to impose Ship-money," (126. B 10—4266) and it is *identically the same holograph with that of these Fifty Psalms,* presenting precisely the same forms and contractions throughout. So that the Scribe of the one must have been the Scribe of the other : no doubt one of Sir John's Secretaries or ' men,' as he himself calls them. I shall give above important historical Paper—which never has been published, or even referred to, so far as I am aware—in my edition of DAVIES' Prose Works. Meanwhile I need not point out how

O let Thy people praise Thy blessed name,
And let all tongues and nations doe the same :
Then shall the Earth [4] bringe forth a rich encrease,
And God shall blesse vs with a fruitfull peace.
Euen God shall bless vs and [5] His holy feare,
Possesse the harts of all men euery where.

PSALM XCI.

1 Who vnder the Most High Himselfe doth hide,
   In most assurèd safety shall abide.

2 Thou art, O Lord, my hope and my defence,
   My God, in Thee is all my confidence.

3 Hee shall preserue thee from the hunter's snare,
   And from the pestilent contagious aier.

valuable is this additional verification of the Davies authorship of our Manuscript—that is in so far as the Psalms up to L. are concerned. I stand in doubt of his authorship of the remainder; but see our Memorial-Introduction on this.

The Psalms that follow have interposed a half-page and one leaf, blank, and another leaf, filled with the secular Poems that succeed them : but it was deemed better to place all the Psalms together. These other Psalms have the same orthography : but the hand-writing is different and plainer. It will be noticed that Psalm L *supra*, is imperfect, extending only to v. 13. G.

4 'Nations' written and erased. G.

5 'Wth' written and erased. G.

4 His winges shall both protect and cherish thee,
5 His faithfull promise shall thy buckler bee.
  Noe terror of the night shall thee dismay,
  Nor Satan's arrow flyinge in the day,
6 Nor mortall plague, which in the darke annoyes,
  Nor that ill angell which at none[6] destroyes.[7]
7 Thousands, ten thousands shall about thee fall,
  Yet noe such ill shall thee approach at all ;
8 Yea with thine eyes thou shalt behould and see,
  The iust reward of such as impious bee ;
9 Thou art my hope, I will on Thee rely,
  Thy tower of safety, Lord, is sett soe high.
10 Noe mischeefe, noe mischance shall thee betide
  No plague come near the place where Thou shalt
    bide.
11 The Lord His angells will Thy keepers make,
  In all Thy righteous wayes which thou shalte take ;
12 They in their hands shall thee sustaine and stay
  That Thou shalt neuer stumble in thy way.
13 Uppon the basilisk and adder's head,
  Dragon and lyon thou shalt safely tread.
14 Thy loue to Mee shall saue thee from mischance,
  Thy knowledge of My name shall thee aduance.

---

[6] Noon ? **G.**   [7] *Sic.* Qu : = departs ? **G.**

15 I will him hear, and help him in His trouble;
I will protect him and his honour duble.
With length of dayes, hee satisfied shall bee,
And hee at last shall My saluation see.

PSALM XCV.[8]

Come let vs hartily reioyce and singe
To God our mightie Sauiour, and our Kinge;
Present the prayse which doth to Him belonge,
And show our gladnes in a cheerfull songe;
For God our Lord, the greatest God is Hee,
And Monarch of all gods that worshipt bee.
The Earth's round globe, Hee holdeth in His hand :
And th' highest mountaynes are at His command.
The sea is His, Hee hath it made of old,
And the dry land His blessed hands did mould :
Come let vs worship then, and humble fall
Before our mightie God which made vs all.
Hee is our Lord, and wee His people bee;
Our shepheard, and His proper sheep are wee.
This day yf you His holy voice will heare,
Let not your hearts bee hardned as they were,
When in the desert you His wrath did moue,
And temptinge Him His mightie power did proue.

---

[8] Written in the centre of the page XCV. G.

Full forty yeeres this nation greeud mee so,
Their erringe harts My wayes would neuer know ;
Therefore displeas'd by oath I did protest
They neuer should possesse my Land of rest.

PSALM C.

BEE ioyfull in the Lord, yee nations all,
Cheer vp your harts in mirth, and songs withall ;
The Lord is God, not wee but Hee alone
Hath made vs all, and feeds vs euery one.
Then enter yee His gates and courts with prayse,
And striue with hart and voice His name to raise.
For why ? the Lord is sweet, His mercy rare,
His truth for euer constant shall endure.

PSALM CIII.

My soule with all thy powers thy Maker praise ;
    Forget not all His benefits to thee,
Who pardons all thy sinnes, and doth thee rayse
    When thou art fal'n through any infirmitie :
Who doth thee saue from mischeifs that would kill thee,
    And crowneth thee with mercies euer more.
And with the best of thinges doth feed and fill thee,
    And egle-like thy youth and strength restore.

When men oppressèd doe to Him appeale,
  Hee righteth euery one against his foe ;
Hee vnto Moses did His lawes reueale,
  And vnto Jacob's care His workes did show.
Hee is more full of grace then wee of sinne ;
  To anger slowe, compassionate and kind ;
Hee doth not euer chide, and never linne,[9]
  Nor keepes displeasure alwayes in His minde,
Nor after our misdeedes doth Hee vs charge ;
  Nor takes Hee of our faults a strict account,
But as the space from earth to heauen is large,
  So farr His mercy doth our sinnes surmount.
As east from west is distant farr away,
  Soe farr doth Hee from us our sinnes remoue :
As fathers, kindnes to their sonnes bewray,
  Soe God to them that feare Him, showes His loue.
For Hee that made vs and knowes all, doth know
  The matter whereof man was made of old ;
That wee were formèd heer on earth below
  Of dust and clay, and of noe better mold.
Man's age doth wither as the fadinge grasse ;
  He flourisheth, but as yᵉ flower in May,
Which when the South-wind ouer it doth passe
  Is gone ; and where it grew no man can say.

  [9] =cease. G.

But God's sweet kindnes⁹ euer doth consist ;
His truth, from age to age, continew shall,
To them that in His righteous lawes persist,
And thinke vppon them to performe them all.
Heauen is God's seat; there doth His glorie dwell,
But ouer all, His empire doth extend ;
Praise Him yee angells which in strength excell,
And His command doe euermore attend.
Praise Him yee hosts of heauen which serue Him there,
Whose seruice with His pleasure doth accord ;
And praise Him all His creatures euery where ;
And thou my soule for thy part, praise the Lord.

PSALM CL.

To Him with trumpets and with flutes,
With cornets, clarions and with lutes ;
With harpes, with organs and with shawmes,
With holy anthems and with psalmes ;
With voice of angells and of men
Sing! Aleluyia! Amen, Amen.

---

¹⁰ 'to mankind for' written here and erased : 'doth consist' and
its corresponding rhyme two lines below, 'persist,' written in a later
hand. Originally the former line read ' But God's sweet kindness to
mankind for euer,' and to rhyme with this, the coreesponding line
ended with 'perseuer.' **G.**

VIII. MISCELLANEOUS POEMS.

HITHERTO UNPUBLISHED.

OF FAITH THE FIRST THEOLOGICALL VERTUE.

FAITH is a sunbeame of th' Æternall light,
That in man's soule infusd by grace doth shine :
Which giues her dazled eye soe cleare a sight
As evidently sees the truith divine ;
This beame that cleares our eyes, inflames our hearts,
And Charitie's kind fire doth there begett :
For sunlike, it both light and heate imparts :
Faith is the light, and Charitie the heate :
This light of faith the noblest wisdome is,
For it the onley truith allowes and a'plyes :
The virgin's lamp, that lights the soule to blisse ;
The Jacob's scales,[1] whereby shee clymes the skyes :
The eye that sees, the hand that apprehends ;
The cause of causes, and the end of ends.

[1] Scala = ladder. G.

A SONGE OF CONTENTION

BETWEENE FOWRE MAIDS CONCERNINGE THAT WHICH
ADDETH MOST PERFECTION TO THAT SEXE.

THE FIRST FOR BEAUTY.

OUR fairest Garland, made of Beautye's flowers,
  Doth of it selfe supplyall other dowers :
Women excell the perfects' men in this,
And therefore herein theire perfection is :
For beautye wee the glorious heauens admire ;
Faire feilds, faire howses, gold and pearle, desire.
Beautye doth alwayes health and youth imploy
  and doth delight the noblest sense, the eye.

THE SECOND FOR WITTE.

Beautye delights the soule, but witte the Reason :
Witte lasts an age, and beautye but a season :
The sense is quickly cloyd with beautye's tast ;
When witt's delight still quicke and fresh doth last :
Beautye, weake eyes with her illusion blindes,
Witte conquers spirits and triumphs ouer minds :
Deade things haue beautye, onely man hath witte,
  and man's perfection doth consist in it.

THE THIRD FOR WEALTH.

Wealth is a power that passeth nature farre :
Makes euery goose a swanne, and sparke a starre :
Queene money, bringes and giues with royall hands
Freinds, kindred, honour, husband, house and lands ;
Not a faire face, but fortune faire, I craue,
 Lett mee want witte soe I fooles' fortune haue.

THE FOURTH FOR VERTUE.

Yet those perfections most imperfect bee,
If there bee wantinge vertuous modestye ;
Vertue's aspect would haue the sweetest grace
If wee could see as wee conceaue her face :
Vertue guids witte, with well-affected will,
Which if witte want, it proues a dangerous ill :
Vertue gaines wealth with her good gouerment,
 If not, sh'is rich, because shee is content.[2]

A MAID'S HYMNE IN PRAISE OF VIRGINITY.

SACRED virginity, vnconquered Queene !
 Whose kingdome never hath invaded beene ;

---

[2] The preceding are in a third handwriting. G.

Of whose sweete rosy crowne noe hand hath power
  Once but to touch, much lesse to plucke a flower :

Gainst whome proud Love—which on the world doth
        raigne,—
With armies of his passions fights in vaine ;
In whome gray Winter neuer doth appeare,
  To whome greene Springtide lasteth all the yeare.

O fresh immortall baye, vntroubled well,
Or violett, which vntoucht doest sweetest smell ;
Faire vine, which without prop [3] doest safely stand,
  Pure gold, new coynd, which neuer past a hand.

O temperance, in the supreame degree
And hiyest pitch that vertue's winges can flee :
O more then humane spirit, of Angells' kind :
  O white, unspotted garment of the mind,

Which first cloathed man, before hee was forlorne ;
And wherein God Himselfe chose to bee borne.
Within my soule, O heavenly vertue rest,
  Untill my soule with heaven it selfe bee blest. [4]

---

[3] Miswritten 'drop' in MS.   G.

[4] At bottom of this page in the MS. 'Thomas Bakewell' is
scribbled twice.   G.

PART OF AN ELEGIE IN PRAISE OF MARRIAGE.

WHEN the first man from Paradise was driven,
 Hee did from thence his onely comfort beare :
Hee still enioyes his wife, which God had giuen,
 Though hee from other joyes deuorcèd were.

This cordiall comfort of societye,
This trueloue knott, that tyes the heart and will,
When man was in th' extremest miserye
 To keepe his heart from breaking, existed still [5]

There is a tale then [6] [when] the world beganne,
Both sexes in one body did remaine :
Till Joue, offended with that double man,
 Caused Vulcan to diuide him into twayne.

In this diuision, hee the hart did seuer,
But cunningly hee did indent the heart,
That if they should be reunited euer,
 Each part might know which was the counterpart :

5 Written ' x'ested. 6 Miswritten ' There is a tale then.' G.

Since when, all men and women thinke it longe,
Each of them their other part haue mett :
Sometimes the[y] meete ye right, sometimes ye wrong,
　This discontent, and that doth ioy begett.

It ioye begetts in there indented harts,
When like indentures they[7] are matcht aright :
Each part to other mutuall joy imparts,
　And thus the man which Vulcan did deuide,

Is nowe againe by Hymen made entire,
And all the ruine is ræedified ;
Two beeinge made one by their diuine desire.
　Sweete marriage is the honny neuer cloyinge ;

The tune, which being still plaid, doth euer please,
The pleasure which is vertue's in inioyinge.
It is the band of peace and yoake of ease,
　It is a yoake, but sweete [and] light it is ;

The fellowship doth take away the trouble,
For euery griefe is made halfe lesse by this,
And euery ioy is by reflection double.
　It is a band, but one of Love's sweete bands,

---

7 Miswritten ' ye.'　G.'

Such as hee binds the world's great parts withall :
Whose wonderous frame by there convention stands,
But beinge disbanded would to ruine fall.[8]

[A FRAGMENT OF A LOVE ELEGIE.]

BUT those impressions by this forme are staynde,
   and blotted out as if they had not beene :
And yet if nothing else in mynde I beare,
  makes me not lesse learn[è]d then before :
For that in her as in a merrour cleare,
I see and learne far better things and more.
   The students of the world and Natur's booke,
   Beauty and order in the world doe noate ;
  She is my little world; on her I looke,
    and doe in her the same p'fections quoate :
For in her eyes the beames of beauty shine,
  and in her sweete behaviour and her grace,
Order apears, and comlines divine,
  Befitting every tyme and every place.

3.

Vnto that sparkling wit, that spirit of fire,
That pointed diomond looke, that ægle's eye

---

[8] Two preceding are apparently in the same handwriting with those before them.   G.

Whose lyghtning makes audacity retire
  and yet drawes on respectiue modesty,
With wings of feare and loue, my spirit doth fly
  and doth therein a flame of fire resemble ;
Which, when it burnes most bright and mounts most
    high,
    then doth it waver most and most doth tremble.
O that my thoughts were words, or could I speake
The tongue of Angells, to expresse my mynde :
For mortall speach is far too faint and weeke
  to utter passion of so high a kynde.
You have a beauty of such life and light
  As it hath power all wandring eyes to stay :
  To move dombe tongues to speake, lame hands to
    write,
  Stayde thoughts to run, hard harts to melt a way :
Yet painters' can of this draw every line
  And every wittles person that hath eyes,
Can se[e] and judg and sweare it is divine :
For in these outwarde formes all fooles are wise.
But that which my admireing spirit doth veiw,
I[n] thought whereof it would for ever dwell,
Eie never saw, the pensill never drew,
Pen neuer coulde describe, tongue never tell :

It is the invisible beauty of your mynde,
Your cleare immagination, lively witt,
So tund, so temp'rd, of such heavenly kind,
As all mens spirits ar charmd and rapt with it.
This life within begetts your lively looke,
As fier doth make all metalls looke like fier ;
Or your quicke soule by choise this body tooke,
As angells wth bright formes themselves attire.
O that my brest might ope, and hart might cleave
That so you might my silent wondring veiw :
O that you might my soreing spirit p'ceive,
How still with trembling wings it waites on you.
Then should you se[e] of thoughts an endles chaine,
Whose links are[9] vertues, and yor vertues bee ;
Then should you see how your faire forme doth raigne
Through all the regions of my fantesie.
  Then should you fynde that I was yours as much
  As ar your sharpe conceits borowd of none ;
  Or as your native beautyes, that are such
  As all the world will sweare it is your owne.

4.

As they that worke in mines, rich vaines beray,
By some few garaines[1] of ore whereon the[y] hit :

---

[9] Miswritten 'yr.' G.   [1] Qu: Grains ? G.

And as one letter found is oft a kay
To many lines that ar in cipher writt ;
  So I by your few loveing lines descry
  Of your long hiden love the golden mine ;
  And reade therein with a true lover's eye
  Of the hart's volume, every secrett line.
But what availes it now, alas to know
That once a blessed man I might haue beene ?
Since I haue lett, by lookeing downe too low
My highest fortunes sore away vnseene :
  And yett if I had raisd my humble eyes
  As high as heauen I could not haue discer[n]d
  Of invisible thoughts which in your hart did rise,
  Vnles of you I had my lesson learnd.
But all was darke and folden vp to me ;
As soon might I my selfe, my selfe haue taught
To read ye blacke records of destiny,
As read the ridles of the silent thought :
  But whereto may I best resemble this ?
  Your loue was like the springing of a tree :
  We cannot see the growing when it is,
  But that it hath sprunge up and growne, we see.
Or it is like to wealth by fairyes brought,
Which they bring still while they invisible goe ;

But all doth vanish and doth turne to nought,
If once a man enricht, those fairyes know :
But now your loue (say you) is dead and gone :
But my strong faith shall giue it life againe.
By strength of fancy miricles are done,
And true beleefe doth seldom hope in vaine.
    Your Phœnix loue is vnto ashes turnd,
    But now the fier of my affection true,
    Which long within my hart hath kyndly burnd,
    Shall spreade such heate as it shall liue anew.
Or if the fyer of your celestiall loue,
Be mounted vp to heauen and cannot dye :
Another slye Prometheus will I proue,
and play the theife to steale it from the skye.
    When you vouchsaft to loue vnworthy me,
    Your loue discended like a shower of raine ;
    Which on the earth, euen senceles though she bee,
    when once it falls, returneth not againe.
Then why should you withdraw the heauenly dew
Which fell sometymes on your despairing lover ?
Though then his earthly spirit full little knew
How good an Angel did about him houer.
O you the glory of your sex and race !
You that all tymes and places hapie make !
You that in beeing vertuous vertue grace,

and make men love it better for your sake :
One sunbeame yet of favour cast on mee,
Let one kinde thought in your cleare fancy rise :
Loue but a thought, or if that may not be
Be pleasd that I may love, it shall suffise.

TO THE Q: [UEENE.]

WHAT Musicke shall we make to you?
    To whome the strings of all men's harts
Make musicke of ten thousand parts :
    In tune and measure true,
    With straines[2] and changes new.

How shall wee fraime a harmony
Worthie your eares, whose princely[3] hands
Keepe harmony in sundry lands :
    Whose people divers be,
    In station and degree ?
      Heauen's tunes may onely please,
      and not such aires as theise.

---

[2] Miswritten 'strainest' in MS. G.
[3] 'heavenly' written and erased. G.

For you which downe from heauen are sent
Such peace vpon the earth to bring,
Haue h[e]ard yᵉ quire of Angells sing :
    and all the sphæres consent,
    like a sweete instrument.

How then should theise harsh tunes you[4] heare
Created of yᵉ trubled ayer,
breed but distast—when you repaire—
    to your celestiall eare ?
    So that this center here
      for you no musicke fynds,
      but harmony of mynds.

[TO FAIRE LADYES.]

LADYES of Founthill,[5] I am come to seeke
    My hart amongst you, which I late did leese ;

---

[4] Spelled here and elsewhere ' yᵘ.' It may be noted here, that throughout these Poems, as with the Psalms, my rule has been to extend mere contraction-forms. The few left have a place for philological ends. A kind of flourish at the end of a number of words, I was disposed to regard as intended to represent ' s,' but instances occur in the MS. to show that it is a mere ornamental addition : and so I leave it unrepresented. G.

[5] Founthill or Fonthill in Wilts. See Prefatory Note to these hitherto unpublished MSS. G.

but many harts may be perhaps alike :
Therefore of mine, the proper markes, are theise.
It is not hard, though true as steele it be,
And like ye diomond, cleare from any spot ;
Transmixt with many darts you shall it se[e],
but all by vertue, not by Cupid, shot ;
It hath no wings, because it needeth none,
Being now arived and settled where it would ;
Wingèd desires and hopes from it gon are,
but it is full of joyes as it can hold.
Faine would I fInd it where it doth remaine,
but would not haue it though I might againe.

UPON A PAIRE OF GARTERS.

G O loveinge woode-bynde, clip with louely grace,
    those two sweet plants which beare ye flowers of loue ;
Go silken vines, those tender elmes embrace,
Which flourish still, although their roots doe moue.
As soone as you possess your blessed places,
You are advancèd and ennobled more
Then dyodemes, which were white silken laces
That ancient kings about there forehead wore :

Sweete bands, take heed lest you vnge[n]tly bynd,
Or with your stricktnes make too deepe a print :
Was neuer tree had such a tinder rynd,
Although her inward hart be hard as flynt ;
And let your knots be fast, and loose at will,
she must be free, though I stand bounden still.

[TO HIS LADY-LOVE.]

I N this sweete booke, yᵉ treasury of witt,
All virtues, beautyes, passions, written be :
And with such life they are sett forth in it
as still methinkes yᵗ which I read I see.
But this booke's Mrs. is a liveing booke,
Which hath indeed those vertues in her mynde,
And in whose face though envey's selfe do looke,
Even envye's eye shall all those beautyes fynd.
Onely yᵉ passions y are printed here,
In her calme thoughts can no impression make :
She will not love, nor hate, nor hope, nor feare,
Though others seeke theise passions for her sake.
So in yᵉ sonne, some say there is no heate
though his reflecting beames doe fire begett.

[TOBACCO.][6]

HOMER[7] of Moly and Nepenthe singes :
    Moly, the gods most soveraigne hearbe divine.
Nepenth Hellen's[8] drink, which gladnes brings,—
Hart's greife repells, and doth ye witts refine.
But this our age another world hath found,
From whence an hearbe of heavenly power is brought :
Moly is not soe soveraigne for a wound
Nor hath Nepenth[e] so great wonders wrought.
It is tobacco : whose sweete subtile fume
The hellish torment of ye teeth doth ease,
By drawing downe and drieing up ye rume[9]
The mother and the nurse of each disease.[1]

---

[6] Cf. Harleian MS. lines 'Of Tobacco' in Epigrams pp. 32-35, *ante.* G.   [7] Miswritten 'Honnour.' G.

[8] Cf. an Epigram ' Of Tobacco,' 36. The first edition thereof in its reading 'Hekens' is an obvious misprint, probably through Davies' ill writing. The reading here 'Nepen ye Hellens' in the MS. is a scribe's misreading of 'Nepen*the* Hellen's'—he having taken the ending ' the ' for the article. Both point to the true reading, ' Nepenthe Helen's drink.' It is impossible that a scholar like Davies could have supposed ' Nepenthe ' to be the drink of the gods, and equally impossible that he could have thought it drink of the Hellenes. G.   [9] Rheum. G.

[1] The handwriting of the six preceding pieces seems to be the same. G.

ELEGIES OF LOUE.

L IKE as the diuers-fretchled[2] Butter-flye,
When Winter's frost is fallne upon his winge,
Hath onely left life's possibility,
    and lies halfe dead untill the cherefull Spring :

But then the Sunne from his all-quickning eye,
Darts forth a sparkle of the liuinge fire :
Which[3] with kinde heate, doth warme the frozen flye
    and with newe spirit his little breast inspire :

Then doth hee lightly rise and spread his winges,
And with the[4] beames that gaue him life doth playe :
Tasts euery flower that on th' earthe's bosoome springs,
    and is in busye motion all the day :

Soe my gaye Muse, which did my heart possesse,
And in my youthful fantasie doth raigne :
Which cleard my forehead with her cheerefullnes
    and gaue a liuely warmth unto my brayne :

---

² =freckled ? G.

³ Miswritten ' with which.'   G.   ⁴ Miswritten ' they.'   G.

With sadder[5] studye, and with graue conceite
Which late my Immagination entertaynd :
Beganne to shrinke, and loose her actiue heate,
and dead as in a læthargy remaynd.

Long in that senseles sleepe congeald shee laye,
Untill euen now another heauenly eye,
And cleare as that which doth begett the daye,
and of a like reuiuinge simpathy :

Did cast into my eyes a subtile beame,
Which peirieinge[6] deepe, into my fancy went,
And did awake my muse out of her dreame,
and unto her new life and vertue lent :

Soe that shee now begins to raise her eyes
Which yett are dazled with her beautye's raye ;
And to record her wonted melodyes,
Although at first shee bee not full so gaye.

---

[5] =more serious. See Vol. I., p. 160, and related Note in Post-script. G.   [6] *Sic : not* peircinge. G.

THE KINGES WELCOME.[7]

O NOWE or never gentle muse be gaye,
  And mount vp higher on thy paper winges,
Then doth the larke when he salutes the daye, .
And to the morne a merrie welcome singes.

Fly swifter then the egle sent by art
From Noremberg, to the Almaine emperour :
A hand lesse cuning, but as true a hart
Sends thee to a prince of greater worth and power.

Rencounter him thowe shalt vpon the waye,
like Phebus midst of all his golden trayne ;
And knowe him too thou shalt at first suruaye
By proper notes and by distinctions plaine.

By his faire outward formes and princely port,
by honours done to him with capp and knee ;
He is decyphred by the vulgar sorte,
but truer caracters will rise to the[e].

---

[7] From the autograph MS. in All Souls' College, Oxford, MS.
155. W. W. 11, 26, fol. 72, *a* and *b*. The contractions of the MS.
have been expanded, but *u* and *v* are reproduced. This full holo-

Thy sight had once an influence devine.
which gave it power the soule of man to viewe ;
wipe and make cleane that dazeled eye of thine,
and thowe shall see his reall markes and true.

Looke ouer all that divers troope, and finde
whoe hath his spirites most Jouiall and free,
whose bodie is best tempred, and whose minde
Is ever best in tune, and that is hee.

See who it is whose actions doe bewraye
that threefold power, which rarely mixt we see ;
A iudgment graue, and yet a fancie gaye,
Joynd with a ritch remembrance, that is hee.

Marke who it is, that hath all noble skill,
which maye to publique good referrèd bee ;
the quickest witt, and best affected will,
whence flowes a streame of vertues, that is hee

graph of 'The Kinge's Welcome,' while it supersedes the short and
imperfect copy from Dr. Laing's MS.—as first printed in our F. W.
L. edition—confirms the authorship thereof. The abbreviated copy is
also given after this one, as it is expedient to reproduce the MS. in
its integrity. G.

If any more then other clearely wise
or wisely iust or iustly valiant be;
If any doe fainte pleasures more despise,
or be more maister of himselfe, 'tis hee

But soft, thie Egletes eye will soone be dym
If thou this rising sunne directly viewe;
looke syde waies on the beames that spread from him;
faire peace, rich plentie, and religion true

Besides a guard of blessed angells houer
about his sacred person, day and night;
and with invisible winges his head doe cover,
that dangers dartes thereon may never light

when by these proper notes thowe shalt him ken,
fly towardes him with winges of love and feare;
like fire which most doth wane and tremble then
when it doth mount most high and burne most cleare.

Yet on; for wingèd time with the[e] goes on,
which like old Æ'son hath his youth renewd;
his hower glase turnèd and his sickle gone,
and all his graye and broken fethers mewd.

On, for the braue yong sonn aboue his head
Comes Northward, that he may his glorie meete ;
whilest the fresh earth in all her pride doth spread
greene veluit carpettes vnderneath his feete.

On, for thee birds will help to fill thic songe,
whereto all english harte stringes doe agree ;
And the Irish harpe stringes, that did iarre soe long
to make the musicke full, nowe tunèd be.

There is noe eye cast downe, there is noe voice
that to pronounce the harte assent, is dombe ;
the world of thinges doth everie where reioyce,
in certaine hope of blessed times to come

Thousandes while they possesse and fill the waies
doth both desire, and hinder his repaire ;
they fill the emptie heaven with praier and praise,
which he requites with demonstrations faire.

Then what hast thowe to doe, and what remaines ?
praie as the people doth, and add but this
This little wish ; that whiles he lives and raignes,
he maye be still the same, that nowe he is.

John Dauis.

TO THE KINGE

UPON HIS MA'TIES FIRST COMMING INTO ENGLAND.

O now or neuer, gentle Muse, be gaye :
And mount up higher with thy paper winges,
Than doth the larke when hee sallutes the daye,
    And to the morne a merry wellcome singes.

Thou must goe meete King James, upon the way
Advanceing Southward, with his golden trayne ;
And know him too thou maist at first survaye,
    by proper noates and by distinctions plaine.

By his faire outward formes, and princely port,
By honour done to him with cap and knee,
Hee is distinguist to the vulgar sort :
    but truer characters will rise to thee.

Thy sight had once an influence divine,
Which gaue it power the Soule of man to vew :
Wipe and make cleare that dazled eye of thine,
    and thou shalt see his reall markes and true.

Looke over all that divers troope, and finde
Who hath his spirits most joviall and free ;
Whose body is best tempred, and whose mind
   is ever best in tune ; and that is he.

See who it is, whose actions doe bewraye
That threefold power, which rarely mixt wee see ;
A judgment grave, and yett a fancy gaye
   joynd with a rich remembrance, That is hee.

Marke who it is, that hath all noble skill,
Which may to publicke good referrèd bee :
The sharpest witte and best affected will,
   whence floes a streame of vertues, That is hee.

If any more than other clearely wise,
Or wisely just, or justly valiant bee ;
If any doe faint pleasure more dispise
   or bee more maister of himselfe, its hee.

But soft, thine eagle's eye will soone bee dim,
If thou this risinge sonne directly vewe :
Looke sidewayes on the beames that spread from him,[7]
   Faire peace, with Plenty, and Religion true.

[8] Miswritten ' them.'   G.

With that strong g'ard of Angells which doe houer
About his sacred person, daye and night :
And with invissible winges his head doe cover,
    that danger's darts thereon may neuer light.

Now on, for wingèd Time with thee goes on,
Which like old Æson hath his youth renewed,
His hower glasse turnd, and his sickle gon,
    and all his graye and broken feathers mewd.

On, for the brave young sonne above his head
Comes North ward, that hee may his glory meete ;
While the fresh Earth in all her pride doth spread,
    greene velvett carpetts underneath his feete.

On, for the birdes will helpe to fill the songe,
Whereto all English hartstringes will agree :
An' th' Irish harpstringes that have jarrd soe longe,
    to make the Musicke full, now tunèd bee.

There is noe eye cast downe, there is no voyce
Which to expresse the harts assent, is dumbe :
The world of thinges doth every where rejoyce
    In certaine hope of blessed times to come.

While thousands doe posses and fill the wayes,
The[y] both desire and hinder his repaire ;
They fill the emptie aire with prayer and praise,
    which hee requitts with demonstrations faire.

TO THE QUEENE AT THE SAME TIME.

I F wee in peace had not received the kinge
    Wee see wee had beene conquered, since wee see
The Queene such armyes doth of beauties bringe
    As all our eyes and hearts her vassals bee.

The Danish armyes once great honnour wonne
Upon this Land ; yett conquered but a part.
But you greate Lady more, alone, haue done ;
    For at first sight you conquer'd every heart.

Starre of the North ! upon these Northerne Realmes
Long may your vertues and your beauties raigne :
Beyond our Cinthiae's yeares, whose golden Beames
    Ar[e] sett with vs, and cannot shine againe :
Well may it bee ; though sunne and moone goe downe
    Seas haue noe power the North pole starre to drowne.[9]

---

[9] The allusion is to the storm on her voyage to Scotland in 1590.
Cf. Constable's Sonnet to the King of Scots. See our Memorial-
Introduction on these Lines. G.

MIRA LOQUOR SOL OCCUBUIT NOX NULLA SECUTA EST.

BY that Eclipse which darkned our Appollo,
Our sunne did sett, and yett noe night did follow ;
For his successor's vertues shone soe bright,
As they continued still, there former light ;   [*their*]
And gaue the world a farther expectation
To adde a greater splendor to our Nation.

CHARLES HIS WAINE.

BRITTAINE doth vnder those bright starres remaine,
Which English Shepheards, Charles his waine, doe
name ;
But more this Ile is Charles, his waine,
Since Charles her royall wagoner became.
For Charles, which now in Arthure's seate doth raigne,
Is our Arcturus, and doth guide the waine.

OF THE NAME OF CHAROLUS, BEING THE DIMINATIVE OF CHARUS.

THE name of Charles, darlinge signifies :
 A name most fitte, for hee was ever such.
Neuer was Prince soe deare in all mens eyes.
Soe highly valued or esteemed soe much :
Edgar was England's darlinge, once wee find,
But Charles the Darlinge is of all mankind.

VERSES SENT TO THE KINGE WITH FIGGES : BY St JOHN DAVIS.

TO add unto the first man's happiness,
 His maker did for him a garden make ;
And placd him there, that hee the same might dresse,
And pleasure great with little labour take.
And this with nature stands, and reason right,
That man who first was formèd of the earth
In trimminge of the earth should take delight,
And her adorne from whom hee tooke his birth.
Nor her for this doth hee ungratefull finde ;
For shee in gardens her best fruites doth yealde.

The Earth in gardens is a mother kinde,
When shee is but a steepdame in the feild.
Sir, in your service God hath mee soe blest
As I haue beene enabled to acquire
A garden, ready planted, trimd and drest,
Whereto in vacant times I doe retire.
This garden, and the fruite thereof, indeede
Are fruites of your great favour unto mee ;
And therefore all the fruites which thence proceed
A proper offeringe to your Highnes bee :
　But if this verse or boldness, meritt blame,
　Those figge leaues, Sʳ I hope shall hide the same.[1]

[LOVE-LINES.]

STAY lovely boy ! why flyest thou mee
　　that languish in theis flames for thee ?
I'me black 'tis true—why so is night,
yet louers in darke shades delight :
the whole World, doe but close thyne eye
will appeare as black as I ;
or open'd, view but what a shade
is by thyne owne fayre body made,

---

[1] The six preceding pieces and the 'Elegiecall Epistle' are in the same handwriting with the 'Maid's hymne in praise of Virginity.' G.

that follows thee where ere thou goe :
Ah, who allow'd would not doe so?
lett mee for euer dwell so nigh,
and thou shalt need no shade but I.

[LOVE-FLIGHT.]

BLACK Mayel, complayne not y^t I flye,
    since fate commaunds antipathy :
prodigious must y^t vnion proue,
where day and night togeather moue :
and the commotion of our lipps
not kisses make but an eclipps ;
where the commixèd blacke and white
portend more terrour then delight :
yet if thou wilt my shaddow bee,
enioy thy deerest wish, but see
that like my shaddow's property
thou hast away as I come nye :
els[e] stay till death hath blinded mee
then I'le bequeath my selfe to thee.[2]

---

[2] These two are in a new and apparently less-trained handwriting. G.

AN ELEGIECALL EPISTLE ON SIR JOHN
DAVIS DEATH.

MORGAN ! to call thee sadd and discontente
    Were to proclaime thee weake; twere an evente
Of more then folly, since the obscurest eye
Is witness of thy magnanimity :
And yett to tell thee that thou hast noe cause
To greife, were to belye thy worth, because
The gapinge wound speakes out the sovldiers fame,
And deepe despites giue fortitude a name.
Tis true hee's dead, and the sterne fates (accurst)
There browes haue wrinkled, and haue done their
    worst
To spite this State and thee, in tearinge hence
That Nature's Accademy, that Starre, from whence
Streamd such full influence, of what the mind
Accounteth quintisentiall ; and the vnkinde
And cruell Death, hath blasted such a flower,
Stolne such a gemme, as makes the sad Earth poore.
And yett alasse[3] hee is not fledd for want
Of what could make the ambitious, proud soule vaunt :

<hr>

[3] This use of 'alas' was common contemporaneously, and especially by the Puritan divines. G.

For whilst hee liv'd hee brocke up Honour's gates,
And pluck't bright fame from snarling Envie's grates
Doomd to obliuion; and his unmatchèd penne
(Drop'd from the winge of some bright Seraphin)
Inculpates him thus to all eternitye
The eldest of the Muses proginie.
Said I hee's dead ? not soe; he could not die,
But findinge that curst lucre, bribery
And puft[4] ambition were the scarlett crimes
Of the Tribunall's tenants, and the times
Not suitinge with his vertues, cause his manner
Was to deserue and not desire, an honour ;
Hee's sor'd aloft, where nought but virtue's pris'd,
And where base Mammon is not idoliz'd :
To that Kinge's Bench where Iustice is not gould,
Nor honours with old Ladies bought and sould ;
To heauen's Exchequer, with intent to paye,
And render thence the Royall subsidaye
Of his rich spirit, which his soueraigne tooke
Without subscription, and crost Nature's booke.

---

[1] I am not quite certain as to this word. It may be 'pust' :
query from pus = poisonous matter ? and so intended to character-
ize ambition?   G.

IX. ENTERTAINMENT OF
QUEEN ELIZABETH AT HAREFIELD BY
COUNTESSE OF DERBY.

NOTE.

This 'Entertainment' has the additional interest of having been that wherein "The Lottery" (pp. 87-95), was introduced. The reasons for our giving the whole to Davies, we have stated in the Memorial-Introduction (II. Critical : Minor Poems). Our text is from Nichols' Progresses of Q. Elizabeth, Vol. III., pp. 586-94. G.

Entertainment of Q. Elizabeth at Harefield by Countesse of Derby.

AFTER the Queene entered (out of the high way) into the Deamesne grounde of Harefielde, near the Dayrie howse, she was mett with 2 persons, the one representing a BAYLIFFE, the other a DAYRIE-MAIDE, with the Speech. Her Majesty, being on horsebacke, stayed under a tree (because it rayned) to heare it.

B. Why, how now, Joane! are you heere? Gods my life, what make you heere, gaddinge and gazinge after this manner? You come to buy gape-seede,[1] doe you? Wherefore come you abroade now I' faith can you tell?

Joa. I come abroade to welcome these Strangers.

B. Strangers? how knew you there would come Strangers?

---

[1] A pun on the open mouth of wonder and curiosity. G.

Jo. All this night I could not sleepe, dreaming of greene rushes; and yesternight the chatting of the pyes, and the chirkinge[2] of the frisketts[3] did foretell as much; and, besides that, all this day my lefte eare glowed,[4] and that is to me (let them all say what they wil) allwaies a signe of Strangers, if it be in the Summer; marye, if it be in the Winter, tis a signe of anger. But what make you in this company, I pray you?

B. I make the way for these Strangers, which the Way-maker himself could not doe; for it is a way was never passed before. Besides, the Mrs. of this faire company, though she know the way to all men's harts, yet she knowes the way but to few men's howses, except she love them very well, I can tell you; and therefore I myselfe, without any comission, have taken upon me to conduct them to the house.

Jo. The house? which house? doe you remember yourselfe? which way goe you?

B. I goe this way, on the right hand. Which way should I goe?

Jo. You say true, and you're a trim man; but I' faith I'll talke noe more to you, except you ware wyser.

---

[2] Imitative word, as the 'chirr' of the grasshopper. G.

[3] An unrecorded word. G.   [4] Folk-lore, as in Herrick, &c. G.

I pray you hartely, 'forsooth, come neare the house, and take a simple lodginge with vs to-night; for I can as- suere you that yonder house that he talks of is but a Pigeon-house, which is very little if it were finisht, and yet very little of it is finisht. And you will believe me, vpon my life, Lady, I saw Carpenters and Brick- layers and other Workmen about it within less than these two howers. Besides, I doubt my Mr. and Mrs. are not at home; or, if they be, you must make your owne provision; for they have noe provision for such Strangers. You should seeme to be Ladies; and we in the country have an old saying, that "halfe a pease a day will serve a Lady." I know not what you are, nether am I acquainted with your dyet; but, if you will goe with me, you shall haue cheare for a Lady: for first you shall haue a dayntie sillibub; next a messe of clowted creame; stroakings,[5] in good faith, redd cowes milk, and they say in London that's restorative: you shall have greene cheeses and creame. (I'll speake a bould word) if the Queene herself (God save her Grace) [were here] she might be seene to eat of it. Wee will not greatly bragge of our possets, but we would be loath to learne to praise: and if you loue frute, for-

---

[5] =the last milk drawn from a cow in milking: same as strip- pings. G.

sooth, wee haue jenitings,[6] paremayns,[7] russet coates,[8] pippines, able-johns,[9] and perhaps a pareplum,[10] a dam- sone, I or an apricocke[1] too, but that they are noe dainties this yeare ; and therefore, I pray, come neare the house, and wellcome heartily, doe soe.

B. Goe to, gossip ; your tongue must be running. If my Mrs. should heare of this, I' faith shee would give you little thankes I can tell you, for offeringe to draw so faire a flight from her Pigeon-house (as you call it) to your Dayrie-house.

Jo. Wisely, wisely, brother Richard ; I' faith as I would vse the matter, I dare say shee would giue me great thankes : for you know my Mrs. charged me earnestly to retaine all idele hearvest-folkes that past this way ; and my meaning was, that, if I could hold them all this night and to-morrow, on Monday morn- ing to carry them into the fields ; and to make them earne their entertaynment well and thriftily ; and to that end I have heere a *Rake* and *Forke,* to deliver to the best Huswife in all this company.

B. Doe soe then : deliver them to the best Hus-

[6] = rennets—a kind of apple? G.   [7] = another kind of apple: see Gerard's Herbal, p. 1459 (1636 edn.) G.   [8] A species of apple like ' rennets.' G.   [9] = apple-johns, as in 1, Henry IV., iii. 3 : 2, Henry IV., ii. 4 *(bis).* G.   [10] Query, a peach ? See Gerard, as before, (p. 1447). Perse-boom is given as the Low-Dutch name of the peach. G.   [1] = Apricot. G.

wife in all this company: for wee shall haue as much vse of her paines and patience there as here. As for the dainties that you talke of, if you have any such, you shall doe well to send them; and as for these strangers, sett thy hart at rest, Joane; they will not rest with [thee] this night, but will passe on to my Mr[s.] house.

Joa. Then, I pray, take this *Rake* and *Forke* with you; but I am ashamed, and woe at my hart, you should goe away soe late. And I pray God you repent you not, and wish yourselves here againe, when you finde you haue gone further and fared worsse.

When her Maiestie was alighted from her horse, and ascended 3 steeps neare to the entering into the house, a carpet and chaire there sett for her; PLACE and TIME present themselves, and vsed this Dialogue:

PLACE *in a partie-colored roabe, like the brick house.*

TIME *with yeollow haire, and in a green roabe, with a hower glasse, stopped, not runninge.*

P. Wellcome, good *Time.*

T. Godden, my little pretie priuat *Place.*

P. Farewell, godbwy *Time;* are you not gone? doe you stay heere? I wonder that *Time* should stay any where; what's the cause?

T. If thou knewest the cause, thou wouldst not wonder; for I stay to entertaine the Wonder of this time; wherein I would pray thee to ioyne mee, if thou wert not too little for her greatnes; for it weare as great a meracle for thee to receive her, as to see the Ocean shut up in a little creeke, or the circumference shrinke vnto the pointe of the center.

P. Too little! by that reason shee should rest in noe *place*, for no *place* is great ynough to receive her. Too little! I haue all this day entertayned the Sunn, which, you knowe, is a great and glorious Guest; hee's but euen now gone downe yonder hill; and now he is gone, methinks, if Cinthia her selfe would come in his place, the place that contaynde him should not be to little to receave her.

T. You say true, and I like your comparison; for the Guest that wee are to entertaine doth fill all places with her divine vertues, as the Sunn fills the World with the light of his beames. But say, poore *Place*, in what manner didst thou entertaine the Sunn?

P. I received his glory, and was fill'd with it : but I must confesse, not according to the proportion of his greatnes, but according to the measure of my capacitie; his bright face (methought) was all day turned vpon mee; neverthcless his beames in infinite abundance weere disperst and spread vpon other places.

T. Well, well; this is noe time for vs to entertaine

one another, when wee should ioine to entertaine her.
Our entertaynment of this Goddesse will be much
alike; for though her selfe shall eclipse her soe much,
as to suffer her brightnes to bee shadowed in this ob-
scuere and narrow *Place*, yet the sunne beames that
follow her, the traine I meane that attends vpon her,
must, by the necessitie of this *Place*, be deuided from
her. Are you ready, *Place?* *Time* is ready.

P. Soe it should seeme, indeed, you are so gaye,
fresh, and cheerfull. You are the present *Time*, are
you not? then what neede you make such haste? Let
me see, your wings are clipt, and, for ought I see, your
hower-glasse runnes not.

T. My wings are clipt indeed, and it is her hands
hath clipt them : and, tis true, my glasse runnes not :
indeed it hath bine stopt a longe time, it can never
rune as long as I waite upon this Mris. I [am] her
Time; and *Time* weare very vngratefull, if it should not
euer stand still, to serue and preserue, cherish and delight her, that is the glory of her time, and makes the
Time happy wherein she liueth.

P. And doth not she make *Place* happy as well as
Time? What if she make thee a contynewall holy-day,
she makes me a perpetuall sanctuary. Doth not the
presence of a Prince make a Cottage a Court, and the

presence of the Gods make euery place Heauen? But, alas, my littlenes is not capable of that happines that her great grace would impart vnto me : but, weare I as large as there harts that are mine Owners, I should be the fairest *Pallace* in the world ; and weere I agreeable to the wishes of there hartes, I should in some measure resemble her sacred selfe, and be in the outward frount exceeding faire, and in the inward furniture exceeding rich.

T. In good time do you remember the hearts of your Owners; for, as I was passing to this place, I found this *Hart*,[2] which, as my daughter *Truth* tould mee, was stolne by owne[3] of the Nymphes from one of the seruants of this Goddesse; but her guiltie conscience enforming her that it did belong only of right vnto her that is Mrs. of all harts in the world, she cast [it] from her for this time; and *Oportunity*, finding it delivered it vnto me. Heere, *Place*, take it thou, and present it vnto her as a pledge and mirror of their harts that owe thee.

P. It is a mirror indeed, for so it is transparent. It is a cleare hart, you may see through it. It hath noe close corners, noe darkenes, noe unbutifull spott in it.

---

[2] A Diamond.   [3] = one. G.

I will therefore presume the more boldly to deliver it; with this assurance, that *Time, Place, Persons,* and all other circumstances, doe concurre alltogether in biddinge her wellcome.

The humble Petition of a guiltlesse Lady, delivered in writing vpon Munday Morninge, when the [robe] of rainbowes was presented to the Q. by the La. WALSINGHAM.

Beauties rose, and vertues booke,
Angells minde, and Angells looke,
    To all Saints and Angells deare,
Clearest Maiestie on earth,
Heauen did smile at your faire birth,
    And since, your daies have been most cleare.

Only poore St. *Swythen* now
Doth heare you blame his cloudy brow :
    But that poore St. deuoutly sweares,
It is but a tradition vaine
That his much weeping causeth raine,
    For S^{ts} in heauen shedd no teares :

But this he saith, that to his feast
Commeth Iris, an vnbidden guest,
    In her moist roabe of collers gay ;

And she cometh, she ever staies,
For the space of fortie daies,
    And more or lesse raines euery day.

But the good St., when once he knew,
This raine was like to fall on you,
    If Sᵗˢ could weepe, he had wept as much
As when he did the Lady leade
That did on burning iron tread :
    To Ladies his respect is such.

He gently first bids Iris goe
Unto the Antipodes below,
    But shee for that more sullen grew.
When he saw that, with angry looke,
From her her rayneie roabes he tooke,
    Which heere he doth present to you.

It is fitt it should with you remaine,
For you know better how to raine.
    Yet if it raine still as before,
St Swythen praies that you would guesse,
That Iris doth more robes possesse,
    And that you should blame him no more.

At her Maiesties departure from Harefield, PLACE, attyred in black mouringe aparell, vsed this farewell followinge :

P. Sweet Maiestie, be pleased to looke vpon a poore Wydow, mourning before your Grace. I am this *Place,* which at your comming was full of ioy ; but now at your departure am as full of sorrow. I was then, for my comfort, accompanied with the present cheerful *Time ;* but now he is to depart with you ; and, blessed as he is, must euer fly before you : But, alas ! I haue no wings, as *Time* hath. My heauiness is such, that I must stand still, amazed to see so greate happines so sone bereft mee. Oh, that I could remoue with you, as other circumstances can ! *Time* can goe with you, *Persons* can goe with you ; they can moue like Heauen ; but I, like dull Earth (as I am indeed) must stand vn-mouable. I could wish my selfe like the inchanted Castle of Loue, to hould you heere for euer, but that your vertues would dissolue all my inchauntments. Then what remedy? As it is against the nature of an Angell to be circumscribed in *Place,* so it is against the nature of *Place* to haue the motion of an Angell. I must stay forsaken and desolate. You may goe with maiestie, joy, and glory. My only suyte, before you goe, is that you will pardon the close imprisonment

which you haue suffred euer since your comminge, im-
putinge it not to mee, but St. Swythen, who of late hath
raysed soe many stormes, as I was faine to prouide this
Anchor,[4] for you, when I did vnderstand you would put
into this creeke. But now, since I perceaue this har-
bour is too little for you, and you will hoyse sayle and
be gone, I beseech you take this Anchor with you. And
I pray to Him that made both *Time* and *Place*, that, in
all places where euer you shall arriue, you may anchor
as safly, as you doe and euer shall doe in the harts of
my Owners.

THE COMPLAINT OF THE V SATYRES AGAINST THE NYMPHS.

Tell me, O Nymphes, why do you
Shune vs that your loues pursue?
What doe the Satyres notes retaine
That should merite your disdaine?

On our browes if hornes doe growe,
Was not Bacchus armèd soe?
Yet of him the Candian maid
Held no scorne, nor was affraid.

---

[4] A Jewell.

Say our colours tawny bee,
Phœbus was not faire to see ;
Yet faire Clymen[1] did not shunn
To bee Mother of his Sonne.

If our beards be rough and long,
Soe had Hercules the strong :
Yet Deianier,[2] with many a kisse,
Joyn'd her tender lipps to his.

If our bodies hayry bee,
Mars as rugged was as wee :
Yet did Ilia[3] think her grac'd,
For to be by Mars imbrac'd.

Say our feet ill-fauored are,
Cripples leggs are worse by farre :
Yet faire Venus, during life,
Was the lymping Vulcan's wife.

Breefly, if by nature we
But imperfect creatures be ;
Thinke not our defects so much,
Since Celestial Powers be such.

---

[1] Clymene. G.   [2] Deianeira, daughter of Oeneus. G.
[3] Mother of Romulus. G.

But you Nymphes, whose veniall loue
Loue of gold alone doth moue,
Though you scorne vs, yet for gold
Your base loue is bought and sold.

                                        finis.

ERRATA.

A very few 'slips' have met my eyes on a final reading. They are—as says an ancient Divine—"as easily corrected as espied." Nevertheless they are here recorded that the Reader of his charity may put them right, and any others that may have escaped Editor and Printer. In *Nosce Teipsum*, the heading and head-line (Vol. I., pp. 25, 26 onward) has 'Immortalitie' misprinted 'Immortalite'—a common contemporary spelling—but it is 'tie' in the title-page (p. 5): *ib.* p. 80, l. 15, read 'be best.' In *Hymnes to Astræa*, *ib.* p. 147, l. 3, remove period (.) after 'rayes.' In *Orchestra*, *ib.* p. 181, st. 53, l. 7, read 'perfect-cunning': p. 185, foot-note 7, put G. at end: p. 192, st. 81, l. 7, 'Ply' =entwine (omitted): p. 194, foot-note 7, it is 'coach,' not 'couch': p. 202, l. 10, 'shoe' was the contemporary spelling: p. 204, st. 113, l. 6, insert 'it' before 'shine.'—G.

CHATTO & WINDUS'S

List of Books.

ON BOOKS AND BOOK-BUYERS.

By John Ruskin, LL.D.

" *I say we have despised literature; what do we, as a nation, care about books?   How much do you think we spend altogether on our libraries, public or private, as compared with what we spend on our horses? If a man spends lavishly on his library, you call him mad—a bibliomaniac. But you never call one a horse-maniac, though men ruin themselves every day by their horses, and you do not hear of people ruining themselves by their books. Or, to go lower still, how much do you think the contents of the bookshelves of the United Kingdom, public and private, would fetch, as compared with the contents of its wine-cellars? What position would its expenditure on literature take as compared with its expenditure on luxurious eating? We talk of food for the mind, as of food for the body: now, a good book contains such food inexhaustibly: it is provision for life, and for the best part of us ; yet how long most people would look at the best book before they would give the price of a large turbot for it! Though there have been men who have pinched their stomachs and bared their backs to buy a book, whose libraries were cheaper to them, I think, in the end, than most men's dinners are. We are few of us put to such a trial, and more the pity; for, indeed, a precious thing is all the more precious to us if it has been won by work or economy; and if public libraries were half as costly as public dinners, or books cost the tenth part of what bracelets do, even foolish men and women might sometimes suspect there was good in reading as well as in munching and sparkling; whereas the very cheapness of literature is making even wiser people forget that if a book is worth reading it is worth buying.*"—Sesame And Lilies, or Kings' Treasures.

A List of Books

PUBLISHED BY

CHATTO & WINDUS,

74 & 75, *PICCADILLY, LONDON, W.*

DVERTISING, A HISTORY OF, from the Earliest Times.
Illustrated by Anecdotes, Curious Specimens, and Biographical Notes
of Successful Advertisers. By HENRY SAMPSON. Crown 8vo, with
Coloured Frontispiece and Illustrations, cloth gilt, 7*s.* 6*d.*

" We have here a book to be thankful for. Among the many interesting illustrations is a photographed copy of the *Times* for January 1st, 1788, which may be easily
read by means of a magnifying glass. We recommend the present volume, which
takes us through antiquity, the Middle Ages, and the present time, illustrating all in
turn by advertisements—serious, comic, roguish, or downright rascally. The chapter on ' swindles and hoaxes ' is full of entertainment ; but of that the volume itself
is full from the first page to the last."—*Athenæum.*

ÆSOP'S FABLES TRANSLATED into HUMAN NATURE.
By C. H. BENNETT. Crown 4to, 24 Plates beautifully printed in Colours, with
descriptive Text, cloth extra, gilt, 6*s.*

" For fun and frolic the new version of Æsop's Fables must bear away the palm.
There are plenty of grown-up children who like to be amused ; and if this new version of old stories does not amuse them they must be very dull indeed, and their situa-
tion one much to be commiserated."—*Morning Post.*

ARTEMUS WARD, COMPLETE.— The Works of CHARLES
FARRER BROWNE, better known as ARTEMUS WARD. With fine Portrait, facsimile of Handwriting, &c. Crown 8vo, cloth extra, 7*s.* 6*d.*

"The author combines the powers of Thackeray with those of Albert Smith. The
salt is rubbed in with a native hand—one which has the gift of tickling."—*Saturday
Review.*

AS PRETTY AS SEVEN, and other Popular German Stories.
Collected by LUDWIG BECHSTEIN. With Additional Tales by the Brothers
GRIMM, and 100 Illustrations by RICHTER. Small 4to, green and gold, 6*s.* 6*d.* ;
gilt edges, 7*s.* 6*d.*

" These tales are pure and healthful ; they will shed over childhood a rosy light,
and strew the path with stars and flowers, the remembrance of which will last through
life."—*Preface.*

ASTLE ON WRITING.—THE ORIGIN AND PROGRESS OF WRITING, as well Hieroglyphic as Elementary, Illustrated by Engravings taken from Marbles, Manuscripts, and Charters, Ancient and Modern ; also Some Account of the Origin and Progress of Printing. By THOMAS ASTLE, F.R.S., F.A.S., late Keeper of Records in the Tower of London. Royal 4to, half-Roxburghe, with 33 Plates (some Coloured), price £1 15s. A few Large Paper copies, roy. folio, half-Roxburghe, the Plates altogether unfolded, £3 3s.

"The completest work on the subject of writing in this or any other language."

AKER.—CLOUDS IN THE EAST : Travels and Adventures on the Perso-Turkoman Frontier. By VALENTINE BAKER. With Maps and Illustrations, coloured and plain, from Original Sketches. Demy 8vo, cloth extra, 18s. *[In the press.*

BANKERS, A HANDBOOK OF LONDON ; with some Account of their Predecessors, the Early Goldsmiths; together with Lists of Bankers, from the Earliest London Directory, printed in 1677, to that of the London Post-Office Directory of 1876. By F. G. HILTON PRICE. Crown 8vo, cloth extra, 7s. 6d.

BARDSLEY'S OUR ENGLISH SURNAMES : Their Sources and Significations. By CHARLES WAREING BARDSLEY, M.A. SECOND EDITION, revised throughout, considerably Enlarged, and partially rewritten. Crown 8vo, cloth extra, 9s.

"Mr. Bardsley has faithfully consulted the original mediæval documents and works from which the origin and development of surnames can alone be satisfactorily traced. He has furnished a valuable contribution to the literature of surnames, and we hope to hear more of him in this field."—*Times.*

BEAUTIFUL PICTURES BY BRITISH ARTISTS: A Gathering of Favourites from our Picture Galleries. In Two Series. The FIRST SERIES including Examples by WILKIE, CONSTABLE, TURNER, MULREADY LANDSEER, MACLISE, E. M. WARD, FRITH, Sir JOHN GILBERT, LESLIE, ANSDELL, MARCUS STONE, Sir NOEL PATON, FAED, EYRE CROWE, GAVIN, O'NEIL, and MADOX BROWN. The SECOND containing Pictures by ARMYTAGE, FAED, GOODALL, HEMSLEY, HORSLEY, MARKS, NICHOLLS, Sir NOEL PATON, PICKERSGILL, G. SMITH, MARCUS STONE, SOLOMON, STRAIGHT, E. M. WARD, and WARREN. All engraved on Steel in the highest style of Art. Edited, with Notices of the Artists, by SYDNEY ARMYTAGE, M.A. Price of each Series, imperial 4to, cloth extra, gilt and gilt edges, 21s. *Each Volume is Complete in itself.*

"This book is well got up, and good engravings by Jeens, Lumb Stocks, and others, bring back to us pictures of Royal Academy Exhibitions of past years."— *Times.*

BLAKE'S WORKS.—A Series of Reproductions in Facsimile of the Works of WILLIAM BLAKE, including the "Songs of Innocence and Experience," "The Book of Thel," "America," "The Vision of the Daughters of Albion," "The Marriage of Heaven and Hell," "Europe, a Prophecy," "Jerusalem," "Milton," "Urizen," "The Song of Los," &c. These Works will be issued both coloured and plain. *[In preparation.*

"Blake is a real name, I assure you, and a most extraordinary man he is, if he still be living. He is the Blake whose wild designs accompany a splendid edition of Blair's 'Grave.' He paints in water-colours marvellous strange pictures— visions of his brain—which he asserts he has seen. They have great merit. I must look upon him as one of the most extraordinary persons of the age."—CHARLES LAMB.

BLANCHARD'S (Laman) POEMS. Now first Collected. Edited, with a Life of the Author (including numerous hitherto unpublished Letters from Lord LYTTON, LAMB, DICKENS, ROBERT BROWNING, and others), by BLANCHARD JERROLD. Crown 8vo, with a Vignette Portrait, cloth extra, 9s.

"His humorous verse is much of it admirable—sparkling with genuine *esprit*, and as polished and pointed as Praed's."—*Scotsman.*

"As Addison and Steele reflected their own generations, so has Laman Blanchard in his sketches mirrored forth the variable and motley peculiarities of the present day ; they have but to be read to be admired."—*Sun.*

BLEWITT.—THE ROSE AND THE LILY: A Story. By
Mrs. OCTAVIAN BLEWITT. With a Frontispiece designed and etched by GEORGE
CRUIKSHANK. Small 8vo, cloth extra, gilt, price 6s. [*In the press.*

BOCCACCIO'S DECAMERON; or, Ten Days' Entertainment.
Translated into English, with Introduction by THOMAS WRIGHT, Esq., M.A.,
F.S.A. With Portrait, and STOTHARD's beautiful Copperplates. Crown 8vo,
cloth extra, gilt, 7s. 6d.

BOUDOIR BALLADS : Vers de Société. By J. ASHBY STERRY.
Crown 8vo, cloth extra. [*In preparation.*

BRAND'S OBSERVATIONS ON POPULAR ANTIQUITIES,
chiefly Illustrating the Origin of our Vulgar Customs, Ceremonies, and Superstitions. With the Additions of Sir HENRY ELLIS. A New Edition, with fine
full-page Illustrations. Crown 8vo, cloth extra, gilt, 7s. 6d. [*In the press.*
"Anyone who will read, on each respective day, the chapter which belongs to it,
will, when he has got through the volume, have a better notion of what English
history is than he will get from almost any other work professedly named a
'history.'"—*Quarterly Review.*

BRET HARTE'S CHOICE WORKS in Prose and Poetry. With
Introductory Essay by J. M. BELLEW, Portrait of the Author, and 50 Illustrations. Crown 8vo, cloth extra, 7s. 6d.
"Not many months before my friend's death, he had sent me two sketches by a
young American writer (Bret Harte), far away in California ('The Outcast of Poker
Flat,' and another), in which he had found such subtle strokes of character as he had
not anywhere else in late years discovered ; the manner resembling himself, but the
matter fresh to a degree that had surprised him ; the painting in all respects masterly,
and the wild rude thing painted a quite wonderful reality. I have rarely known
him more honestly moved."—FORSTER'S *Life of Dickens.*

BREWSTER'S (Sir David) MARTYRS OF SCIENCE. A
New Edition, in small crown 8vo, cloth extra, gilt, with full-page Portraits, 4s. 6d.

BREWSTER'S (Sir David) MORE WORLDS THAN ONE,
the Creed of the Philosopher and the Hope of the Christian. A New Edition, in
small crown 8vo, cloth extra, gilt, with full-page Astronomical Plates, 4s. 6d.
"There does certainly exist a wide-spread desire to know, so far as can be known,
the extent of God's living, responsible creation. The planet which we inhabit is but
one vessel in the midst of a fleet sailing on through the vast ocean of space, under
convoy of the sun. Far on the distant horizon what seem to be a great many other
convoy ships appear, though such is their remoteness that even our best glasses
enable us to know very little regarding them. But in the vessels of the same group
as ourselves, we see evolutions similar to those which our own ship performs· ·we
see them maintain relations similar to our own to the great guardian vessel in the
midst—we see them regulated by her in all their movements, and that when night
falls dark most of them have their sets of lanthorns hoisted up to give them light ;
and there is a desire among us to know somewhat respecting the crews of these
neighbouring vessels of ours, and whether—as we all seem bound on a common
voyage—the expedition, as it is evidently under one and the same control, may not
have a common purpose or object to accomplish."—HUGH MILLER.

BRIC-À-BRAC HUNTER (The) ; or, Chapters on Chinamania.
By Major H. BYNG HALL. With Photographic Frontispiece. Crown 8vo, cloth,
full gilt (from a special and novel design), 10s. 6d.
"This is a delightful book. His hints respecting marks, texture, finish, and character of various wares will be useful to amateurs. By all who are interested in
chinamania will be most warmly appreciated a very amusing and chatty volume."
Standard.

BRILLAT SAVARIN'S PHYSIOLOGY OF TASTE. Translated
into English, with an Introduction and Notes. Crown 8vo, cloth extra.
[*In the press.*

BUNYAN'S PILGRIM'S PROGRESS. Edited by Rev. T. SCOTT.

With 17 beautiful Steel Plates by STOTHARD, engraved by GOODALL; and numerous Woodcuts. Crown 8vo, cloth extra, gilt, 7s. 6d.

"The style of Bunyan is delightful to every reader, and invaluable as a study to every person who wishes to obtain a wide command over the English language. The vocabulary is the vocabulary of the common people. There is not an expression, if we except a few technical terms of theology, which would puzzle the rudest peasant. Yet no writer has said more exactly what he meant to say. For magnificence, for pathos, for vehement exhortation, for subtle disquisition, for every purpose of the poet, the orator, and the divine, this homely dialect—the dialect of plain working men—was perfectly sufficient. There is no book in our literature on which we could so readily stake the fame of the old unpolluted English language; no book which shows so well how rich that language is in its own proper wealth, and how little it has been improved by all that it has borrowed. . . . . We are not afraid to say that, though there were many clever men in England during the latter half of the seventeenth century, there were only two great creative minds. One of those minds produced the 'Paradise Lost,' the other, the 'Pilgrim's Progress.'"—MACAULAY.

BYRON'S (Lord) LETTERS AND JOURNALS. With

Notices of his Life. By THOMAS MOORE. A Reprint of the Original Edition, newly revised, complete in a thick Volume of 1060 pp., with Twelve full-page Plates. Crown 8vo, cloth extra, gilt, 7s. 6d.

"We have read this book with the greatest pleasure. Considered merely as a composition, it deserves to be classed among the best specimens of English prose which our age has produced. . . . The style is agreeable, clear, and manly, and, when it rises into eloquence, rises without effort or ostentation. Nor is the matter inferior to the manner. It would be difficult to name a book which exhibits more kindness, fairness, and modesty."—MACAULAY, in the *Edinburgh Review.*

ANOVA'S WORKS IN SCULPTURE AND MODEL-

LING. 150 Plates, exquisitely engraved in Outline by MOSES, and printed on an India tint. With Descriptions by the Countess ALBRIZZI, a Biographical Memoir by CICOGNARA, and Portrait by WORTHINGTON. A New Edition. Demy 4to, cloth extra, gilt, gilt edges, 31s. 6d.

"The fertility of this master's resources is amazing, and the manual labour expended on his works would have worn out many an ordinary workman. The outline engravings are finely executed. The descriptive notes are discriminating, and in the main exact."—*Spectator.*

"A very handsome volume. . . . The graceful designs of the original are rendered by the engraver with exquisite fidelity. As a gift-book, the volume deserves to be placed beside the 'Outlines' of a very kindred genius—Flaxman."—*Graphic.*

CARTER'S ANCIENT ARCHITECTURE OF ENGLAND.

Including the Orders during the British, Roman, Saxon, and Norman Eras; and also under the Reigns of Henry III. and Edward III. Illustrated by 103 large Copperplate Engravings, comprising upwards of Two Thousand Specimens. Edited by JOHN BRITTON. Royal folio, half-morocco extra, £2 8s.

"Mr. Carter was the first to point out to the public the right way of delineating and representing the component and detached parts of the old buildings of England. His national work on Ancient Architecture occupied him in drawing, etching, arranging, and publishing, more than twenty years. It is highly valuable."—JOHN BRITTON.

CATLIN'S ILLUSTRATIONS OF THE MANNERS, CUS-

TOMS, AND CONDITION OF THE NORTH AMERICAN INDIANS, written during Eight Years of Travel and Adventure among the Wildest and most Remarkable Tribes now existing. Containing 360 Coloured Engravings from the Author's original Paintings. Two Vols. imperial 8vo, cloth extra, gilt, the Plates beautifully printed in Colours, £3 3s.

"One of the most admirable observers of manners who ever lived among the aborigines of America."—HUMBOLDT'S *Cosmos.*

CATLIN'S NORTH AMERICAN INDIAN PORTFOLIO. Containing Hunting Scenes, Amusements, Scenery, and Costume of the Indians of the Rocky Mountains and Prairies of America, from Drawings and Notes made by the Author during Eight Years' Travel. A series of 31 magnificent Plates (6 now first published), beautifully coloured in facsimile of the Original Drawings exhibited at the Egyptian Hall. With Letterpress Descriptions, imperial folio, half-morocco, gilt, £7 10s.

CHAMBERLAINE'S IMITATIONS OF DRAWINGS FROM THE GREAT MASTERS in the Royal Collection. Engraved by BARTOLOZZI and others. 74 fine Plates, mostly tinted ; including, in addition, "Ecce Homo," after GUIDO, and the scarce Series of 7 Anatomical Drawings. Imperial folio, half-morocco, gilt edges, £5 5s.

CLAUDE, BEAUTIES OF, containing 24 of his choicest Landscapes, beautifully Engraved on Steel, by BROMLEY, LUPTON, and others. With Biographical Sketch and Portrait. Royal folio, in a portfolio, £1 5s.

CLAUDE'S LIBER VERITATIS. A Collection of 303 Prints after the Original Designs of CLAUDE. Engraved by RICHARD EARLOM. With a descriptive Catalogue of each Print, Lists of the Persons for whom, and the Places for which, the original Pictures were first painted, and of the present Possessors of most of them. London : published by Messrs. Boydell and Co., Cheapside. Printed by W. Bulmer and Co., Cleveland Row, 1777. Three Vols. folio, half-morocco extra, gilt edges, £10 10s.

COLMAN'S HUMOROUS WORKS.—Broad Grins, My Night-gown and Slippers, and other Humorous Works, Prose and Poetical, of GEORGE COLMAN. With Life and Anecdotes by G. B. BUCKSTONE, and Frontispiece by HOGARTH. Crown 8vo, cloth extra, gilt, 7s. 6d.

"What antic have we here, in motley livery of red and yellow, with cap on head, and dagger of lath in hand? It is the king's jester, a professed droll, strangely gifted in all grimace, who pulls faces, and sells grins by the yard. For the impudent joke he has scarcely an equal."—*Westminster Review.*

CONEY'S ENGRAVINGS OF ANCIENT CATHEDRALS, Hôtels de Ville, Town Halls, &c., including some of the finest Examples of Gothic Architecture in France, Holland, Germany, and Italy. 32 large Plates, imperial folio, half-morocco extra, £3 13s. 6d.

CONSTABLE'S GRAPHIC WORKS. Comprising 40 highly finished Mezzotinto Engravings on Steel, by DAVID LUCAS; with descriptive Letterpress by C. R. LESLIE, R.A. Folio, half-morocco, gilt edges, £2 2s.

COTMAN'S ENGRAVINGS OF THE SEPULCHRAL BRASSES IN NORFOLK AND SUFFOLK. With Letterpress Descriptions, an Essay on Sepulchral Memorials by DAWSON TURNER, Notes by Sir SAMUEL MEYRICK, ALBERT WAY, and Sir HARRIS NICOLAS, and copious Index. New Edition, containing 173 Plates, two of them Illuminated. Two Volumes, small folio, half-morocco extra, £6 6s.

"Cotman's work on Sepulchral Brasses is by far the most important work on the subject."—DAWSON TURNER.

COTMAN'S ETCHINGS OF ARCHITECTURAL REMAINS, chiefly Norman and Gothic, in various Counties in England, but principally in Norfolk, with Descriptive Notices by DAWSON TURNER, and Architectural Observations by THOMAS RICKMAN. Two Vols. imperial folio, containing 240 spirited Etchings, half-morocco, top edges gilt, £8 8s.

COTMAN'S LIBER STUDIORUM. A Series of Landscape Studies and Original Compositions, for the Use of Art Students, consisting of 48 Etchings, the greater part executed in "soft ground." Imperial folio, half-morocco, £1 11s. 6d.

CREASY.—MEMOIRS OF EMINENT ETONIANS; with

Notices of the Early History of Eton College. By Sir EDWARD CREASY, Author of " The Fifteen Decisive Battles of the World." A New Edition, brought down to the Present Time, with 13 Illustrations. Crown 8vo, cloth extra, gilt, *7s. 6d.*

" A new edition of *Creasy's Etonians* will be welcome. The book was a favourite a quarter of a century ago, and it has maintained its reputation. The value of this new edition is enhanced by the fact that Sir Edward Creasy has added to it several memoirs of Etonians who have died since the first edition appeared. The work is eminently interesting."—*Scotsman.*

CRUIKSHANK'S COMIC ALMANACK. Complete in Two

SERIES: The FIRST from 1835 to 1843 ; the SECOND from 1844 to 1853. A Gathering of the BEST HUMOUR of THACKERAY, HOOD, MAYHEW, ALBERT SMITH, A'BECKETT, ROBERT BROUGH, &c. With 2000 Woodcuts and Steel Engravings by CRUIKSHANK, HINE, LANDELLS, &c. Crown 8vo, cloth gilt, two very thick volumes, 15s.; or, separately, *7s. 6d.* per volume.

CUSSANS' HANDBOOK OF HERALDRY. With Instructions

for Tracing Pedigrees and Deciphering Ancient MSS.; Rules for the Appointment of Liveries, Chapters on Continental and American Heraldry, &c. &c. By JOHN E. CUSSANS. Illustrated with 360 Plates and Woodcuts. Crown 8vo, cloth extra, gilt and emblazoned, *7s. 6d.*

CUSSANS' HISTORY OF HERTFORDSHIRE. A County

History, got up in a very superior manner, and ranging with the finest works of its class. By JOHN E. CUSSANS. Illustrated with full-page Plates on Copper and Stone, and a profusion of small Woodcuts. Parts I. to X. now ready, 21s. each.

" The amount of labour Mr. Cussans bestows to obtain original information is immense ; his anxiety for accuracy is intense, and the painstaking care with which he investigates statements and peruses old documents is remarkable. The result of his industry is a work abounding in new and curious information. It differs from ' Clutterbuck ' in this respect, that whereas that well-patronised and expensive book had most care and attention bestowed on the first volume—(that part of Hertford-shire where the author resided)—each successive portion of Mr. Cussans' history is manifestly an improvement on the earlier portions. Nothing can ever repay the author for the very great care, pains, and time he has devoted to this work, which must have been truly a labour of love to him ; but he has sure reward in the esteem of those who can appreciate aright earnestness, diligence, and perseverance in the accomplishment of a useful and valuable object."—*Herts Guardian.*

CYCLOPÆDIA OF COSTUME ; or, A Dictionary of Dress—Regal,

Ecclesiastical, Civil, and Military—from the Earliest Period in England to the reign of George the Third. Including Notices of Contemporaneous Fashions on the Continent, and preceded by a General History of the Costumes of the Principal Countries of Europe. By J. R. PLANCHÉ, Somerset Herald. To be Completed in Twenty-four Parts, quarto, at Five Shillings each, profusely illustrated by Coloured and Plain Plates and Wood Engravings.—A Prospectus will be sent upon application. *[In course of publication.*

" There is no subject connected with dress with which ' Somerset Herald' is not as familiar as ordinary men are with the ordinary themes of everyday life. The gathered knowledge of many years is placed before the world in this his latest work, and, when finished, there will exist no work on the subject half so valuable. The numerous illustrations are all effective—for their accuracy the author is responsible ; they are well drawn and well engraved, and, while indispensable to a proper comprehension of the text, are satisfactory as works of art."—*Art Journal.*

" These numbers of a Cyclopædia of Ancient and Modern Costume give promise that the work, when complete, will be one of the most perfect works ever published upon the subject. The illustrations are numerous and excellent, and would, even without the letterpress, render the work an invaluable book of reference for information as to costumes for fancy balls and character quadrilles. . . . Beautifully printed and superbly illustrated."—*Standard.*

" Those who know how useful is Fairholt's brief and necessarily imperfect glossary will be able to appreciate the much greater advantages promised by Mr. Planché's book."—*Athenæum.*

IBDIN'S (T. F.) BIBLIOMANIA; or, Book-Madness: A Bibliographical Romance. With numerous Illustrations. A New Edition, with a Supplement, including a Key to the Assumed Characters in the Drama. Demy 8vo, half-Roxburghe. 21s.; a few Large Paper copies, half-Roxburghe, the edges altogether uncut, at 42s.

"I have not yet recovered from the delightful delirium into which your 'Bibliomania' has completely thrown me. Your book, to my taste, is one of the most extraordinary gratifications I have enjoyed for many years. You have glued me down to two hundred pages at a sitting, and I can repeat the pleasure without losing it."—ISAAC DISRAELI.

DEMOCRACY (THE). A Novel. By WHYTE THORNE. Three Vols., crown 8vo, 31s. 6d.

DIXON.—WHITE CONQUEST: AMERICA IN 1875. By W. HEPWORTH DIXON. Two Vols. 8vo, cloth extra, 30s.

"The best written, most instructive, and most entertaining book that Mr. Dixon has published since 'New America.'"—Athenæum.

"'White Conquest' is no whit inferior to the author's other writings; indeed, in some respects it may be said to be superior. It has all the old brilliancy of description, the same sense of humour, and the wonderful accumulation of facts, historical and otherwise, to which Mr. Hepworth Dixon has accustomed his admirers; and besides these merits the volumes acquire an additional charm from the fact that they deal with romantic and comparatively unknown regions; and a special value, because they deal with the gravest of modern social problems."—Morning Post.

DRURY'S ILLUSTRATIONS of FOREIGN ENTOMOLOGY. Containing, in 150 beautifully Coloured Plates, upwards of 600 Exotic Insects of the East and West Indies, China, New Holland, North and South America, Germany, &c. With important Additions and Scientific Indexes, by J. O. WESTWOOD, F.L.S. Three Vols. 4to, half-morocco extra, £5 5s.

"Drury's work has not been surpassed in beauty and accuracy of execution by any of the sumptuous efforts of the present day."—Encyclopædia Britannica.

DUNRAVEN'S (Earl of) THE GREAT DIVIDE: A Narrative of Travels in the Upper Yellowstone in the Summer of 1874. With Maps and numerous striking full-page Illustrations by VALENTINE W. BROMLEY. Demy 8vo, cloth gilt, 18s.

"There has not for a long time appeared a better book of travel than Lord Dunraven's 'The Great Divide.' . . . The book is full of clever observation, and both narrative and illustrations are thoroughly good." Athenæum.

"A jolly, rollicking narrative of adventure and sport, mixed up with a great deal of useful information concerning one of the most interesting regions in the American continent."—Nature.

"Under the title of 'The Great Divide' the Earl of Dunraven tells a pleasant tale of an excursion, half as hunter, half as tourist, to the region first made known a year or two ago to the world as the 'marvellous country of the Yellowstone.' . . . The reader will find in Lord Dunraven the most genial and unaffected of guides; while, on more serious matters, the Indian question, &c., his book, in its light way, has some claims to rank as an authority."—Graphic.

 ARLY ENGLISH POETS. Edited, with Introductions and copious Notes, by the Rev. A. B. GROSART. Crown 8vo, cloth boards, 6s. per Volume: a few Large Paper copies (only 50 printed), at 12s. The following are now ready:

THE WORKS OF GILES FLETCHER. One Vol.
THE WORKS OF SIR JOHN DAVIES. Two Vols.

"Mr. Grosart has spent the most laborious and the most enthusiastic care on the perfect restoration and preservation of the text; and it is very unlikely that any other edition of the poet can ever be called for . . . . From Mr. Grosart we always expect and always receive the final results of most patient and competent scholarship."—Examiner.

To be followed by

ROBERT HERRICK.
SIR PHILIP SYDNEY.

JOHN DONNE.
And others.

EMANUEL ON DIAMONDS AND PRECIOUS STONES;

Their History, Value, and Properties; with Simple Tests for ascertaining their Reality. By HARRY EMANUEL, F.R.G.S. With numerous Illustrations, Tinted and Plain. A New Edition, crown 8vo, cloth extra, gilt, 6s.

EMERSON'S NEW WORK.—LETTERS & SOCIAL AIMS.

By RALPH WALDO EMERSON. Second Edition. Crown 8vo, cloth extra, 7s. 6d.
"His method of work is that of great thinkers. Gradually he absorbs and assimilates whatever science or history can furnish, and slowly and reflectively he gives us the result of his thoughts."—*Athenæum.*
"Will be eagerly welcomed by his numerous admirers on both sides of the Atlantic. . . . These latest essays and lectures of the American sage contain the matured fruits of earnest and deep thought wrapt up in language always clear and incisive, often happily epigrammatic. They present the author's ripest opinions on literature and society. Every part of the work breathes the free air which belongs to a free country, and is redolent of hope and youth. The happy knack which Emerson always possessed of illustrating his meaning by apposite anecdotes has not failed him in his old age; and in these pages light is often flashed upon an obscure or abstruse proposition from a pithy and pointed story. Without any pedantic show of learning, every page bears witness to the author's wide, one might almost say encyclopædic, acquaintance with the literature of all ages and of all races. Not only has Emerson been a great reader, but he has, so to speak, got at the very innermost core of the books which he has devoured."—*Scotsman.*

ENGLISH GENTLEMAN'S LIBRARY. Demy 8vo, cloth extra

(uniform binding), Illustrated :—

D'Arblay's(Madame) Diary and Letters. Edited by her Niece, CHAR- LOTTE BARRETT. A New Edition, illustrated by numerous fine Portraits engraved on Steel. Four Vols. 8vo., cloth extra, 36s.

Grammont (Count), Memoirs of. By ANTHONY HAMILTON. A New Edition, with a Biographical Sketch of Count Hamilton, numerous Historical and Illustrative Notes by Sir WALTER SCOTT, and 64 Copper-plate Portraits by EDWARD SCRIVEN. 8vo, cloth extra, 15s.

Maxwell's Life of the Duke of Wellington. Three Vols. 8vo, with numerous highly finished Line and Wood Engravings by Eminent Artists. Cloth extra, gilt, £1 7s.

Montagu's(LadyMaryWortley) Letters and Works. Edited by Lord WHARNCLIFFE. With important Additions and Corrections, derived from the Original Manuscripts, and a New Memoir. Two Vols. 8vo, with fine Steel Portraits, cloth extra, 18s.

Roscoe's Life of Lorenzo de' Medici, called "THE MAGNIFICENT." A New and much improved Edition. Edited by his Son, THOMAS ROSCOE. Demy 8vo, with Portraits and nume-rous Plates, cloth extra, 9s.

Roscoe's Life and Pontificate of Leo the Tenth. Edited by his Son, THOMAS ROSCOE. Two Vols. 8vo. with Portraits and numerous Plates, cloth extra, 18s.

Saint-Simon (Memoirs of the Duke of), during the Reign of Louis the Fourteenth and the Regency. Translated from the French and Edited by BAYLE ST. JOHN. A New Edition. Three Vols. 8vo., cloth extra, 27s.

Walpole's (Horace) Anecdotes of Painting in England. With some Account of the principal English Artists, and incidental Notices of Sculptors, Carvers, Enamellers, Architects, Medallists, Engravers, &c. With Additions by Rev. JAMES DALLAWAY. Edited, with Additional Notes, by RALPH N. WORNUM. Three Vols. 8vo, with upwards of 150 Portraits and Plates, cloth extra, £1 7s.

Walpole's (Horace) entire Correspondence. Chronologically ar-ranged, with the Prefaces and Notes of CROKER, Lord DOVER, and others; the Notes of all previous Editors, and Additional Notes by PETER CUNNINGHAM. Nine Vols. 8vo, with numerous fine Portraits en-graved on Steel, cloth extra, £4 1s.

Walpole's (Horace) Royal and Noble Authors of England, Scotland, and Ireland; with Lists of their Works. A New Edition, Annotated, considerably Enlarged, and brought down to the Present Time. Illus-trated by nearly 200 Copperplate Portraits. Six Vols. 8vo, cloth extra.
[*In preparation.*

ENGLISHMAN'S HOUSE (The): A Practical Guide to all interested in Selecting or Building a House, with full Estimates of Cost, Quantities, &c. By C. J. RICHARDSON. Third Edition. With nearly 600 Illustrations. Crown 8vo, cloth extra, 7s. 6d.

AIRHOLT.—TOBACCO: Its History and Associations; including an Account of the Plant and its Manufacture; with its Modes of Use in all Ages and Countries. By F. W. FAIRHOLT, F.S.A. A New Edition, with Coloured Frontispiece and upwards of 100 Illustrations by the Author. Crown 8vo, cloth extra, 6s.

" A very pleasant and instructive history of tobacco and its associations, which we cordially recommend alike to the votaries and to the enemies of the muchmaligned but certainly not neglected weed. . . . Full of interest and information."—*Daily News.*

" A delightful reprint. . . . A more complete and dainty book on a subject which some still think unsavoury it would not be easy to call t. mind."—*Graphic.*

FARADAY'S CHEMICAL HISTORY OF A CANDLE. Lectures delivered to a Juvenile Audience. A New Edition, Edited by W. CROOKES, Esq., F.C.S., &c. Crown 8vo, cloth extra, with numerous Illustrations, 4s. 6d.

FARADAY'S VARIOUS FORCES OF NATURE. A New Edition, Edited by W. CROOKES, Esq., F.C.S., &c. Crown 8vo, cloth extra, with numerous Illustrations, 4s. 6d.

" For many years the English public had the privilege of listening to the discourses and speculations of Professor Faraday, at the Royal Institution, on Matter and Forces; and it is not too much to say that no lecturer on Physical Science, since the time of Sir Humphrey Davy, was ever listened to with more delight The pleasure which all derived from the expositions of Faraday was of a somewhat different kind from that produced by any other philosopher whose lectures we have attended. It was partially derived from his extreme dexterity as an operator: with him we had no chance of apologies for an unsuccessful experiment—no hanging fire in the midst of a series of brilliant demonstrations, producing that depressing tendency akin to the pain felt by an audience at a false note from a vocalist. All was a sparkling stream of eloquence and experimental illustration. We would have defied a chemist loving his science, no matter how often he might himself have repeated an experiment, to feel uninterested when seeing it done by Faraday."—W. CROOKES.

FIGUIER'S PRIMITIVE MAN: A Popular Manual of the prevailing Theories of the Descent of Man as promulgated by DARWIN, LYELL, Sir JOHN LUBBOCK, HUXLEY, E. B. TYLOR, and other eminent Ethnologists. Translated from the last French edition, and revised by E. B. T. With 263 Illustrations. Demy 8vo, cloth extra, gilt, 9s.

" An interesting and essentially popular resumé of all that has been written on the subject. M. Figuier has collected together the evidences which modern researches have accumulated, and has done this with a considerable amount of care He endeavours to separate the inquiry respecting Primitive Man from the Mosaic account of Man's creation, and does not admit that the authority of Holy Writ is in any way questioned by those labours which aim at seeking the real epoch of Man's first appearance upon earth. . . . An interesting book, with 263 illustrations, of which thirty are full-page engravings, confessedly somewhat fanciful in their combinations, but which will be found on examination to be justified by that soundest evidence, the actual discovery of the objects of which they represent the use."—*Athenæum.*

FINGER-RING LORE: Historical, Legendary, and Anecdotal. Earliest Notices; Superstitions; Ring Investiture, Secular and Ecclesiastical; Betrothal and Wedding Rings; Ring-tokens; Memorial and Mortuary Rings; Posy-Rings; Customs and Incidents in Connection with Rings; Remarkable Rings, &c. &c By WILLIAM JONES, F.S.A With Hundreds of Illustrations of Curious Rings of all Ages and Countries. Crown 8vo, cloth extra, 7s. 6d.   [*In the press.*

ELL AND GANDY'S POMPEIANA; or, The Topography, Edifices, and Ornaments of Pompeii. With upwards of 100 Line Engravings by GOODALL, COOKE, HEATH, PYE, &c. Demy 8vo, cloth extra, gilt, 18s.

GEMS OF ART : A Collection of 36 Engravings, after Paintings by REMBRANDT, CUYP, REYNOLDS, POUSSIN, MURILLO, TENIERS, CORREGGIO, GAINSBOROUGH, NORTHCOTE, &c., executed in Mezzotint by TURNER, BROMLEY, &c. Folio, in Portfolio, £1 11s. 6d.

GILBERT (W. S.), ORIGINAL PLAYS by : "A Wicked World," "Charity," "Palace of Truth," "Pygmalion," "Trial by Jury," &c. One Vol. crown 8vo, cloth extra, 9s.

"His workmanship is in its way perfect ; it is very sound, very even, very well sustained, and excellently balanced throughout."—*Observer*.

"A book which not only the modern playgoer, but those who do not frequent the theatre, can read with equal pleasure."—*Era*.

"Mr. Gilbert has done well and wisely to publish in a collected form some of his best plays. The *Palace of Truth* and *Pygmalion* may be read and enjoyed as poems by persons who have never entered the walls of a theatre."—*Standard*.

GILLRAY'S CARICATURES. Printed from the Original Plates, all engraved by Himself between 1779 and 1810; comprising the best Political and Humorous Satires of the Reign of GEORGE THE THIRD, in upwards of 600 highly spirited Engravings. Atlas folio, half-morocco extra, gilt edges, £7 10s.—There is also a Volume of SUPPRESSED PLATES, atlas folio, half-morocco, 31s. 6d.—Also, a VOLUME OF LETTERPRESS DESCRIPTIONS, comprising a very amusing Political History of the Reign of GEORGE THE THIRD, by THOS. WRIGHT and R. H. EVANS. Demy 8vo, cloth extra, 15s. ; or half-morocco, £1 1s.

GILLRAY, THE CARICATURIST : The Story of his Life and Times, and Anecdotal Descriptions of his Engravings. Edited by THOMAS WRIGHT, Esq., M.A., F.S.A. With 83 full-page Plates, and numerous Wood Engravings. Demy 4to, 600 pages, cloth extra, 31s. 6d.

"High as the expectations excited by this description [in the Introduction] may be, they will not be disappointed. The most inquisitive or exacting reader will find ready gathered to his hand, without the trouble of reference, almost every scrap of narrative, anecdote, gossip, scandal, or epigram, in poetry or prose, that he can possibly require for the elucidation of the caricatures."—*Quarterly Review*.

GOSSE (Edmund W.)—KING ERIK: A Tragedy. With a Vignette by W. B. SCOTT. Small 8vo, cloth gilt, 6s.

"The author's book, *On Viol and Flute*, displayed such a singular ear for music, such a singular poetic interpretation of flowers and trees, and such-like children of Flora, and, above all, such a distinct and individual poetic savour, that it would have been a pity indeed had these good gifts been wasted in any wrong direction. In this case there is happily no cause for such pity. We have seldom seen so marked an advance in a second book beyond a first. . . . The faults of *King Erik* are but slight matters ; its merits are solid, and of a very high order."—*Academy*.

GOSSE (Edmund W.)—ON VIOL AND FLUTE. Second Edition. With a Vignette by W. B. SCOTT. Small 8vo, cloth gilt, 5s.

GREENWOOD'S NEW NOVEL. — DICK TEMPLE. By JAMES GREENWOOD. Three Vols. crown 8vo, 31s. 6d.   [*In the press*.

GREENWOOD'S (James) LOW-LIFE DEEPS : An Account of the Strange Fish to be found there ; including "The Man and Dog Fight," with much additional and confirmatory evidence ; "With a Tally-Man," "A Fallen Star," "The Betting Barber," "A Coal Marriage," &c. With Illustrations in tint by ALFRED CONCANEN. Crown 8vo, cloth extra, gilt, 7s. 6d.

"The book is interesting reading. It shows that there are many things in London life not dreamt of by most people. It is well got up, and contains a number of striking illustrations."—*Scotsman*.

GREENWOOD'S WILDS OF LONDON ; Descriptive Sketches, from Personal Observations and Experience of Remarkable Scenes, People, and Places in London. By JAMES GREENWOOD, the "Lambeth Casual." With 12 Tinted Illustrations by ALFRED CONCANEN. Crown 8vo, cloth extra, gilt, 7s. 6d.

"Mr. James Greenwood presents himself once more in the character of 'one whose delight it is to do his humble endeavour towards exposing and extirpating social abuses and those hole-and-corner evils which afflict society.'"—*Saturday Review.*

GOLDEN LIBRARY. Square 16mo (Tauchnitz size), cloth extra, price 2s. per Volume.

Book of Clerical Anecdotes: The Humours and Eccentricities of "the Cloth."

Byron's Don Juan.

Carlyle (Thomas) on the Choice of Books. With a Memoir. [1s. 6d.]

Godwin's (William) Lives of the Necromancers.

Holmes's Autocrat of the Breakfast Table. With an Introduction by GEORGE AUGUSTUS SALA.

Holmes's Professor at the Breakfast Table.

Hood's Whims and Oddities. Both Series Complete in One Volume, with all the original Illustrations.

Irving's (Washington) Tales of a Traveller.

Irving's (Washington) Tales of the Alhambra.

Jesse's (Edward) Scenes and Occupations of Country Life; with Recollections of Natural History.

Lamb's Essays of Elia. Both Series Complete in One Vol.

Leigh Hunt's Essays: A Tale for a Chimney Corner, and other Pieces. With Portrait, and Introduction by EDMUND OLLIER.

Mallory's (Sir Thomas) Mort D'Arthur: The Stories of King Arthur and of the Knights of the Round Table. Edited by B. M. RANKING.

Pascal's Provincial Letters. A New Translation, with Historical Introduction and Notes, by T. M'CRIE, D.D., LL.D.

Pope's Complete Poetical Works.

Rochefoucauld's Maxims and Moral Reflections. With Notes, and an Introductory Essay by SAINTE-BEUVE.

St. Pierre's Paul and Virginia, and the Indian Cottage. Edited, with Life, by the Rev. E. CLARKE.

Shelley's Early Poems and Queen Mab, with Essay by LEIGH HUNT.

Shelley's Later Poems: Laon and Cythna, &c.

Shelley's Posthumous Poems, the Shelley Papers, &c.

Shelley's Prose Works, including a Refutation of Deism, Zastrozzi, St. Irvyne, &c.

White's Natural History of Selborne. Edited, with additions, by THOMAS BROWN, F.L.S.

"A series of excellently printed and carefully annotated volumes, handy in size, and altogether attractive."—*Bookseller.*

GOLDEN TREASURY OF THOUGHT. An Encyclopædia of Quotations from Writers of all Times and all Countries. Selected and Edited by THEODORE TAYLOR. Crown 8vo, cloth gilt, and gilt edges, 7s. 6d.

GRIMM.—GERMAN POPULAR STORIES. Collected by the Brothers GRIMM, and Translated by EDGAR TAYLOR. Edited, with an Introduction, by JOHN RUSKIN. With 22 Illustrations after the inimitable designs of GEORGE CRUIKSHANK. Both Series Complete. Square crown 8vo, 6s. 6d.; gilt leaves, 7s. 6d.

"The illustrations of this volume . . . . are of quite sterling and admirable art, of a class precisely parallel in elevation to the character of the tales which they illustrate ; and the original etchings, as I have before said in the Appendix to my 'Elements of Drawing,' were unrivalled in masterfulness of touch since Rembrandt (in some qualities of delineation, unrivalled even by him). . . . . To make somewhat enlarged copies of them, looking at them through a magnifying glass, and never putting two lines where Cruikshank has put only one, would be an exercise in decision and severe drawing which would leave afterwards little to be learnt in schools."—*Extract from Introduction by* JOHN RUSKIN.

GUYOT'S EARTH AND MAN; or, Physical Geography in its Relation to the History of Mankind. With Additions by Professors AGASSIZ, PIERCE, and GRAY. With 12 Maps and Engravings on Steel, some Coloured, and a copious Index. A New Edition. Crown 8vo, cloth extra, gilt, 4s. 6d.

HAKE'S (T. GORDON) NEW SYMBOLS: Poems. By the Author of " Parables and Tales." Crown 8vo, cloth extra, 6s.
"The entire book breathes a pure and ennobling influence, shows welcome originality of idea and illustration, and yields the highest proof of imaginative faculty and mature power of expression."—*Athenæum*.

HALL'S (Mrs. S. C.) SKETCHES OF IRISH CHARACTER. With numerous Illustrations on Steel and Wood, by DANIEL MACLISE, Sir JOHN GILBERT, W. HARVEY, and G. CRUIKSHANK. 8vo, cloth extra, gilt, 7s. 6d.
"The Irish sketches of this lady resemble Miss Mitford's beautiful English Sketches in 'Our Village,' but they are far more vigorous and picturesque and bright."—*Blackwood's Magazine*.

HARRIS'S AURELIAN: A Natural History of English Moths and Butterflies, and the Plants on which they feed. A New Edition. Edited, with Additions, by J. O. WESTWOOD. With about 400 exquisitely Coloured Figures of Moths, Butterflies, Caterpillars, &c., and the Plants on which they feed. Small folio, half-morocco extra, gilt edges, £3 13s. 6d.

HAWKER (MEMORIALS OF THE LATE REV. ROBERT STEPHEN), sometime Vicar of Morwenstow, in the Diocese of Exeter. Collected, arranged, and edited by the Rev. FREDERICK GEORGE LEE, D.C.L., Vicar of All Saints', Lambeth. With Photographic Portrait, Pedigree, and Illustrations. Demy 8vo, cloth extra, 12s.

HAYDON'S (B. R.) CORRESPONDENCE & TABLE-TALK. With a Memoir by his Son, FREDERIC WORDSWORTH HAYDON. Comprising a large number of hitherto Unpublished Letters from KEATS, WILKIE, SOUTHEY, WORDSWORTH, KIRKUP, LEIGH HUNT, LANDSEER, HORACE SMITH, Sir G. BEAUMONT, GOETHE, Mrs. SIDDONS, Sir WALTER SCOTT, TALFOURD, JEFFREY, Miss MITFORD, MACREADY, Mrs. BROWNING, LOCKHART, HALLAM, and others. With 23 Illustrations, including Facsimiles of many interesting Sketches, Portraits of HAYDON by KEATS and WILKIE, and HAYDON'S Portraits of WILKIE, KEATS, and MARIA FOOTE. Two Vols., 8vo, cloth extra, 36s.
"As a defence of the painter's character and career the work before us will possibly meet with as much criticism as approval; but there can, we think, be no question of its interest in a purely biographical sense, or of its literary merit. The letters and table-talk form in themselves a most valuable contribution to the social and artistic history of the time, and would be very welcome even without the memoir which precedes them."—*Pall Mall Gazette*.
"The volumes are among the most interesting produced or likely to be produced by the present season."—*Examiner*.
"One of the most moving histories that has been published in modern days. . . Haydon's case has never before been fairly laid before the public; the man has never been shown as he was in truth, through the medium of his correspondence, his diaries, sayings and actions. . . . Charming correspondence, and still more charming table-talk."—*Morning Post*.
"Here we have a full-length portrait of a most remarkable man. . . . His son has done the work well—is clear and discriminating on the whole, and writes with ease and vigour. Over and above the interest that must be felt in Haydon himself, the letters afford us the opportunity of studying closely many of the greatest men and women of the time. . . . We do not hesitate to say that these letters and table-talk form a most valuable contribution to the history of art and literature in the past generation. The editor has selected and arranged them with uncommon judgment, adding many notes that contain *ana* and anecdotes. Every page has thus its point of interest. The book will no doubt have a wide audience, as it well deserves."—*Nonconformist*.

HISTORICAL PORTRAITS; Upwards of 430 Engravings of Rare Prints. Comprising the Collections of RODD, RICHARDSON, CAULFIELD, &c. With Descriptive Text to every Plate, giving a brief outline of the most important Historical and Biographical Facts and Dates connected with each Portrait, and references to original Authorities. In Three Vols., royal 4to, half-morocco, full gilt back and edges, price £7 7s.

THE ORIGINAL HOGARTH.

HOGARTH'S WORKS. ENGRAVED BY HIMSELF. 153 fine Plates, with elaborate Letterpress Descriptions by JOHN NICHOLS. Atlas folio, half-morocco extra, gilt edges, £7 10s.

" I was pleased with the reply of a gentleman who, being asked which book he esteemed most in his library, answered ' Shakespeare ' ; being asked which he esteemed next best, answered ' Hogarth.' "—CHARLES LAMB.

HOLBEIN'S PORTRAITS OF THE COURT OF HENRY THE EIGHTH. A Series of 84 exquisitely beautiful Tinted Plates, engraved by BARTOLOZZI, COOPER, and others, and printed on Tinted Paper, in imitation of the Original Drawings in the Royal Collection at Windsor. With Historical Letterpress by EDMUND LODGE, Norroy King of Arms. Imperial 4to, half-morocco extra, gilt edges, £5 15s. 6d.

" A very charming, costly, and captivating performance."—DIBDIN.

HOLBEIN'S PORTRAITS OF THE COURT OF HENRY VIII. CHAMBERLAINE'S Imitations of the Original Drawings, mostly engraved by BARTOLOZZI. London: printed by W. BULMER & Co., Shakespeare Printing Office, 1792. 92 splendid Portraits (including 8 additional Plates), elaborately tinted in Colours, with Descriptive and Biographical Notes, by EDMUND LODGE, Norroy King of Arms. Atlas folio, half-morocco, gilt edges, £20.

** The graceful and delicate colouring preserves all the effect of the original highly-finished drawings, and at the same time communicates an enchanting animation to the features. Not more than ten of the subjects are included in " Lodge's Portraits," and still fewer are to be found in any other collection.

HOOD'S (Thomas) CHOICE WORKS, in Prose and Verse. Including the CREAM OF THE COMIC ANNUALS. With Life of the Author, Portrait, and over Two Hundred original Illustrations. Crown 8vo, cloth extra, gilt, 7s. 6d.

" Not only does the volume include the better-known poems by the author, but also what is happily described as ' the cream of the Comic Annuals.' Such delicious things as ' Don't you smell Fire ? ' ' The Parish Revolution,' and ' Huggins and Duggins,' will never want readers."—*Graphic.*

"The volume, which contains nearly 800 pages, is liberally illustrated with facsimile cuts of Hood's own grotesque sketches, many of them pictorial puns, which always possess a freshness, and never fail to raise a genuine laugh. We have here some of Hood's earlier attempts, and his share of the ' Odes and Addresses to Great People.' Then we have the two series of ' Whims and Oddities,' which ought to be prescribed for nervous and hypochondriacal people : for surely more mirth was never packed into the same compass before, more of the rollicking abandonment of a rich, joyous humour, or more of the true geniality of nature which makes fun so delightful and leaves no after-taste of unkindness in the mouth. ' The Plea of the Midsummer Fairies ' will be found here in unabridged form, together with ' Hero and Leander,' a number of ' Minor Poems,' among which we meet with some very pretty fancies the well-known ' Retrospective Review,' and ' I Remember, I Remember '-- Hood's contributions to the *Gem*, including ' The Dream of Eugene Aram,' ' The Cream of the Comic Annuals '-- in itself a fund of merriment large enough to dispel the gloom of many a winter's evening --and the ' National Tales.' This is a fair representative selection of Hood's works, many of which have been hitherto inaccessible except at high prices. Most of the best known of his comic effusions -- those punning ballads in which he has never been approached --are to be found in the liberal collection Messrs. Chatto & Windus have given to the public."—*Birmingham Daily Mail.*

HOOD'S (Tom) HUMOROUS WORKS. Edited, with a Memoir, by his Sister, FRANCES FREELING BRODERIP. Crown 8vo, cloth extra, with numerous Illustrations, 6s. [*In the press.*

HOOD'S (Tom) FROM NOWHERE TO THE NORTH POLE: A Noah's Arkæological Narrative. By TOM HOOD. With 25 Illustrations by W. BRUNTON and E. C. BARNES. Square crown 8vo, in a handsome and specially-designed binding, gilt edges, 6s.

"Poor Tom Hood! It is very sad to turn over the droll pages of 'From Nowhere to the North Pole,' and to think that he will never make the young people, for whom, like his famous father, he ever had such a kind, sympathetic heart, laugh or cry any more. This is a birthday story, and no part of it is better than the first chapter, concerning birthdays in general, and Frank's birthday in particular. The amusing letterpress is profusely interspersed with the jingling rhymes which children love and learn so easily. Messrs. Brunton and Barnes do full justice to the writer's meaning, and a pleasanter result of the harmonious co-operation of author and artist could not be desired."—*Times.*

HONE'S SCRAP-BOOKS: The Miscellaneous Collections of WILLIAM HONE, Author of "The Table-Book," "Every-Day Book," and "Year-Book"; being a Supplement to those works. With Notes, Portraits, and numerous Illustrations of curious and eccentric objects. Crown 8vo. [*In preparation.*

"He has deserved well of the naturalist, the antiquarian, and the poet."

HOOK'S (THEODORE) CHOICE HUMOROUS WORKS, including his Ludicrous Adventures, Bons-mots, Puns, and Hoaxes. With a new Life of the Author, Portraits, Facsimiles, and Illust. Crown 8vo, cloth extra, gilt, 7s. 6d.

"His name will be preserved. His political songs and *jeux d'esprit,* when the hour comes for collecting them, will form a volume of sterling and lasting attraction; and after many clever romances of this age shall have sufficiently occupied public attention, and sunk, like hundreds of former generations, into utter oblivion, there are tales in his collection which will be read with even a greater interest than they commanded in their novelty."—J. G. LOCKHART.

HOPE'S COSTUME OF THE ANCIENTS. Illustrated in upwards of 320 Outline Engravings, containing Representations of Egyptian, Greek, and Roman Habits and Dresses. A New Edition. Two Vols., royal 8vo, with Coloured Frontispieces, cloth extra, £2 5s.

"The substance of many expensive works, containing all that may be necessary to give to artists, and even to dramatic performers and to others engaged in classical representations, an idea of ancient costumes sufficiently ample to prevent their offending in their performances by gross and obvious blunders."

HORNE.—ORION. An Epic Poem, in Three Books. By RICHARD HENGIST HORNE. With Photographic Portrait. TENTH EDITION. Crown 8vo, cloth extra, 7s.
"Orion will be admitted, by every man of genius, to be one of the noblest, if not the very noblest poetical work of the age. Its defects are trivial and conventional, its beauties intrinsic and supreme."—EDGAR ALLAN POE.

ITALIAN MASTERS (DRAWINGS BY THE): Autotype Facsimiles of Original Drawings. With Critical and Descriptive Notes by J. COMYNS CARR. Atlas folio, half-morocco, gilt. [*In preparation.*

ARDINE'S (Sir Wm.) NATURALIST'S LIBRARY. 42
vols. fcap. 8vo, illustrated by over 1200 Coloured Plates, with numerous
Portraits and Memoirs of eminent Naturalists, half (imitation) calf, full
gilt, top edges gilt, £9 9s. ; or, separately, red cloth extra, 4s. 6d. per
Vol., as follows :—
Vols. 1 to 4. British Birds; 5. Sun Birds; 6 and 7. Humming Birds; 8. Game
Birds ; 9. Pigeons ; 10. Parrots ; 11 and 12. Birds of West Africa ; 13. Fly
Catchers ; 14. Pheasants, Peacocks, &c.; 15. Animals—Introduction ; 16. Lions
and Tigers ; 17. British Quadrupeds ; 18 and 19. Dogs ; 20. Horses ; 21 and 22.
Ruminating Animals ; 23. Elephants, &c. ; 24. Marsupialia ; 25. Seals, &c. ; 26.
Whales, &c. ; 27. Monkeys ; 28. Insects—Introduction ; 29. British Butterflies ;
30. British Moths, &c.; 31. Foreign Butterflies ; 32. Foreign Moths ; 33. Beetles ;
34. Bees ; 35. Fishes—Introduction, and Foreign Fishes ; 36 and 37. British
Fishes ; 38. Perch, &c. ; 39 and 40. Fishes of Guiana ; 41. Smith's Natural History
of Man ; 42. Gould's Humming Birds.
"The book is perhaps the most interesting, the most beautiful, and the cheapest
series ever offered to the public."—*Athenæum.*

JENNINGS' (Hargrave) THE ROSICRUCIANS : Their
Rites and Mysteries. With Chapters on the Ancient Fire and Serpent Wor-
shipers, and Explanations of Mystic Symbols in Monuments and Talismans
of Primeval Philosophers. Crown 8vo, with 300 Illustrations, 10s. 6d.

JOSEPHUS (The Works of). Translated by WHISTON. Containing both the "Antiquities of the Jews," and the "Wars of the Jews." Two
Vols. 8vo, with 52 Illustrations and Maps, cloth extra, gilt, 14s.
"This admirable translation far exceeds all preceding ones, and has never been
equalled by any subsequent attempt of the kind."—LOWNDES.

AVANAGH.—THE SILVER FISH, and other Fairy
Stories. By BRIDGET and JULIA KAVANAGH. With Thirty Illustrations
by J. MOYR SMITH. Small 8vo, cloth, full gilt, 6s. [*In the press.*

KINGSLEY'S (Henry) FIRESIDE STUDIES. Two Vols.
crown 8vo, 21s.
*** The titles of the Essays contained in these volumes are as follows :—THE
FATHERS OF THE SPECTATOR—TWO OLD SUSSEX WORTHIES—AN OLD-FASHIONED
MEMBER—THE MASTER OF THE "MERMAID"—THE FATHER OF IRREGULAR
DRAMA—FLETCHER AND BEAUMONT—SIR PHILIP SIDNEY.

KINGSLEY'S (Henry) NEW NOVEL. — THE GRANGE
GARDEN. Three Vols. crown 8vo, 31s. 6d. [*Nearly ready.*

AMB'S (Charles) COMPLETE WORKS, in Prose and
Verse, reprinted from the Original Editions, with many pieces now first
included in any Edition, and Notes and Introduction by R. H. SHEPHERD.
With Two Portraits and facsimile of a page of the " Essay on Roast Pig."
Crown 8vo, cloth extra, gilt, 7s. 6d.
"The genius of Mr. Lamb, as developed in his various writings, takes rank with
the most original of the age. As a critic he stands *facile princeps* in the subject he
handled. Search English literature through, from its first beginnings until now, and
you will find none like him. There is not a criticism he ever wrote that does not
directly tell you a number of things you had no previous notion of. In criticism he
was indeed, in all senses of the word, a discoverer—like Vasco Nunez or Magellan. In
that very domain of literature with which you fancied yourself most variously and
closely acquainted, he would show you ' fresh fields and pastures new,' and these the
most fruitful and delightful. For the riches he discovered were richer that they had
lain so deep—the more valuable were they, when found, that they had eluded the
search of ordinary men. As an essayist, Charles Lamb will be remembered in years
to come with Rabelais and Montaigne, with Sir Thomas Browne, with Steele and
with Addison. He unites many of the finest characteristics of these several writers.
He has wisdom and wit of the highest order, exquisite humour, a genuine and cordial
vein of pleasantry, and the most heart-touching pathos. In the largest acceptation
of the word, he is a humanist."—JOHN FORSTER.

LAMB (Mary and Charles) : THEIR POEMS, LETTERS, and
REMAINS. With Reminiscences and Notes by W. CAREW HAZLITT. With
HANCOCK's Portrait of the Essayist, Facsimiles of the Title-pages of the rare First
Editions of Lamb's and Coleridge's Works, and numerous Illustrations. Crown
8vo, cloth extra, 10s. 6d.
" Must be consulted by all future biographers of the Lambs."—*Daily News.*
" Very many passages will delight those fond of literary trifles ; hardly any
portion will fail in interest for lovers of Charles Lamb and his sister."—*Standard.*

LANDSEER'S (Sir Edwin) ETCHINGS OF CARNIVOROUS
ANIMALS. Comprising 38 subjects, chiefly Early Works, etched by his Brother
THOMAS or, his Father, with Letterpress Descriptions. Royal 4to, cloth extra,
15s.

LAMONT.—YACHTING IN THE ARCTIC SEAS ; or, Notes
of Five Voyages of Sport and Discovery in the Neighbourhood of Spitzbergen
and Novaya Zemlya. By JAMES LAMONT, F.G.S., F.R.G.S. Author of "Seasons
with the Sea-Horses." Edited, with numerous full-page Illustrations, by
WILLIAM LIVESAY, M.D. Demy 8vo, cloth extra, with Maps and numerous
Illustrations, 18s.
" After wading through numberless volumes of icy fiction, concocted narrative,
and spurious biography of Arctic voyagers, it is pleasant to meet with a real and
genuine volume. . . . . He shows much tact in recounting his adventures, and
they are so interspersed with anecdotes and information as to make them anything
but wearisome. . . . . The book, as a whole, is the most important addition made
to our Arctic literature for a long time."—*Athenæum.*
" Full of entertainment and information."—*Nature.*
" Mr. Lamont has taken a share distinctively his own in the work of Arctic discovery, and the value of his labours as an ' amateur explorer ' is to be attributed to
the systematic manner in which he pursued his investigations, no less than to his
scientific qualifications for the task. . . . The handsome volume is full of valuable
and interesting information to the sportsman and naturalist—it would be difficult to
say which of the two will enjoy it most."—*Scotsman.*

LEE (General Robert) : HIS LIFE AND CAMPAIGNS. By
his Nephew, EDWARD LEE CHILDE. With Steel-plate Portrait by JEENS, and
a Map. Post 8vo, 9s.
" A valuable and well-written contribution to the history of the Civil War in the
United States."—*Saturday Review.*
" As a clear and compendious survey of a life of the true heroic type, Mr. Childe's
volume may well be commended to the English reader."—*Graphic.*

LIFE IN LONDON ; or, The Day and Night Scenes of Jerry
Hawthorn and Corinthian Tom. With the whole of Cruikshank's very Droll
Illustrations, in Colours, after the Originals. Crown 8vo, cloth extra, gilt,
7s. 6d.

LINTON'S (Mrs. E. Lynn) JOSHUA DAVIDSON, Christian
and Communist. SIXTH EDITION, with a New Preface. Small crown 8vo, cloth
extra, 4s. 6d.
" In a short and vigorous preface, Mrs. Linton defends her notion of the logical
outcome of Christianity as embodied in this attempt to conceive how Christ would
have acted, with whom He would have fraternised, and who would have declined to
receive Him, had He appeared in the present generation."—*Examiner.*

LOST BEAUTIES OF THE ENGLISH LANGUAGE. An
Appeal to Authors, Poets, Clergymen, and Public Speakers. By CHARLES
MACKAY, LL.D. Crown 8vo, cloth extra, 6s. 6d.

LONDON.—WILKINSON'S LONDINA ILLUSTRATA; or, Graphic and Historical Illustrations of the most Interesting and Curious Architectural Monuments of the City and Suburbs of London and Westminster (now mostly destroyed). Two Vols. imperial 4to, containing 207 Copperplate Engravings, with historical and descriptive Letterpress, half-bound morocco, top edges gilt, £5 5s.

⁎ *An enumeration of a few of the Plates will give some idea of the scope of the Work:*—St. Bartholomew's Church, Cloisters, and Priory, in 1393 ; St. Michael's, Cornhill, in 1421 ; St. Paul's Cathedral and Cross, in 1616 and 1656; St. John's of Jerusalem, Clerkenwell, 1660; Bunyan's Meeting House, in 1687; Guildhall, in 1517; Cheapside and its Cross, in 1547, 1585, and 1641 ; Cornhill, in 1599; Merchant Taylors' Hall, in 1599; Shakespeare's Globe Theatre, in 1612 and 1647; Alleyne's Bear Garden, in 1614 and 1647 ; Drury Lane, in 1792 and 1814; Covent Garden, in 1732, 1794, and 1809; Whitehall, in 1638 and 1697; York House, with Inigo Jones's Water Gate, circa 1626 ; Somerset House, previous to its alteration by Inigo Jones, circa 1600 : St James's Palace, 1660; Montagu House (now the British Museum) before 1685, and in 1804.

LONGFELLOW'S PROSE WORKS, Complete. Including "Outre Mer," "Hyperion," "Kavanagh," "The Poets and Poetry of Europe," and "Driftwood." With Portrait and Illustrations by VALENTINE BROMLEY. 800 pages, crown 8vo, cloth extra, 7s. 6d.

LONGFELLOW'S POETICAL WORKS. With numerous fine Illustrations. Crown 8vo, cloth extra, gilt, 7s. 6d.

"Longfellow, in the 'Golden Legend,' has entered more closely into the temper of the Monk, for good and for evil, than ever yet theological writer or historian, though they may have given their life's labour to the analysis."—RUSKIN.

"We shall only say that he is the most popular of American poets, and that this popularity may safely be assumed to contain in itself the elements of permanence, since it has been fairly earned, without any of that subservience to the baser tastes of the public which characterises the quack of letters. His are laurels honourably gained and gently worn. Without comparing him with others, it is enough if we declare our conviction that he has composed poems which will live as long as the language in which they are written."—JAMES RUSSELL LOWELL.

MACLISE'S GALLERY OF ILLUSTRIOUS LITERARY CHARACTERS. (THE FAMOUS FRASER PORTRAITS.) With Notes by the late WILLIAM MAGINN, LL.D. Edited, with copious Additional Notes, by WILLIAM BATES, B.A. The volume contains 83 CHARACTERISTIC PORTRAITS, now first issued in a complete form. Demy 4to, cloth gilt and gilt edges, 31s. 6d.

"One of the most interesting volumes of this year's literature."—*Times.*

"Deserves a place on every drawing-room table, and may not unfitly be removed from the drawing-room to the library."—*Spectator.*

MADRE NATURA versus THE MOLOCH OF FASHION. By LUKE LIMNER. With 32 Illustrations by the Author. FOURTH EDITION, revised and enlarged. Crown 8vo, cloth, extra gilt, 2s. 6d.

"Agreeably written and amusingly illustrated. Common sense and erudition are brought to bear on the subjects discussed in it."—*Lancet.*

MAGNA CHARTA. An exact Facsimile of the Original Document in the British Museum, printed on fine plate paper, nearly 3 feet long by 2 feet wide, with the Arms and Seals of the Barons emblazoned in Gold and Colours. Price 5s. A full Translation, with Notes, on a large sheet, 6d.

MARK TWAIN'S CHOICE WORKS. Revised and Corrected throughout by the Author. With Life, Portrait, and numerous Illustrations. 700 pages, cloth extra, gilt, 7s. 6d.

MARK TWAIN'S PLEASURE TRIP on the CONTINENT of EUROPE. Post 8vo, illustrated boards, 2s.

MARSTON'S (Dr. Westland) DRAMATIC and POETICAL WORKS. Collected Library Edition, in Two Vols. crown 8vo, 18*s.*

"'The Patrician's Daughter' is an oasis in the desert of modern dramatic literature, a real emanation of mind. We do not recollect any modern work in which states of thought are so freely developed, except the 'Torquato Tasso' of Goethe. The play is a work of art in the same sense that a play of Sophocles is a work of art ; it is one simple idea in a state of gradual development."—*Times.*

MARSTON'S (Philip Bourke) SONG TIDE, and other Poems. Second Edition. Crown 8vo, cloth extra, 8*s.*

"This is a first work of extraordinary performance and of still more extraordinary promise. The youngest school of English poetry has received an important accession to its ranks in Philip Bourke Marston."—*Examiner.*

MARSTON'S (P. B.) ALL IN ALL : Poems and Sonnets. Crown 8vo, cloth extra, 8*s.*

"Many of these poems are leavened with the leaven of genuine poetical sentiment, and expressed with grace and beauty of language. A tender melancholy, as well as a penetrating pathos, gives character to much of their sentiment, and lends it an irresistible interest to all who can feel."—*Standard.*

MEYRICK'S PAINTED ILLUSTRATIONS OF ANCIENT ARMS AND ARMOUR : A Critical Inquiry into Ancient Armour as it existed in Europe, but particularly in England, from the Norman Conquest to the Reign of Charles II. ; with a Glossary, by Sir S. R. MEYRICK. New and greatly improved Edition, corrected throughout by the Author, with the assistance of ALBERT WAY and others. Illustrated by more than 100 Plates, splendidly Illuminated in gold and silver ; also an additional Plate of the Tournament of Locks and Keys. Three Vols. imperial 4to, half-morocco extra, gilt edges, £10 10*s.*

"While the splendour of the decorations of this work is well calculated to excite curiosity, the novel character of its contents, the very curious extracts from the rare MSS. in which it abounds, and the pleasing manner in which the author's antiquarian researches are prosecuted, will tempt many who take up the book in idleness, to peruse it with care. No previous work can be compared, in point of extent, arrangement, science, or utility, with the one now in question. 1st. It for the first time supplies, to our schools of art, correct and ascertained data for costume, in its noblest and most important branch—historical painting. 2nd. It affords a simple, clear, and most conclusive elucidation of a great number of passages in our great dramatic poets—ay, and in the works of those of Greece and Rome—against which commentators and scholiasts have been trying their wits for centuries. 3rd. It throws a flood of light upon the manners, usages, and sports of our ancestors, from the time of the Anglo-Saxons down to the reign of Charles the Second. And lastly, it at once removes a vast number of idle traditions and ingenious fables, which one compiler of history, copying from another, has succeeded in transmitting through the lapse of four or five hundred years.

MEYRICK'S ENGRAVED ILLUSTRATIONS OF ANCIENT ARMS AND ARMOUR. 154 highly finished Etchings of the Collection at Goodrich Court, Herefordshire, engraved by JOSEPH SKELTON, with Historical and Critical Disquisitions by Sir S. R. MEYRICK. Two Vols. imperial 4to, with Portrait, half-morocco extra, gilt edges, £4 14*s.* 6*d.*

"We should imagine that the possessors of Dr. Meyrick's former great work would eagerly add Mr. Skelton's as a suitable illustration. In the first they have the history of Arms and Armour ; in the second work, beautiful engravings of all the details, made out with sufficient minuteness to serve hereafter as patterns for artists or workmen."—*Gentleman's Magazine.*

MUSES OF MAYFAIR : Vers de Société of the Nineteenth Century. Including Selections from TENNYSON, BROWNING, SWINBURNE, ROSSETTI, JEAN INGELOW, LOCKER, INGOLDSBY, HOOD, LYTTON, C.S.C., LANDOR, AUSTIN DOBSON, HENRY LEIGH, &c. &c. Edited by H. CHOLMONDELEY-PENNELL. Crown 8vo, cloth extra, gilt, gilt edges, 7*s.* 6*d.*

LD DRAMATISTS. Crown 8vo, cloth extra, with Vignette Portraits, price 6s. per vol.

Ben Jonson's Works. With Notes, Critical and Explanatory, and a Biographical Memoir by WILLIAM GIFFORD. Edited by Lieut. Col. F. CUNNINGHAM. Three Vols.

Chapman's (George) Complete Works. Now first Collected. Three Vols. Vol I. contains the Plays complete, including the doubtful ones ; Vol. II. the Poems and Minor Translations, with an Introductory Essay by ALGERNON CHARLES SWINBURNE ; Vol. III. the Translations of the Iliad and Odyssey.

Marlowe's Works. Including his Translations. Edited, with Notes and Introduction, by Col. CUNNINGHAM. One Vol.

Massinger's Plays. From the Text of WILLIAM GIFFORD. With the addition of the Tragedy of " Believe as You List." Edited by Col. CUNNINGHAM. One Vol.

O'SHAUGHNESSY'S (Arthur) AN EPIC OF WOMEN, and other Poems. Second Edition. Fcap. 8vo, cloth extra, 6s.

O'SHAUGHNESSY'S LAYS OF FRANCE. (Founded on the " Lays of Marie.") Second Edition. Crown 8vo, cloth extra, 10s. 6d.

O'SHAUGHNESSY'S MUSIC AND MOONLIGHT : Poems and Songs. Fcap. 8vo, cloth extra, 7s. 6d.

" It is difficult to say which is more exquisite, the technical perfection of structure and melody, or the delicate pathos of thought. Mr. O'Shaughnessy will enrich our literature with some of the very best songs written in our generation."—*Academy*.

LUTARCH'S LIVES, Complete. Translated by the LANGHORNES. New Edition, with Medallion Portraits. In Two Vols. 8vo, cloth extra, 10s. 6d.

" When I write, I care not to have books about me ; but I can hardly be without a ' Plutarch.' "—MONTAIGNE.

POE'S (Edgar Allan) CHOICE PROSE AND POETICAL WORKS. With BAUDELAIRE'S " Essay." 750 pages, crown 8vo, Portrait and Illustrations, cloth extra, 7s. 6d.

" Poe's great power lay in writing tales, which rank in a class by themselves, and have their characteristics strongly defined."—*Fraser's Magazine*.

" Poe stands as much alone among verse-writers as Salvator Rosa among painters."—*Spectator*.

PROUT, FATHER.—THE FINAL RELIQUES OF FATHER PROUT. Collected and edited, from MSS. supplied by the family of the Rev. FRANCIS MAHONY, by BLANCHARD JERROLD. Crown 8vo, cloth extra, with Portrait and Facsimiles, 12s. 6d.

" We heartily commend this handsome volume to all lovers of sound wit, genuine humour, and manly sense."—*Spectator*.

" Sparkles all over, and is full of interest. Mahony, like Sydney Smith, could write on no subject without being brilliant and witty."—*British Quarterly Review*.

" A delightful collection of humour, scholarship, and vigorous political writing. It brings before us many of the ' Fraser ' set—Maginn, Dickens, Jerrold, and Thackeray. Maginn described himself better than any critic could do, when he wrote of himself as ' an Irish potato seasoned with Attic salt.' "—*Edinburgh Daily Review*.

" It is well that the present long delayed volume should remind a younger generation of his fame. . . . The charming letters from Paris, Florence, and Rome . . . are the most perfect specimens of what a foreign correspondence ought to be."—*Academy*.

ICCADILLY NOVELS (The): Popular Stories by the Best Authors. Crown 8vo, carefully printed on creamy paper, and tastefully bound in cloth for the Library, price 6s. each.

WILKIE COLLINS.

THE WOMAN IN WHITE. Illustrated by Sir J. GILBERT and F. A. FRASER.

ANTONINA. Illustrated by Sir J. GILBERT and ALFRED CONCANEN.

BASIL. Illustrated by Sir JOHN GILBERT and M. F. MAHONEY.

THE DEAD SECRET. Illustrated by Sir JOHN GILBERT and H. FURNISS.

QUEEN OF HEARTS. Illustrated by Sir J. GILBERT and A. CONCANEN.

THE MOONSTONE. Illustrated by G. DU MAURIER and F. A. FRASER.

HIDE AND SEEK. Illustrated by Sir JOHN GILBERT and M. F. MAHONEY.

MAN AND WIFE. Illustrated by WILLIAM SMALL.

POOR MISS FINCH. Illustrated by G. DU MAURIER and EDWARD HUGHES.

MISS OR MRS. ? Illustrated by S. L. FILDES and HENRY WOODS.

THE NEW MAGDALEN. Illustrated by DU MAURIER and C. S. R.

THE FROZEN DEEP. Illustrated by DU MAURIER and M. F. MAHONEY.

MY MISCELLANIES. With Steel Portrait, and Illustrations by CONCANEN.

THE LAW and THE LADY. Illustrated by S. L. FILDES and S. HALL.

"Like all the author's works, full of a certain power and ingenuity. . . . It is upon such suggestions of crime that the fascination of the story depends. . . . The reader feels it his duty to serve to the end upon the inquest on which he has been called by the author."—*Times*, in review of "The Law and the Lady."

"The greatest master the sensational novel has ever known."—*World*.

E. LYNN LINTON.

PATRICIA KEMBALL. With Frontispiece by DU MAURIER.

"A very clever and well-constructed story, original and striking, and interesting all through. A novel abounding in thought and power and interest."—*Times*.

"Displays genuine humour, as well as keen social observation. Enough graphic portraiture and witty observation to furnish materials for half-a-dozen novels of the ordinary kind."—*Saturday Review*.

KATHARINE S. MACQUOID.

THE EVIL EYE, AND OTHER STORIES. Illustrated by THOMAS R. MACQUOID and PERCY MACQUOID.

"For Norman country life what the 'Johnny Ludlow' stories are for English rural delineation, that is, cameos delicately, if not very minutely or vividly wrought, and quite finished enough to give a pleasurable sense of artistic ease and faculty. A word of commendation is merited by the illustrations."—*Academy*.

HENRY KINGSLEY.

NUMBER SEVENTEEN.

"Quite sufficient plot and enough originality to form a charming story."—*Echo*.

FLORENCE MARRYAT.

OPEN! SESAME! Illustrated by F. A. FRASER.

"A story which arouses and sustains the reader's interest to a higher degree than, perhaps, any of its author's former works. . . . A very excellent story." *Graphic*.

PICCADILLY NOVELS, *continued.*

MRS. OLIPHANT.

WHITELADIES. With Illustrations by A. HOPKINS & H. WOODS.

"Is really a pleasant and readable book, written with practical ease and grace."
—*Times.*

JAMES PAYN, Author of "Lost Sir Massingberd."

| **THE BEST OF HUSBANDS.** | **WALTER'S WORD.** Illus- |
| Illustrated by J. MOYR SMITH. | trated by J. MOYR SMITH. |

"His novels are always commendable in the sense of art. They also possess another distinct claim to our liking : the girls in them are remarkably charming and true to nature, as most people, we believe, have the good fortune to observe nature represented by girls." · *Spectator.*

ANTHONY TROLLOPE.

THE WAY WE LIVE NOW. With Illustrations.

"Mr. Trollope has a true artist's idea of tone, of colour, of harmony ; his pictures are one, and seldom out of drawing ; he never strains after effect, is fidelity itself in expressing English life, is never guilty of caricature." —*Fortnightly Review.*

T. A. TROLLOPE.

DIAMOND CUT DIAMOND; and other Stories.

"The indefinable charm of Tuscan and Venetian life breathes in his pages."—*Times.*
"Full of life, of interest, of close observation, and sympathy. . . . When Mr. Trollope paints a scene, it is sure to be a scene worth painting."—*Saturday Review.*

JOHN SAUNDERS, Author of "Abel Drake's Wife."

| **BOUND TO THE WHEEL.** | **ONE AGAINST THE** |
| **GUY WATERMAN.** | **WORLD**; or, Reuben's War. |

Authors of "Gideon's Rock" and "Abel Drake's Wife."

THE LION IN THE PATH: An Historical Romance.

"A carefully written and beautiful story—a story of goodness and truth, which is yet as interesting as though it dealt with the opposite qualities. . . The author of this really clever story has been at great pains to work out all its details with elaborate conscientiousness, and the result is a very vivid picture of the ways of life and habits of thought of a hundred and fifty years ago. . . . Certainly a very interesting book."—*Times.*

OUIDA.

Uniform Edition, crown 8vo, red cloth extra, 5s. each.

FOLLE FARINE.	**PASCAREL**: Only a Story.
IDALIA: A Romance.	**PUCK:** His Vicissitudes, Adven-
CHANDOS: A Novel.	tures, &c.
UNDER TWO FLAGS.	**A DOG OF FLANDERS.**
TRICOTRIN.	**STRATHMORE.**
CECIL CASTLEMAINE'S	**TWO LITTLE WOODEN**
GAGE.	SHOES.
HELD IN BONDAGE.	**SIGNA.**

"Keen poetic insight, an intense love of nature, a deep admiration of the beautiful in form and colour, are the gifts of Ouida."—*Morning Post.*

PUGIN'S ARCHITECTURAL WORKS:—

Apology for the Revival of Christian Architecture. Illustrated by 10 large Etchings. Small 4to, cloth extra, 5s.

Examples of Gothic Architecture, selected from Ancient Edifices in England. 225 fine Engravings by LE KEUX, with descriptive Letterpress by E. J. WILLSON Three Vols. 4to, half-morocco, gilt back, £3 13s. 6d.

Floriated Ornaments. 31 Plates handsomely printed in Gold and Colours, with introductory Letterpress, royal 4to, half-morocco, £1 16s.

Gothic Ornaments. 90 Plates, by J. D. HARDING and others. Royal 4to, half-morocco, £1 16s.

Ornamental Timber Gables. 30 Plates. Royal 4to, half-mor., 18s.

Specimens of Gothic Architecture, from Ancient Edifices in England. 114 Outline Plates by LE KEUX and others. With descriptive Letterpress and Glossary by E. J. WILLSON. Two Vols., 4to half-mor., £1 16s.

True Principles of Pointed or Christian Architecture. With 87 Illustrations. Small 4to, 10s. 6d.

PURSUIVANT OF ARMS (The); or, Heraldry founded upon Facts. A Popular Guide to the Science of Heraldry. By J. R. PLANCHÉ, Esq., Somerset Herald. To which are added, Essays on the BADGES OF THE HOUSES OF LANCASTER AND YORK. With Coloured Frontispiece, five full-page Plates, and about 200 Illustrations. Crown 8vo, cloth extra, gilt, 7s. 6d.

ABELAIS' WORKS. Faithfully translated from the French, with variorum Notes, and numerous Characteristic Illustrations by GUSTAVE DORÉ. Crown 8vo, cloth extra, 700 pages, 7s. 6d.

ROLL OF BATTLE ABBEY; or, A List of the Principal Warriors who came over from Normandy with William the Conqueror, and Settled in this Country, A.D. 1066-7. Printed on fine plate paper, nearly three feet by two, with the principal Arms emblazoned in Gold and Colours. Price 5s.

ROLL OF CAERLAVEROCK, the Oldest Heraldic Roll; including the Original Anglo-Norman Poem, and an English Translation of the MS. in the British Museum. By THOMAS WRIGHT, M.A. The Arms emblazoned in Gold and Colours. In 4to, very handsomely printed, extra gold cloth, 12s.

ROWLANDSON (Thomas): HIS LIFE AND TIMES; The History of his Caricatures, and the Key to their Meaning. With very numerous full-page Plates and Wood Engravings. Demy 4to, cloth extra, gilt and gilt edges, 31s. 6d.   *[In preparation.*

ALA (George Augustus) ON COOKERY IN ITS HIS-TORICAL ASPECT. With very numerous Illustrations by the AUTHOR. Crown 4to, cloth extra, gilt.   *[In preparation.*

SANDWITH (Dr.) OF KARS.—MINSTERBOROUGH. An English Tale. By HUMPHRY SANDWITH, C.B., D.C.L. Three Vols. crown 8vo, 31s. 6d.

SEVEN GENERATIONS OF EXECUTIONERS.

SANSON FAMILY, Memoirs of the, compiled from Private Documents in the possession of the Family (1688-1847), by HENRI SANSON. Translated from the French, with an Introduction by CAMILLE BARRÈRE. Two Vols. 8vo, cloth extra, 18s.

" A faithful translation of this curious work, which will certainly repay perusal,— not on the ground of its being full of horrors, for the original author seems to be rather ashamed of the technical aspect of his profession, and is commendably reticent as to its details, but because it contains a lucid account of the most notable *causes célèbres* from the time of Louis XIV. to a period within the memory of persons still living. . . . The Memoirs, if not particularly instructive, can scarcely fail to be extremely entertaining."—*Daily Telegraph.*

SHAKESPEARE.—THE LANSDOWNE EDITION. Beautifully printed in red and black, in small but very clear type. Post 8vo, with engraved facsimile of DROESHOUT'S Portrait, and 37 beautiful Steel Plates, after STOTHARD, cloth extra, gilt, gilt edges, 18*s*.

SHAKESPEARE, THE SCHOOL OF. Including "The Life and Death of Captain Thomas Stukeley," with a New Life of Stucley, from Unpublished Sources; "A Warning for Fair Women," with a Reprint of the Account of the Murder; "Nobody and Somebody;" "The Cobbler's Prophecy;" "Histrio-mastix;" "The Prodigal Son," &c. Edited, with Introductions and Notes, by R. SIMPSON, Author of "An Introduction to the Philosophy of Shakespeare's Sonnets." Two Vols., crown 8vo, cloth extra. [*In the press.*

SHAKESPEARE.—THE FIRST FOLIO. Mr. WILLIAM SHAKE-SPEARE'S Comedies, Histories, and Tragedies. Published according to the true Original Copies. London, Printed by ISAAC IAGGARD and ED. BLOUNT, 1623.—An exact Reproduction of the extremely rare Original, in reduced facsimile by a photographic process—ensuring the strictest accuracy in every detail. Small 8vo, hf. Roxburghe, 10*s.* 6*d. A full Prospectus will be sent upon application.*

"To Messrs. Chatto & Windus belongs the merit of having done more to facilitate the critical study of the text of our great dramatist than all the Shakespeare clubs and societies put together. A complete facsimile of the celebrated First Folio edition of 1623 for half-a-guinea is at once a miracle of cheapness and enterprise. Being in a reduced form, the type is necessarily rather diminutive, but it is distinct as in a genuine copy of the original, and will be found to be as useful and far more handy to the student than the latter."—*Athenæum.*

"**SECRET OUT**" **SERIES.** Crown 8vo, cloth extra, profusely Illustrated, price 4*s.* 6*d.* each.

Art of Amusing: A Collection of Graceful Arts, Games, Tricks, Puzzles, and Charades. By FRANK BELLEW. 300 Illustrations.

Hanky-Panky: Very Easy Tricks, Very Difficult Tricks, White Magic, Sleight of Hand. Edited by W. H. CREMER. 200 Illustrations.

Magician's Own Book: Performances with Cups and Balls, Eggs, Hats, Handkerchiefs, &c. All from Actual Experience. Edited by W. H. CREMER. 200 Illustrations.

Magic no Mystery: Tricks with Cards, Dice, Balls, &c., with fully descriptive Directions; the Art of Secret Writing; the Training of Performing Animals, &c. With Coloured Frontispiece and numerous Illusts.

Merry Circle (The): A Book of New Intellectual Games and Amusements. By CLARA BELLEW. Numerous Illustrations.

Secret Out: One Thousand Tricks with Cards, and other Recreations; with entertaining Experiments in Drawing-room or "White Magic." By W. H. CREMER. 300 Engravings.

SLANG DICTIONARY (The): Etymological, Historical, and Anecdotal. An ENTIRELY NEW EDITION, revised throughout, and considerably Enlarged. Crown 8vo, cloth extra, gilt, 6*s.* 6*d.*

"We are glad to see the Slang Dictionary reprinted and enlarged. From a high scientific point of view this book is not to be despised. Of course it cannot fail to be amusing also. It contains the very vocabulary of unrestrained humour, and oddity, and grotesqueness. In a word, it provides valuable material both for the student of language and the student of human nature."—*Academy.*

"In every way a great improvement on the edition of 1864. Its uses as a dictionary f the very vulgar tongue do not require to be explained."—*Notes and Queries.*

"Compiled with most exacting care, and based on the best authorities."—*Standard.*

SHAW AND BRIDGENS' DESIGNS FOR FURNITURE, with Candelabra and Interior Decoration. 60 Plates, royal 4to, half-morocco £1 11*s.* ; Large Paper, imperial 4to, the Plates Coloured, half-morocco, £2 8*s.*

SHAW'S ILLUMINATED WORKS :—

Ancient Furniture, drawn from existing Authorities. With Descriptions by Sir S. R. MEYRICK. 4to, 74 Plates, half-morocco, £1 11s. 6d.; or, with some Plates Coloured, 4to, half-morocco, £2 2s.; Large Paper copies, impl. 4to, all the Plates extra finished in opaque Colours, half-morocco extra, £4 14s. 6d.

Dresses and Decorations of the Middle Ages, from the Seventh to the Seventeenth Centuries. 94 Plates, beautifully Coloured, a profusion of Initial Letters, and Examples of Curious Ornament, with Historical Introduction and Descriptive Text. Two Vols. imperial 8vo, half-Roxburghe, £5 5s.; large paper copies, the whole illuminated in body-colours, heightened with gold and silver, £14 14s.

Luton Chapel: A Series of 20 highly-finished Line Engravings of Gothic Architecture and Ornaments. Imperial folio, India Proofs, half-morocco, £2 8s.

Illuminated Ornaments of the Middle Ages, from the Sixth to the Seventeenth Century. Selected from Missals, MSS., and early printed Books. 66 Plates, carefully coloured from the Originals, with Descriptions by Sir F. MADDEN, Keeper of MSS., Brit. Mus. 4to, half-Roxburghe, £3 13s. 6d.; Large Paper copies, the Plates beautifully finished with opaque Colours and illuminated with Gold, imperial 4to, half-Roxburghe, £7 7s.

Ornamental Metal Work: A Series of 50 Copperplates, several Coloured. 4to, half-morocco, 18s.

Encyclopædia of Ornament. Select Examples from the purest and best Specimens of all kinds and all Ages. 4to, 59 Plates, half-morocco, £1 1s.; Large Paper copies, imperial 4to, with all the Plates Coloured, half-morocco, £2 12s. 6d.

SHERIDAN'S COMPLETE WORKS, with Life and Anecdotes. Including his Dramatic Writings, printed from the Original Editions, his Works in Prose and Poetry, Translations, Speeches, Jokes, Puns, &c.; with a Collection of Sheridaniana. Crown 8vo, cloth extra, gilt, with 10 full-page Tinted Illustrations, 7s. 6d.

"Whatever Sheridan has done, has been, *par excellence*, always the *best* of its kind. He has written the best comedy (School for Scandal), the *best* drama (the Duenna), the *best* farce (the Critic), and the *best* address (Monologue on Garrick); and, to crown all, delivered the very best oration (the famous Begum Speech) ever conceived or heard in this country."—BYRON.

"The editor has brought together within a manageable compass not only the seven plays by which Sheridan is best known, but a collection also of his poetical pieces which are less familiar to the public, sketches of unfinished dramas, selections from his reported witticisms, and extracts from his principal speeches. To these is prefixed a short but well-written memoir, giving the chief facts in Sheridan's literary and political career; so that with this volume in his hand, the student may consider himself tolerably well furnished with all that is necessary for a general comprehension of the subject of it."—*Pall Mall Gazette.*

SILVESTRE'S UNIVERSAL PALÆOGRAPHY; or, A Collection of Facsimiles of the Writings of every Age. Containing upwards of 300 large and beautifully executed Facsimiles, taken from Missals and other MSS., richly Illuminated in the finest style of art. A New Edition, arranged under the direction of Sir F. MADDEN, Keeper of MSS., Brit. Mus. Two Vols. atlas folio, half-morocco, gilt, £31 10s.

Also, a Volume of HISTORICAL AND DESCRIPTIVE LETTERPRESS, by CHAMPOLLION FIGEAC and CHAMPOLLION, Jun. Translated, with Additions, by Sir F. MADDEN. Two Vols. royal 8vo, half-morocco, gilt, £2 8s.

"This great work contains upwards of three hundred large and beautifully executed facsimiles of the finest and most interesting MSS. of various ages and nations, illuminated in the highest style of art. The cost of getting up this splendid publication was not far from £20,000."—*Allibone's Dictionary.*

"The great work on Palæography generally—one of the most sumptuous works of its class ever published."—*Chambers's Encyclopædia.*

SIGNBOARDS: Their History. With Anecdotes of Famous Taverns and Remarkable Characters. By JACOB LARWOOD and JOHN CAMDEN HOTTEN. With nearly 100 Illustrations. SEVENTH EDITION. Crown 8vo, cloth extra, 7s. 6d.

"Even if we were ever so maliciously inclined, we could not pick out all Messrs. Larwood and Hotten's plums, because the good things are so numerous as to defy the most wholesale depredation."—*The Times*.

SMITH'S HISTORICAL AND LITERARY CURIOSITIES:
Containing Facsimiles of Autographs, Scenes of Remarkable Events, Interesting Localities, Old Houses, Portraits, Illuminated and Missal Ornaments, Antiquities, &c. 4to, with 100 Plates (some Illuminated), half-morocco extra, £2 5s.

SMOKER'S TEXT-BOOK. By J. HAMER, F.R.S.L. Exquisitely printed from "silver-faced" type, cloth, very neat, gilt edges, 2s. 6d.

SOWERBY'S MANUAL OF CONCHOLOGY: A Complete Introduction to the Science. Illustrated by upwards of 650 etched Figures of Shells and numerous Woodcuts. With copious Explanations, Tables, Glossary, &c. 8vo, cloth extra, gilt, 15s. ; or, the Plates beautifully Coloured, £1 8s.

"Sowerby has illustrated the conchological system of Lamarck in a very useful and popular manner; and has not only suggested many judicious improvements, but has defined several new genera with judgment and precision."—SWAINSON.

STEDMAN'S (Edmund Clarence) **VICTORIAN POETS:** Critical Essays. Crown 8vo, cloth extra, 9s.

"The book is, on the whole, generous and enlightened, and bears the stamp of unfailing honesty. . . . Mr. Stedman has not approached his task in a light spirit, nor without the preparation of due pains and culture."—*Academy*.

"We ought to be thankful to those who do critical work with competent skill and understanding, with honesty of purpose, and with diligence and thoroughness of execution. And Mr. Stedman, having chosen to work in this line, deserves the thanks of English scholars by these qualities and by something more ; . . . . he is faithful, studious, and discerning."—*Saturday Review*.

STOTHARD'S MONUMENTAL EFFIGIES OF GREAT BRITAIN, from William I. to Henry VIII., selected from our Cathedrals and Churches. With Historical Description and Introduction, by JOHN KEMPE, F.S.A. A NEW EDITION, with a large body of Additional Notes by JOHN HEWITT. Imperial 4to, containing 150 beautifully finished full-page Engravings and Nine Vignettes, all Tinted, and some Illuminated in Gold and Colours, half-morocco, £9 9s.; Large Paper, royal folio, with all the coats of arms illuminated in gold and colours, and the plates very carefully finished in body-colours, heightened with gold in the very finest style, half-morocco, £15 15s.

"No English library should be without this unique and important publication. Charles Stothard is the model which every antiquarian artist must follow, if he wishes to excel. His pencil was always guided by his mind, and we may safely assert that no one ever united equal accuracy and feeling." *Quarterly Review*

"It is only in the beautiful work on Monumental Effigies, by Stothard, that everything has been done which fidelity and taste could effect."—SHAW.

STOW'S SURVEY OF LONDON. Edited by W. J. THOMS, F.S.A. A New Edition, with Copper-plate Illustrations, large 8vo, half-Roxburghe, price 9s.

"Carefully reproduced."—*Quarterly Review*.

STRUTT'S DRESSES AND HABITS OF THE ENGLISH, from the Establishment of the Saxons in Britain to the Present Time. With an Historical Inquiry into every branch of Costume, Ancient and Modern. New Edition, with Explanatory Notes by J. R. PLANCHÉ, Somerset Herald. Two Vols. royal 4to, with 153 Engravings from the most Authentic Sources, beautifully Coloured, half-Roxburghe, £6 6s. ; or the Plates splendidly Illuminated in Silver and Opaque Colours, in the Missal style, half-Roxburghe, £15 15s.

STRUTT'S SPORTS AND PASTIMES OF THE PEOPLE

OF ENGLAND; including the Rural and Domestic Recreations, May Games, Mummeries, Shows, Processions, Pageants, and Pompous Spectacles, from the Earliest Period to the Present Time. With 140 Illustrations. Edited by WILLIAM HONE. Crown 8vo, cloth extra, 7s. 6d.—A few LARGE PAPER COPIES, uniform with the "Dresses," with an extra set of Copperplate Illustrations, carefully Coloured by hand, from the Originals, 50s.

"The amusing pages of Strutt entitle his memory to great respect; and, borrowing the idea of Dr. Johnson, I will boldly affirm that he who wishes to be informed of the curious and interesting details connected with Ancient Manners and Customs, Costumes, Regal and Ecclesiastical Antiquities, must devote his days and his nights to the volumes of Strutt."—*Dibdin's Decameron.*

STRUTT'S REGAL AND ECCLESIASTICAL ANTIQUITIES

OF ENGLAND: Authentic Representations of all the English Monarchs, from Edward the Confessor to Henry the Eighth; with many Great Personages eminent under their several Reigns. New Edition, with critical Notes by J. R. PLANCHÉ, Somerset Herald. Royal 4to, with 72 Engravings from Manuscripts, Monuments, &c., beautifully Coloured, half-Roxburghe, £3 3s.; or the Plates splendidly Illuminated in Gold and Colours, half-morocco, £10 10s.

MR. SWINBURNE'S NEW POEM.

ERECHTHEUS: A Tragedy. By ALGERNON CHARLES SWINBURNE. SECOND EDITION. Crown 8vo, cloth extra, 6s.

"The harmony of all the parts is perfect. . . . Our *Erechtheus* is as living to us now as it could have been to an Athenian. . . . To such altitudes, rarely scaled by the feet of poets in the modern age, has he ascended. . . . *Erechtheus* is, in truth, a masterpiece . . . a poem which appeals to men of all nations and of all times."—*Academy.*

"Matured thought and ripened power are brought to the task of reclothing old fables. Our extracts, copious as they are, fail to convey an idea of the sustained strength and beauty of the entire work, which we are inclined to rank as Mr. Swinburne's masterpiece."—*Athenæum.*

"Mr. Swinburne has written nothing near so good as this since he wrote 'Atalanta in Calydon.'. . . . It would be difficult, in our opinion, to find a nearer approach to the terse and weighty dialogue of the Sophoclean tragedy than Mr. Swinburne gives us in the dialogue of his play. Exquisite sweetness and melody."—*Spectator*

MR. SWINBURNE'S OTHER WORKS.

Queen Mother and Rosamond. Fcap. 8vo, 5s.

Atalanta in Calydon. A New Edition. Crown 8vo, 6s.

Chastelard. A Tragedy. Fcap. 8vo, 7s.

Poems and Ballads. Fcap. 8vo, 9s.

Notes on "Poems and Ballads." 8vo, 1s.

Essays and Studies. Crown 8vo, 12s.

Songs before Sunrise. Crown 8vo, 10s. 6d.

Bothwell: A Tragedy. Two Vols. crown 8vo, 12s. 6d.

George Chapman: An Essay. Crown 8vo, 7s.

Songs of two Nations: DIRÆ, A SONG OF ITALY, ODE ON THE FRENCH REPUBLIC. Crown 8vo, 6s.

William Blake: A Critical Essay. With Facsimile Paintings, Coloured by Hand, after Drawings by BLAKE and his Wife. Demy 8vo, 16s.

Also,

Rossetti's (W. M.) Criticism upon Swinburne's "Poems and Ballads." Fcap. 8vo, cloth extra, 3s. 6d.

SWIFT'S CHOICE WORKS, in Prose and Verse. With Memoir, Portrait, and Facsimiles of the Maps in the Original Edition of "Gulliver's Travels." Crown 8vo, cloth extra, gilt, 7s. 6d.

"The 'Tale of a Tub' is, in my apprehension, the masterpiece of Swift : certainly Rabelais has nothing superior, even in invention, nor anything so condensed, so pointed, so full of real meaning, of biting satire, of felicitous analogy. The 'Battle of the Books' is such an improvement of the similar combat in the Lutrin that we can hardly own it as an imitation."—HALLAM.

"In humour and in irony, and in the talent of debasing and defiling what he hated, we join with the world in thinking the Dean of St. Patrick's without a rival."—LORD JEFFREY.

"Swift's reputation as a poet has been in a manner obscured by the greater splendour, by the natural force and inventive genius, of his prose writings ; but, if he had never written either the 'Tale of a Tub' or 'Gulliver's Travels,' his name merely as a poet would have come down to us, and have gone down to posterity, with well-earned honours."—HAZLITT.

SYNTAX'S (Dr.) THREE TOURS, in Search of the Picturesque, in Search of Consolation, and in Search of a Wife. With the whole of ROWLANDSON's droll full-page Illustrations, in Colours, and Life of the Author by J. C. HOTTEN. Medium 8vo, cloth extra, gilt, 7s. 6d.

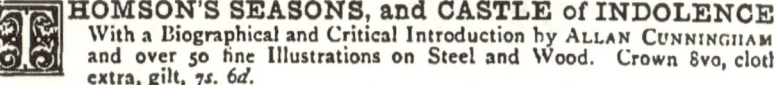

THOMSON'S SEASONS, and CASTLE of INDOLENCE. With a Biographical and Critical Introduction by ALLAN CUNNINGHAM, and over 50 fine Illustrations on Steel and Wood. Crown 8vo, cloth extra, gilt, 7s. 6d.

THACKERAYANA : Notes and Anecdotes. Illustrated by a profusion of Sketches by WILLIAM MAKEPEACE THACKERAY, depicting Humorous Incidents in his School-life, and Favourite Characters in the books of his everyday reading. Large post 8vo, with Hundreds of Wood Engravings and Five Coloured Plates, from Mr. Thackeray's Original Drawings, cloth, full gilt, gilt top, 12s. 6d.

"It would have been a real loss to bibliographical literature had copyright difficulties deprived the general public of this very amusing collection. One of Thackeray's habits, from his schoolboy days, was to ornament the margins and blank pages of the books he had in use with caricature illustrations of their contents. This gave special value to the sale of his library, and is almost cause for regret that it could not have been preserved in its integrity. Thackeray's place in literature is eminent enough to have made this an interest to future generations. The anonymous editor has done the best that he could to compensate for the lack of this. He has obtained access to the principal works thus dispersed, and he speaks, not only of the readiness with which their possessors complied with his request, but of the abundance of the material spontaneously proffered to him. He has thus been able to reproduce in facsimile the five or six hundred sketches of this volume. They differ, of course, not only in cleverness but in finish ; but they unquestionably establish Thackeray's capability of becoming, if not an eminent artist, yet a great caricaturist. A grotesque fancy, an artistic touch, and a power of reproducing unmistakable portraits in comic exaggerations, as well as of embodying ludicrous ideas pictorially, make the book very amusing. Still more valuable is the descriptive, biographical, and anecdotal letterpress, which gives us a great accumulation of biographical information concerning Thackeray's works, reading, history, and habits. Without being a formal biography, it tells us scores of things that could scarcely have come into any biography. We have no clue to the sources of information possessed by the editor. Apparently he has been a most diligent student of his hero, and an indefatigable collector of scraps of information concerning his entire literary career. We can testify only to the great interest of the book, and to the vast amount of curious information which it contains. We regret that it has been published without the sanction of his family, but no admirer of Thackeray should be without it. It is an admirable addendum, not only to his collected works, but also to any memoir of him that has been, or that is likely to be, written."—*British Quarterly Review.*

THORNBURY'S (Walter) HISTORICAL AND LEGENDARY BALLADS AND SONGS. Illustrated by J. WHISTLER, JOHN TENNIEL, A. F. SANDYS, W. SMALL, M. J. LAWLESS, J. D. WATSON, G. J. PINWELL, F. WALKER, T. R. MACQUOID, and others. Handsomely printed, crown 4to, cloth extra, gilt and gilt edges, 21s.

"Mr. Thornbury has perceived with laudable clearness that one great requisite of poetry is that it should amuse. He rivals Goethe in the variety and startling incidents of his ballad-romances : he is full of vivacity and spirit, and his least impassioned pieces ring with a good out-of-doors music of sword and shield. Some of his mediæval poems are particularly rich in colour and tone ; the ' Lady Witch,' ' John of Padua,' and, above all, 'The Jester's Moral,' are admirable cabinet pictures. The old Norse ballads, too, are worthy of great praise. Best of all, however, we like his Cavalier songs ; there is nothing of the kind in English more spirited, masculine, and merry."—*Academy*.

"Will be welcomed by all true lovers of art. . . . We must be grateful that so many works of a school distinguished for its originality should be collected into a single volume."—*Saturday Review.*

"Who has not thrilled over such songs as ' Trample, trample, went the roan,' or 'The death of King Warwolf' ?—and who needs to be told that the illustrations are above price when they are by such men as Tenniel, Sandys, Whistler, and the lamented Fred Walker? The book is beautifully got up."—*Morning Post.*

TOURNEUR'S (Cyril) COLLECTED WORKS, including a unique Poem, entitled " The Transformed Metamorphosis ; " and " Laugh and Lie Down ; or, The World's Folly." Edited, with Critical Preface, Introductions, and Notes, by J. CHURTON COLLINS. Post 8vo, 10s. 6d.   [*In the press.*

TURNER'S (J. M. W.) LIFE AND CORRESPONDENCE. Founded upon Letters and Papers furnished by his Friends and Fellow-Academicians. By WALTER THORNBURY. New Edition, entirely rewritten and considerably enlarged. With numerous Illustrations. Two Vols. demy 8vo, cloth extra.   [*In the press.*

TURNER GALLERY (The) : A Series of Sixty Engravings from the Principal Works of JOSEPH MALLORD WILLIAM TURNER. With a Memoir and Illustrative Text by RALPH NICHOLSON WORNUM, Keeper and Secretary, National Gallery. Handsomely half-bound, India Proofs, royal folio, £10 ; Large Paper copies, Artists' India Proofs, elephant folio, £20.—*A Descriptive Pamphlet will be sent upon application.*

"To those whose memories are old enough to go back through any considerable portion of Turner's life, or who may have seen the majority of the pictures he painted during so many years of loving labour, it will be at once manifest that no better selection could have been made of paintings which could be got at by any reasonable means. Many of his grandest productions are in this series of engravings, and the ablest landscape engravers of the day have been employed on the plates, among which are some that, we feel assured, Turner himself would have been delighted to see. These proof impressions constitute a volume of exceeding beauty, which deserves to find a place in the library of every man of taste. The number of copies printed is too limited for a wide circulation, but, on that account, the rarity of the publication makes it the more valuable.

"A series of engravings from Turner's finest pictures, and of a size and quality commensurate with their importance, has not till now been offered to the public ; nor, indeed, could it have been produced but for the glorious legacy bequeathed to the country. During his lifetime he exercised supreme control over his works, and would allow none to be engraved but what he chose ; the large sums, moreover, paid to him for 'touching the proofs,' which he considered equivalent to what he would have received for copyright, acted almost as a prohibition to such engravings getting into the hands of any but the opulent.

"It is not too much to affirm that a more beautiful and worthy tribute to the genius of the great painter does not exist, and is not likely to exist at any future time."—*Art Journal.*

TIMBS' CLUBS AND CLUB LIFE IN LONDON. With

ANECDOTES of its FAMOUS COFFEE HOUSES, HOSTELRIES, and TAVERNS. By JOHN TIMBS, F.S.A. Numerous Illustrations. Crown 8vo, cloth extra, gilt, 7s. 6d.

"The book supplies a much-felt want. The club is the avenue to general society at the present day, and Mr. Timbs gives the *entrée* to the club. The scholar and antiquary will also find the work a repertory of information on many disputed points of literary interest, and especially respecting various well-known anecdotes, the value of which only increases with the lapse of time."—*Morning Post.*

TIMBS' ENGLISH ECCENTRICS and ECCENTRICITIES:

Stories of Wealth and Fashion, Delusions, Impostures and Fanatic Missions, Strange Sights and Sporting Scenes, Eccentric Artists, Theatrical Folks, Men of Letters, &c. By JOHN TIMBS, F.S.A. With nearly 50 Illustrations. Crown 8vo, cloth extra, 7s. 6d.

"The reader who would fain enjoy a harmless laugh in some very odd company might do much worse than take an occasional dip into 'English Eccentrics.' The illustrations are admirably suited to the letterpress."—*Graphic.*

TROLLOPE'S (Anthony) THE WAY WE LIVE NOW. Il-

lustrated Library Edition. Two Vols. 8vo, cloth extra, with 40 full-page Plates, 12s. See also "Piccadilly Novels."

AGABONDIANA; or, Anecdotes of Mendicant Wanderers

through the Streets of London; with Portraits of the most Remarkable, drawn from the Life by JOHN THOMAS SMITH, late Keeper of the Prints in the British Museum. With Introduction by FRANCIS DOUCE, and Descriptive Text. With the Woodcuts and the 32 Plates, from the original Coppers. Crown 4to, half-Roxburghe, 12s. 6d.

ALTON AND COTTON, ILLUSTRATED.—THE COM-

PLETE ANGLER; or, The Contemplative Man's Recreation: Being a Discourse of Rivers, Fish-ponds, Fish and Fishing, written by IZAAK WALTON; and Instructions how to Angle for a Trout or Grayling in a clear Stream, by CHARLES COTTON. With Original Memoirs and Notes by Sir HARRIS NICOLAS, K.C.M.G. With the 61 Plate Illustrations, precisely as in Pickering's two-volume Edition. Complete in One Volume, large crown 8vo, cloth antique, 7s. 6d.

"Among the reprints of the year, few will be more welcome than this edition of the 'Complete Angler,' with Sir Harris Nicolas's Memoirs and Notes, and Stothard and Inskipp's illustrations."—*Saturday Review.*

"As a book, the volume before us is neatly trimmed and winsome to the eye. There is room for it in the world among its predecessors, and in the getting up the publishers have done it every justice."—*Academy.*

WELLS' JOSEPH AND HIS BRETHREN: A Dramatic Poem.

By CHARLES WELLS. With an Introductory Essay by ALGERNON CHARLES SWINBURNE. Crown 8vo, with Vignette Portrait, cloth extra, 9s.

"The author of 'Joseph and his Brethren' will some day have to be acknowledged among the memorable men of the second great period in our poetry. . . . There are lines even in the overture of his poem which might, it seems to me, more naturally be mistaken even by an expert in verse for the work of the young Shakspeare, than any to be gathered elsewhere in the fields of English poetry."—SWINBURNE.

"In its combination of strength and delicacy, in sweet liquid musical flow, in just cadence, and in dramatic incisiveness of utterance, the language throughout keeps closer to the level of the Elizabethan dramatists than that of any dramatist of subsequent times. . . . Mr. Swinburne does not praise the character of Phraxanor over-much when he places it only behind the Cleopatra of Shakspeare, and adds that all women in literature after these two seem coarse or trivial when they touch on anything sensual. A poet has been saved from oblivion, and the present and future . by a work they could ill afford to lose."—*Athenæum.*

WARRANT TO EXECUTE CHARLES I. An exact Facsimile of this important Document, with the Fifty-nine Signatures of the Regicides, and corresponding Seals, on paper to imitate the Original, 22 in. by 14 in. Price 2s.

WARRANT TO EXECUTE MARY QUEEN OF SCOTS. An exact Facsimile of this important Document, including the Signature of Queen Elizabeth and Facsimile of the Great Seal, on tinted paper, to imitate the Original MS. Price 2s.

WILD'S CATHEDRALS. Select examples of the Ecclesiastical Architecture of the Middle Ages ; arranged in Two Series (the First FOREIGN, the Second ENGLISH). Each Series containing Twelve fine Plates, mounted upon Cardboard, and carefully Coloured, after the Original Drawings by CHARLES WILD. In a portfolio, £4 4s. each series.

"These splendid plates are unequalled, whether bound as a volume, treasured in a portfolio, or framed for universal admiration."—*Athenæum.*

WILSON'S AMERICAN ORNITHOLOGY ; or, Natural History of the Birds of the United States ; with the Continuation by Prince CHARLES LUCIAN BONAPARTE. NEW AND ENLARGED EDITION, completed by the insertion of above One Hundred Birds omitted in the original Work, and Illustrated by valuable Notes, and Life of the Author, by Sir WILLIAM JARDINE. Three Vols., 8vo, with a fine Portrait of WILSON, and 103 Plates, exhibiting nearly four hundred figures of Birds accurately engraved and beautifully printed in Colours, cloth extra, gilt, £3 3s. Also, a few Large Paper copies, quarto, with the Plates all carefully Coloured by hand, at £6 6s.

"The History of American Birds by Alexander Wilson is equal in elegance to the most distinguished of our own splendid works on Ornithology."—CUVIER.

"With an enthusiasm never excelled, this extraordinary man penetrated through the vast territories of the United States, undeterred by forests or swamps, for the sole purpose of describing the native birds."—LORD BROUGHAM.

"By the mere force of native genius, and of delight in nature, he became, without knowing it, a good, a great writer."—*Blackwood's Magazine.*

WRIGHT'S CARICATURE HISTORY of the GEORGES (House of Hanover). With 400 Pictures, Caricatures, Squibs, Broadsides, Window Pictures, &c. By THOMAS WRIGHT, Esq., M.A., F.S.A. Crown 8vo, cloth extra, 7s. 6d.

"Emphatically one of the liveliest of books, as also one of the most interesting. Has the twofold merit of being at once amusing and edifying."—*Morning Post.*

WRIGHT'S HISTORY OF CARICATURE AND OF THE GROTESQUE IN ART, LITERATURE, SCULPTURE, AND PAINTING, from the Earliest Times to the Present Day. By THOMAS WRIGHT, M.A., F.S.A. Profusely Illustrated by F. W. FAIRHOLT, F.S.A. Large post 8vo, cloth extra, gilt, 7s. 6d.

"Almost overwhelms us with its infinite research. Mr. Wright dexterously guides the reader to a full survey of our English caricature, from its earliest efforts to the full-blown blossoms of a Rowlandson or a Gillray. The excellent illustrations of Mr. Fairholt add greatly to the value of the volume."—*Graphic.*

"A very amusing and instructive volume."—*Saturday Review.*